MURDER KNOWS
NO BOUNDARIES

MURDER KNOWS NO BOUNDARIES

GEORGE ENCIZO

Columbus, Ohio

Murder Knows No Boundaries

Published by Gatekeeper Press
2167 Stringtown Rd. Suite 109
Columbus, OH 43123-2989
www.GatekeeperPress.com

ISBN – 9781642377859
ISBN – 9781642377866

Library of Congress Control Number: 2019952665

Cover design by Elizabeth Babski

"Anger is an acid that can do more harm to the vessel in which it is stored than to anything on which it is poured."

Mark Twain

CHAPTER 1

Beware, when a messenger of ill will rears its ugly head as it did late one night on a deserted stretch of highway.

July 21, 2018

As one of his newest deputies, Sheriff, JD Pickens, assigned Jason Conlon to patrol county road 325 weekends from four in the afternoon until midnight. The highway wound through farm country and crossed into the next county. It was mostly used in the daytime by farmers and ranchers as an access road to their properties. Those drivers who used the highway at night complained that it was dangerous to travel because high school teenagers were using it as a drag racing strip. Conlon's assignment was to act as a deterrent, and it seemed to be working.

Friday night went without an incident, but Saturday night around nine-thirty Conlon's headlights shined on a deer in the road. He slowed to a stop and waited for the deer to cross, but it simply turned its head in Conlon's direction and looked at him as if to say "This is my territory and you're infringing on it." Conlon turned on the flashers expecting the deer would move. When he turned the lights on, the dash cam automatically came on. Finally, the deer scampered off. Conlon decided it was a good time to pull to the side of the road and take a coffee break. His wife had filled the thermos she bought him as a present for graduating from the Florida Law Enforcement Academy.

Suddenly, a black vehicle sped past him and didn't bother to slow down. Conlon turned the flashes back on and his brights. Then he radioed that he was in pursuit and chased after the vehicle. He caught up with it and signaled for the driver to pull over—which it did. Conlon radioed that he had pulled the vehicle over and did a license plate search to determine if it was a stolen vehicle. The plate belonged to Myra Peterson in Highlands County, Florida but it was for a 2004 Honda CRV. Conlon could see the vehicle he pulled over wasn't a CRV and radioed the info to the dispatcher.

Conlon's patrol car had the latest GPS, so the dispatcher knew precisely where Conlon's location was. He also had a bodycam and shoulder radio. Both were turned on when he opened the door. The equipment was a new addition to all the patrol cars and was purchased by Sheriff Pickens, along with two deputies with the help of a law enforcement grant from the DOJ. With the additional deputies, Pickens now had five deputies, two sergeants, and a corporal. That was not many when compared to surrounding cities and counties.

Conlon used the car's speaker and told the driver to roll down the window and place both hands out the window. After the driver did, Conlon eased himself from the patrol car, checking to make sure his bodycam was on. He used the radio clipped to his shoulder to let dispatch know he was approaching the other vehicle with his weapon out.

Conlon was nervous, but he had served three tours in Afghanistan and had been in many situations like this, so he remained calm, but alert.

Suddenly, the passenger's door opened, and someone stepped out and fired at Conlon. One shot hit him center mass, and another hit him in the arm. Conlon fell backward but managed to get off a shot. Fortunately, Conlon was wearing his bulletproof vest as required at night by Sheriff Pickens for all his deputies. The shooter got back in the car, and the driver sped off, leaving Deputy Conlon on the ground. Conlon managed to radio *10:24*—the code for an "Officer Down."

The emergency operator immediately called for an ambulance and gave them the coordinates for Conlon's location. Then she sent Deputy Lea Abrue, who was on duty to provide backup.

Since the Warfield office was the closest to where Conlon was, after calling for backup, the operator called Sergeant Mia Dunne, then called Sheriff JD Pickens.

Dunne was at home when she received the call and immediately left for the scene, knowing backup would be there.

Sergeant Dunne, an African American female, was married with two children, and a retired army military police officer. Dunne was a no-nonsense officer and a stickler for protocol. She had recently received a bump in paygrade. She knew Pickens would also arrive at the scene.

Sheriff JD Pickens was watching television with his wife, Dr. Marge Davids the county medical examiner, and his eleven-year-old daughter Sara when he received the call that an officer was down. The emergency call had gone right to his cell phone.

Pickens kissed his wife and daughter, grabbed his gun and holster, and drove to the scene following the GPS coordinates sent by the dispatcher.

*   *   *

When Pickens arrived at the scene, Sergeant Dunne and a deputy were there as were the EMTs who were working on Deputy Conlon. Pickens expected the worst as he walked over to speak to Dunne. He already had a limited number of deputies and couldn't afford to lose Conlon. Pickens recalled his interview with the young man and how he admired that Conlon was a devoted family man. It was for that reason that Pickens had hired Conlon. He had also interviewed Conlon's wife and noted her devotion to her husband and her support of his becoming a deputy assigned to Pickens. The one thing Pickens never expected was that he might have to one day tell her that her husband died in the line of duty. It would be the first time he had to inform a spouse of that.

Pickens greeted Dunne. "How bad was it?"

"It's not that bad," said Dunne. Pickens breathed a sigh of relief. "The vest saved him, but his chest will be sore awhile. The EMTs bandaged his arm. Fortunately, it was only a flesh wound. Conlon is tough. He'll survive this."

"Is he up for talking?"

Dunne pointed to the rear of the ambulance where Conlon sat with an EMT who was bandaging his arm.

"Sure, but he may be a little embarrassed that it happened."

"There's nothing to be embarrassed about. He was just doing his job. Let's talk to him."

Pickens and Dunne walked over to the ambulance.

Deputy Conlon shook his head. "Sorry, Sheriff, I screwed up."

Pickens waved his hand. "Hold on, Deputy, you didn't screw up. You were doing your duty. There's nothing to apologize for."

Conlon breathed a heavy sigh. "I should have been more careful and told the driver to turn on the overhead light. If I had, I might've seen the passenger and been more cautious." Conlon breathed. "I didn't see whoever it was until they fired at me. The overhead light didn't come on when they opened the door."

"Hold on, Conlon," said Dunne. "If the light didn't come on, then they planned on attacking you." Dunne turned to Pickens. "It was *deliberate*."

"I agree," said Pickens. "We'll review the dash cam and your bodycam footage later. Right now, you need to take the rest of the night off. Can you drive?"

Conlon turned to the EMT.

"It's up to him," said the EMT. "As long as he drives carefully."

"Don't worry, I will," said Conlon and stroked his chest. "Shirley's gonna be pissed when she sees my battle scars."

"It could've been worse, Deputy," said Dunne.

"Yeah, that's what we said in Afghanistan after returning from a skirmish where no one got shot." Conlon shook his head. "What I don't understand was why they didn't try to outrun me. They could have made it to the next county before I caught up to them."

"Because," said Pickens, "as Sergeant Dunne said, it was *deliberate*. Don't beat yourself up. Go home and be with your family. We'll talk tomorrow if you're up to it."

"I'll be up to it. It's not my first close call. Shirley doesn't know about those, but I guess I can't keep this one from her," he said with a gesture toward his chest where bruises would be forming.

Conlon was twenty-seven years old. He and his wife, Shirley, had two children ages four and six, and Shirley, had one in the oven. He and Shirley married right after high school. After he mustered out of the army, Conlon enrolled in the Florida Law Enforcement Academy and had been hired by Pickens along with Lea Abrue, a twenty-three-year-old African American female. Conlon was three months out of the academy.

"Wise decision, Deputy," said Dunne.

The EMT held up two fingers with the slug from Conlon's vest. "Here's a souvenir for you."

"I'll take that," said Pickens as he took the slug. "If it's from a .38 revolver, there won't be any casings. It's evidence anyway, and I'll need your vest. You can get a new one when you're ready to go back on duty. Abrue will follow you home to make sure you get there. Oh, and we'll need your bodycam and an incident report. Type one up tomorrow and send it to Billy with copies to Sergeant Dunne and me."

"Will do, Sheriff."

"Now go home," said Pickens.

Conlon stood. As he walked to his patrol car, Deputy Abrue followed him.

"Way to go, rookie," said Abrue. "Didn't you learn anything in the academy? You should have waited for back up, especially if the overhead light wasn't lit." Abrue grinned, "You better not tell Shirley about the light."

Conlon shot her a bird. "Shut up, rookie."

Both laughed, then got in their patrol cars, and Abrue followed Conlon home.

Pickens and Dunne used their flashlights to search the area and took pictures of the crime scene with their phones, including the drag marks the shooter's vehicle left behind when it sped away from the scene.

Pickens checked his watch. "It's late, Sergeant. Let's go home. We'll process what we have tomorrow and get a criminalist to finish processing the scene. Come to my office in the morning."

"Sure thing." Dunne blew out a sigh. "Thank goodness you got that grant for the vests and the new equipment."

"Yeah, thank goodness."

"I think this may have been a planned attack on us. I'll put my deputies on alert status."

"Good idea. I'll do the same. For now, if we patrol this stretch of road again, there'll be two deputies in a car." Pickens frowned. "Goodnight, Sergeant."

"Goodnight, Sheriff."

Pickens watched Dunne drive away before starting his own vehicle.

Pickens decided instead of going home; he'd stop at the office and leave the slug and Conlon's vest locked in his office. First thing in the morning, he'd get them to the medical examiner's office for processing. The sheriff's office didn't have the resources to do forensics; that was the medical examiner's role since only they had the equipment and personnel.

Pickens said goodnight to the dispatcher and told him he'd done a good job and that Conlon was going to be okay.

CHAPTER 2

WHEN PICKENS GOT home, Marge was waiting for him. Sarah was tucked in bed. Marge immediately noticed Pickens' frown, something he did when he was wary. After over ten years of marriage, Pickens and Marge had learned to understand each other's moods. Pickens was known to frown and for outbursts when he was angry or frustrated, whereas Marge was more logical and capable of seeing both sides of a situation.

Marge put her arms around him. He hugged her.

"How bad was it?" said Marge.

Pickens let out a deep breath. "It could have been worse. Thank goodness Conlon had on his vest. He'll be sore for a few days, especially with the wound to his arm."

"But he's going to be okay, right?" asked Marge.

"Yes." Pickens then told her what happened. "I'm upset because if we don't catch the guy, then it sends a message to the whole county that people can shoot at deputies with no consequences." Pickens exhaled. "The sheriff's office will lose their sense of authority. The county used to be peaceful. What happened to it? In just the past three years, we've had a serial killer who worked in my office and threatened my family. Then we find four bodies off Grange Road. One was a young mother murdered by her husband and dumped in a field like garbage.

A teenager savagely killed his parents and ten-year-old sister, and buried them in the same field and then went on a rampage across the country with his partner killing others. Now, this—someone deliberately ambushed my deputy." Pickens shook his head. "What's next?"

"It seems worse than it is," said Marge. "Those last two cases didn't occur on your watch, but you solved them." She placed her hand on his cheek. "You helped a mother and her two grandchildren have closure after twenty years. And you solved a thirty-year-old murder that ended the reign of two vicious serial killers." She rubbed his cheek. "We'll get through this. We always do."

Pickens kissed the palm of her hand. "Yeah, I guess we will. Oh, I locked Deputy Conlon's vest, his bodycam, and the slug from the weapon in my office. They'll be safe until Monday when I can get them to you."

"If you'd like, I can have someone get them tomorrow and start the forensics."

"I wouldn't mind, but I don't want anyone to give up their weekend."

She squeezed his shoulder. "I'll do it myself."

Pickens placed his hand on her shoulder. "Thanks, but what about Sarah? If you're going to work, so am I."

She smiled. "I'll drop her off at your parents' house. It will just be a short while. I don't need much time to process the evidence. If you'd like, I can start the forensics or wait until Monday for the criminalists to do it."

"Just process it. Let the criminalist do the forensics." Pickens smiled. "Right now, I'd like to play football with the medical examiner and forget about tonight."

"Let's go quarterback and make sure you score a touch-down."

"I'll do better than a touchdown. I'll even go for the two-point conversion."

Pickens took her hand and led her to their bedroom.

*   *   *

Sunday morning after breakfast, Pickens left for the office and Marge took Sarah to Pickens's parents before going to Pickens' office to retrieve the evidence.

Pickens was surprised to see Sergeant Amy Tucker and Corporal Billy Thompson at their desks. He guessed like him; they were not only shaken up about Conlon but also worried about themselves. It might explain why they were there.

Tucker was Pickens' oldest deputy and recently given the title of Detective Sergeant. She was considered the mama bear by the other deputies because she was old enough to be their mother. Her streaked, dirty-blonde hair was always tied in a ponytail and tucked under a sheriff's ball cap, and her nice figure made quite an impression in a uniform. She was also a licensed family counselor. Thompson had been promoted to corporal at the same time as Tucker made detective.

"What are you two doing here?" said Pickens.

"Same thing as you, JD," said Amy. "The Conlon thing and we're as concerned as you are. Who'll be the lead on the case, me or Sergeant Dunne?"

"It's not a case yet. It's an incident. And just to be clear, it's not gonna be a pissing contest. Since Conlon works for Dunne, she'll be involved. And since you're our only detective, so will you. And Billy . . ."

Billy interrupted him with a cough.

"Corporal Thompson will work his computers. Marge's . . ."

Just then, Marge entered the room and coughed.

Pickens shook his head. "Dr. Davids' team will handle the

forensics." Now, all three were grinning. "I'm glad you think it's funny because I don't."

"We don't either," snapped Amy. "Why do you think we're here on Sunday? We're a team, and when one of us is attacked, we're all attacked."

"Sheriff Pickens," said Marge, "why don't you give me that evidence from your office." She nodded toward his office.

Pickens turned, walked to his office, and unlocked the door.

Once inside the office, Marge said, "JD, ease up. Can't you tell they're just as concerned as you? That's why they're here. They're your team and a damn good one."

He pursed his lips. "You're right. I'm an asshole."

"Yes, you are."

Pickens' head snapped back.

"But you're my asshole. Now give me that evidence." He handed it to her. She took the vest and Conlon's shells but handed the bodycam back to him. "See if Billy can identify the shooter." She winked at him. "Now do your job, Sheriff, and don't apologize. Just let them know they're on your team." She turned and left.

Pickens exhaled. Armed with Conlon's bodycam, he left his office, strolled over to Billy, and handed him the bodycam.

"Upload Conlon's data and see if you can identify the shooter. Amy and I will start a board in case this wasn't an isolated incident."

Pickens and Amy rolled out the whiteboard, and he wrote *Shooting Incident 7/21/2018.* Underneath that he wrote *Deputy Justin Conlon.*

"Once we get the ballistics, we'll add the caliber of weapon, and hopefully the forensics team will match the slug to a weapon used in another shooting, something that could help identify its owner."

"If Billy identifies the shooter," said Amy, "we'll add a name."

"Let's hope so. Then you can do some detective work and get whoever it was. Sorry about before, Amy."

"Don't apologize. We're all upset. Conlon's a good guy and a family man. Whoever did this, we'll find them." She gritted her teeth. "It's personal with us."

Unfortunately, Billy couldn't identify the shooter from Conlon's bodycam or the dash cam. The shooter's arms concealed the face. And although he was able to identify the make of the vehicle as a Mercury Cougar, he couldn't tell the year. All he knew was that it wasn't older than 2002 since Mercury stopped making the Cougar after that. And then there was the license plate—but it belonged to another vehicle and owner.

With no other evidence available besides Conlon's report, the incident became an open case. Pickens ordered every deputy to be on the alert when making traffic stops or answering 911 calls. He also canceled the Friday and Saturday night drag racing patrols.

After several days of convalescence and a mandatory counseling session, Deputy Conlon was cleared to return to duty.

Although no one spoke about the case, the heavy sense of foreboding that none of them were truly safe, hung over the office.

CHAPTER 3

Two weeks later

EDWARD BUXTON AND his wife Paula were enjoying a leisurely glass of wine in the den when the doorbell rang. Edward went to open the door. He was surprised to see the couple standing there. Edward and his wife weren't expecting company, especially this couple. The Buxtons had only met them once—months ago.

The Buxtons had other plans for the evening, but when the man held the packet in front of Edward's face, he welcomed the couple into his home.

After pleasantries, the contents of the packet were emptied onto the kitchen island top. The Buxtons and their guests took turns snorting the lines of white powder.

Without asking, Mrs. Buxton led her male guest to her bedroom.

Mr. Buxton and his female guest exchanged some brief erotic conversation and decided to join his wife and her companion in the bedroom.

Buxton grew excited when he saw the look of desire in his guest's eyes, then gasped as the knife cut across his throat. Buxton clutched his throat, stumbled backward, and fell to the floor.

In the bedroom, Mrs. Buxton didn't see the face of her guest as the bullet penetrated the back of her head.

The two uninvited guests made sure they left nothing behind that would identify them and held hands as they left the Buxton home the same way they entered.

CHAPTER 4

ARLY SATURDAY MORNING, Deputies Zeke Jackson and Jason Conlon were on patrol together. Since the Conlon incident, Pickens decided that for nighttime 911 calls two deputies would respond in one car. Since Jackson was the senior deputy, Conlon rode shotgun. So far things had been quiet, but Saturday shortly after one in the morning, they were advised to respond to a domestic disturbance call on Foley Circle in the Harmony Hill subdivision at the northern edge of the city. The subdivision was a blue-collar neighborhood consisting of fifteen homes on three streets.

When Jackson turned onto Foley Circle, the deputies noticed that there were only four houses. All had their lights off. Two homes had cars parked in the driveway. In front of one house was a parked car on the street. There was no streetlight.

As he pulled up to the address, Jackson radioed the dispatcher and asked if they had the correct address. The dispatcher confirmed they did. Jackson turned on the spotlight and shined it at the house, searching for a house number. He located the number but noticed the front door was ajar. Sensing something was wrong, Jackson angled the car at the house so the headlights lit it up. Next, he turned the flashers on and the dash cam. Both deputies turned on their bodycams.

"Be careful, Conlon," said Jackson. "This could be a setup."

Conlon nodded, then slowly opened the passenger side door and exited with his weapon drawn. Jackson also got out with his gun drawn. Conlon looked left then right and cautiously approached the house. In his peripheral vision to his right, Conlon saw a vehicle moving. He turned just as someone opened fire. Conlon got off three shots before he was hit and went down.

Jackson returned fire from behind the hood of the patrol car and radioed, "Shots fired. Officer down. Shots fired. Officer down. Need backup."

Jackson continued firing but the shooter was was in a moving vehicle, and it sped off with its lights off. Jackson immediately went to the aid of his partner. Conlon was on the ground bleeding. His weapon was still in his hand.

"Hang on, Conlon, help is on its way." Jackson lifted Conlon's head. "Look at me, dammit. Open your eyes. Say something, anything, please." But Conlon's eyes were closed and he said nothing. Jackson worried he was gone. He stood and went to the trunk, opened it, and took out the First Aid kit. Then he ran around to the front of the vehicle, took bandages from the First Aid kit, and placed them over the wounds, attempting to stop the bleeding.

Jackson heard sirens approaching. "Stay with me, Conlon, help is coming."

Lights came on in the nearby houses, and a few people opened their doors and stood in the doorways to see what the commotion was. One neighbor was alert enough to call 911 and report the incident.

An ambulance and a patrol car pulled up beside Jackson's vehicle with lights flashing. Two EMTs rushed over to aid Conlon.

"We'll take it from here, Deputy," said a female EMT.

Jackson stepped aside and watched the EMTs administer aid to Conlon.

A male EMT shook his head. "It's bad," he said. "Let's get him in the ambulance and to the hospital." They put him on a stretcher and loaded Conlon into the ambulance.

"Can I go with him?" said Jackson.

"No," said Deputy Richie Ortiz, who had arrived at the same time the ambulance did. "You have to stay here and give your report of what happened. After that, we'll both go to the hospital."

Reluctantly Jackson agreed and both deputies watched as the ambulance left.

* * *

At the sheriff's office, the dispatcher had received both Jackson's call and the 911 call. He sent an ambulance to the scene and backup. Then he called Sheriff Pickens.

Pickens was sound asleep when his phone chirped. Marge woke and shook him.

"JD, your phone's ringing. Wake up."

He rubbed his hand over his forehead and exhaled. "Now what?" He grabbed his phone and bolted upright when he saw it was the dispatcher. "Shit, it's gonna be bad news. I know it." He answered the call and got out of bed. "Another officer down. I gotta go." He kissed her, dressed, grabbed his weapon, and left.

As Pickens drove to the scene, his thoughts were the same as they'd been during the first incident—he'd lost a deputy. When he arrived, the street was lit up by five patrol cars with their lights flashing. All the houses were lit up.

Besides Jackson's patrol car, the patrol cars for deputies Tucker, Thompson, Abrue, and Ortiz's were already there.

When the dispatcher issued the *Officer Down* notification, every officer and deputy who was part of Pickens' team had responded.

Pickens got out of his vehicle and found Amy talking to Billy. He interrupted her.

"How bad is it?" Pickens said.

"Bad," said Amy. "Conlon was rushed to the hospital. Dunne's on her way there."

"Fill me in." Pickens listened as she told him what Jackson had told her. "How is he?"

"He's shaken, but he's anxious to get to the hospital to see Conlon."

"We all are, but we got a job to do. I'll talk to him." Pickens tilted his head. "Who's the civilian?"

"Orville Walsh. He's the neighbor who called 911 as soon as he heard shooting. We got his info. Abrue and Ortiz policed the area and found shells in the street and bagged them. They also bagged the shells from Zeke's weapon. Conlon's weapon and the shells from it were also bagged separately."

"Good. Where's Jackson?"

"He's over there leaning against his vehicle." She pointed at Jackson's patrol car.

Pickens walked over to the vehicle, and Amy followed.

Jackson stood against his patrol car. His shirt had Conlon's blood on it.

"How ya doing, Zeke?"

"Okay, Sheriff. But Conlon, he's . . ." Jackson's hands trembled. "It's bad, Sheriff." He slammed his fist on the roof of his patrol car. "We were ambushed. As soon as we were out of the car, all hell broke out."

Pickens put his hand on Jackson's shoulder. "Take a deep breath and tell me what happened."

"It was like a fucking drive-by. Sorry Sergeant."

Amy waved him off.

"Conlon was hit, and I returned fire. We didn't see the shooter until it was too late, and it all happened so fast. I can't tell you what the vehicle looked like except it was black."

"That's okay. Hopefully, it will be in your bodycam footage. Why did you get out of your vehicle with your weapons drawn?"

Before Jackson could answer, Amy's phoned chimed.

"It's Dunne," she said. Amy listened and nodded. "Okay, keep us posted. He's here. I'll let him know. Thanks."

"Is Conlon okay?" said Jackson.

"He's in surgery. No word yet. His wife's there. Sergeant Dunne brought her and will call when she has an update."

"That's good for now," said Pickens. He turned back to Jackson. "Zeke, why'd you get out of your vehicle with weapons drawn?"

"It was the door. It was open."

"It was open?" Pickens turned to Amy. "Did anyone check the house, Amy?"

"I was about to send Billy and Abrue to do it," she answered.

Before Pickens could say anything else, all the car radios blasted.

"Emergency, emergency. Anyone. Need help. The sheriff's office is under attack. Need help." Then the emergency operator said, "The shooting has stopped. Please send help."

Amy said, "I can get this. You stay here."

Pickens was tempted to go, but he wanted to investigate the crime scene while it was still fresh.

"Okay, Amy, you and Billy go," said Pickens.

"I'm going, too," said Deputy Ortiz. "I was on duty there, so I need to be there."

"Get going, Ritchie. We'll handle things here," said Pickens. He pointed to Amy. "Be careful. I don't want to lose another deputy and give me an update as soon as you can."

"Don't worry. We'll be extra careful."

Amy flashed a salute, and the three left with their sirens and flashers on.

Pickens addressed Jackson. "Zeke, you up for investigating?"

"Damn right I am."

"First let's find out who owns the house." Pickens turned and yelled. "Mr. Walsh, got a moment?"

"Sure thing, Sheriff." Walsh stood by his wife still in pajama bottoms and a t-shirt. He brushed his comb-over with his hand. His wife also had on pajamas. Both hadn't bothered to dress since it was a hot night with the temperature in the eighties and humid.

Pickens approached the couple. "Thanks for calling 911."

Walsh waved him off. "Wish I coulda done more, but the shooting was over by the time I dialed. Hell, I thought I was back in Nam by the way it sounded."

"Did you see anything?"

"No, unfortunately. When I turned the porch light on, whoever attacked your deputies was gone. Sorry."

"No problem. How well do you know your neighbors?"

"Edward and Paula Buxton? Not that much. They keep to themselves. Occasionally I see them in the morning after their run." Walsh put his hand to his cheek and leaned. "She's a looker, especially in her tight running outfits." Pickens feigned a grin. "Once in a while, we have a brief conversation, mostly about their run. A few times I saw another couple go into their house, but those were rare occasions. Last week, Edward asked me if I would watch their house when they went on vacation and water their plants. They were supposed to leave this morning, but I guess they decided to leave a day early. He works for the county, and she's a nurse. Other than that, we had no contact."

"Did they give you a key?"

"Sure did. You want it?"

"If you don't mind."

"Cecilia, get their key."

Mrs. Walsh turned, went into the house, and returned with the key.

"Thanks, hon. Here you are, Sheriff."

"Do they have a dog or children?"

"Neither. Don't even have a security system. Edward thinks that sign," Walsh said, gesturing toward a sign in the front yard, "is enough to keep burglars away. Me, I got the best money can buy."

"Smart man," said Pickens. "Is there a back door and does the key unlock it?"

"Both. The door opens into the garage, and you get into the house by the door to the kitchen. Same key unlocks it."

"Thanks. Best if you and your wife go back into your house while we check out your neighbors." The Walshes left without an argument. Pickens shouted to the other neighbors. "Folks, please go inside. We don't want anything to happen. We're gonna search the house." The neighbors all complied.

"Zeke," Pickens called.

"Yeah, Sheriff?"

"Take this key and go around back and enter the house. Abrue and I will go in the front. We'll wait thirty seconds to allow you time to get in." Pickens explained how Jackson would enter the house. "Use your flashlight, and we'll use ours. We don't want to end up in a shootout with each other."

Pickens had chosen Abrue to enter the house with him. He wasn't about to send a rookie and the youngest deputy around back by herself and risk losing another rookie.

Jackson didn't laugh. He knew how serious the sheriff was. He took the key and went around back.

"Let's go, Abrue."

"Let me go first," said Abrue.

Pickens hesitated. He worried she was too new and wouldn't be cautious enough. He didn't want to lose another deputy.

"I can handle it, Sheriff. I may be a rookie, but I know what to do."

"Okay. But go in low and at the slightest movement or sound, you drop to the floor. You understand?"

"Understood."

Both turned their flashlights on and then Abrue approached the front door and opened it. She shined her light into the house, then cautiously entered.

Pickens entered behind Abrue and noticed that the door wasn't forced open. Both shined their lights around what was the living room.

"Clear," said Abrue, and she moved down a hallway to the bedrooms.

"You take the master," said Pickens. "I'll take the other rooms."

While Pickens and Abrue were searching the bedrooms, Jackson had entered the kitchen crouched down. He spotted something on the floor in the beam of his flashlight and approached.

"Jesus," Jackson said. "Got a body," he yelled.

Pickens froze and yelled, "Don't touch it and clear the room."

Pickens cleared the spare bedroom and an office.

Abrue entered the master bedroom and shined her light around the room. She almost dropped the flashlight when she saw the body of a woman slumped over the bed face down. Blood covered the back of her head. Her legs dangled over the side, and her underwear was pulled down below her knees.

"Oh, God," said Abrue. "Sheriff, you gotta see this. It's bad."

Pickens entered the room and shined his flashlight at the bed.

"Sonofabitch," said Pickens. "Back out, Abrue. Slowly, and don't touch anything."

Jackson was behind Pickens. "Another body?" he said.

"Yeah," said Pickens. "Out, now, and don't touch anything." Pickens took out his handkerchief and closed the bedroom door. They backed down the hall to the living room. "What'd you find in the kitchen?"

"Another body on the floor in front of the kitchen island. Probably the husband. His throat was slit, and he sat on the floor in a pool of his blood. It also looked like someone shot him in the head."

"Did you touch anything?" said Pickens.

"No. I stayed away from the body as you said to, then I cleared the room and joined you two."

"Okay. Outside, let's go. I'll call the ME, and an ambulance, and then Sergeant Tucker."

They carefully backed out of the house and stood on the walkway to the front entrance. Pickens dialed his wife.

Marge answered after the second ring.

"Are you at the hospital?" she said.

"No. I'm still at the house." Pickens exhaled. "We've got a problem." He explained about the shooting of Conlon, the attack on his office, and the bodies. "It started as a domestic abuse call, and now it's a homicide. I need someone here."

A crime scene investigation was in the purview of the ME's office since they had the manpower and the expertise to do it.

"I'll be there. Call your parents and tell them I'm dropping Sarah and Bailey off with them."

"You don't have to come here. Can't Tom handle it?"

Tom Morgan was the assistant medical examiner and had worked a number of crime scenes.

"He can, but I'm still coming. I'll wake my team and have them get there."

"Your whole team?"

"My whole team. How's Conlon?"

"Last I heard he was still in surgery. I'm gonna call Amy and see if she's heard anything. She's at the office, and I need to know if my dispatcher was hurt. Thanks for this. And, Marge, don't let any of your team go in the master bedroom until you have."

"It's that bad?"

"You'll see when you get here. I called for an ambulance. And . . ."

"I know. I do, too," Marge said.

Pickens didn't have to finish his statement. She knew what he'd say.

Pickens then called Amy. He hoped she didn't have bad news, and the emergency operator wasn't hurt.

*   *   *

When Amy, Billy and Ritchie arrived at the sheriff's office, the street was deserted. They got out of their patrol cars and approached the entrance. The windows were shattered, and the door and walls were riddled with bullet holes. It looked like the after effect of a firefight.

"What the hell happened here?" said Billy.

"I ain't seen anything like this since my time in Afghanistan," said Ritchie.

"Let's hope the emergency operator wasn't hurt," said Amy. "Butler, you okay?" she yelled.

Twenty-three-year-old Joey Butler was the nighttime emergency operator. Butler was a grad student by day and the emergency operator at night to pay his school expenses. He was the one who issued the all-out emergency call.

"Yeah, I'm fine," Butler called back from inside.

Amy and the deputies entered the office.

"Where the hell are you?" shouted Billy. Corporal Billy Thompson was in charge of the emergency operators and dispatchers.

Butler stood from the desk he was hiding behind. "Over here. Are they gone?"

"They're gone," said Amy. "What happened?"

"One minute it was quiet, and I was listening to the chatter from you guys. Then all hell broke out." Butler exhaled. "First the windows shattered and that's when I hit the floor. Can't say how many shooters there were, but it seemed like there was an army out there. It wasn't long after I sent my distress call before it ended." Butler looked down. "I almost peed my pants."

Billy and Ritchie grinned.

"It's not funny. You guys are trained for this. I'm a fucking college student."

"We're just glad you're okay," said Billy. "And for your info, we're not trained for something like this. Maybe Ritchie was in the marines. But not me."

"Maybe I should find another job."

"Hell no," said Amy. "We couldn't replace you. Hopefully, this was an isolated incident."

"I know. Besides, except for lately, I get to study when I'm on duty. This is a sweet gig, and I ain't giving it up."

"You hear that, Billy? A sweet gig for a sweet guy."

Ritchie blew Butler a kiss.

"Screw you, Ritchie."

Amy ignored their crude remarks. If it helped relieve the stress of the situation, it was fine with her. The office damage could be repaired, but the shock of being caught in a firestorm if you're not used to it could damage one's psyche.

"Okay, boys, that's enough for now. We got things to do. Billy, get the camera and take pictures of the damage here and get shots of the exterior. Then you and Ritchie police the sidewalk and street for shells. Also, check for witnesses. Maybe someone saw the shooters. At this hour, I doubt it but check anyway. And be careful, the shooter might be waiting to shoot more of us."

"What the hell's going on, Amy?" asked Ortiz. "Why would someone want to take us out?"

Amy took a deep breath. "I wish I knew, Ritchie, that's why I said, be careful."

"We'll be extra careful," said Billy.

Amy raised an index finger. "While you're at it, check Lydia's Bakery. Someone may have come in early to get things ready, and they may have a camera outside."

"What about me?" said Butler.

"You're still on duty. Check your radio and make sure it's working. Then help clean up this mess. I'm gonna call the sheriff."

*   *   *

Pickens was anxiously awaiting an update from Amy. He was about to call her when his phone chirped.

"It's about time, Amy. What happened?"

"Shit happened, that's what." She told him what Butler had said and that he was okay, and that Billy and Ritchie were policing the street. "Everyone is concerned for their safety and being extra cautious."

"Sonofabitch," said Pickens.

"Yeah," replied Amy. "How are things there?"

"Not good. We entered the house and found two bodies. I'm waiting for the ME."

"Want me to come there?"

"No. I'll handle it. You finish up there, then go to the hospital. Have you heard from Dunne?"

"Not yet. I'll call her and have her call you. Is there anything we can do on this end?"

"Yeah. Have Billy run the names of the homeowners. He can get the address from Butler. Have him get the time of the first 911 call and the phone number it came from. Butler should have that info. Start a board. List all three incidents and their times. When I get there, we'll put it all together. Maybe we can trace the first 911 call and get a name."

"You staying there till the ME finishes?"

"Got no choice. You got your situation, I got mine, and someone has to go to the hospital. I'll go after I finish here."

"Okay, JD. We need someone on the street. Abrue or Zeke? Ritchie's on duty here."

"Neither. I'm sending Abrue home and Zeke to the hospital to relieve Dunne after we finish here. If anything happens, Ritchie can handle it, or you or Billy. I'd do it myself, but I've got to be here and then at the hospital. Conlon . . ."

"Yeah, Conlon and his wife need to see you. Billy and I can handle things if necessary.

"Thanks, Amy."

"Any idea why someone is targeting us?"

"Not a clue. But like I said, we all need to be extra cautious."

CHAPTER 5

WHEN TOM MORGAN and the two criminalists, Betty-Jean Carr and Andy Doring, arrived at the Buxton house, an ambulance was already there. Morgan directed the criminalists to process the scene except for the master bedroom, as Marge had instructed.

"Tom," said Pickens. "As soon as you can, can you send Billy all the crime scene photos?"

"Don't worry, JD," said Marge, who had just arrived, "he knows the drill." Morgan gave them a thumbs-up. "Let us do our jobs, JD, and stay out of our way."

Pickens raised both palms.

"I'm going to check the master bedroom. Is it really that bad?"

Pickens shook his head. "You'll see."

Marge nodded then entered the house and went to the master bedroom. She gasped when she saw the victim. She had seen a number of horrible crime scenes, but this one disturbed her because of its violent nature. Marge set aside her feelings, put on latex gloves and a mask, took a camera from her bag, and took pictures of the victim and the entire room. Next, she carefully processed the victim, again, taking pictures as she did. She removed the woman's underwear and put them in an evidence bag and completed a rape kit. She checked the bed for possible DNA evidence.

After she finished in the master bedroom, Marge stepped out and called for Morgan.

"Yes, Marge," Morgan said, then glanced into the room. "Was it bad?"

"Yes, she was sodomized. I don't want Betty-Jean or Andy to see her. You and I will bag her."

Morgan nodded. "The body in the kitchen may be her husband. He was shot point blank in the forehead. Based on the position of the body, I'd say the shot was post mortem after the killer slit his throat." Morgan exhaled. "Sick bastard."

"Or bastards," said Marge. "I didn't find any shells. Were there any in the kitchen?"

"Unfortunately, no."

"We'll tell JD. And, Tom . . ."

"Yeah, I know. You're gonna work the bodies when we get to the morgue."

"I have to start working them. It's necessary. Can you help me?"

Morgan grinned. "Wouldn't think otherwise. I'll ask the criminalists if they can. We owe JD and his team that much."

"Thanks, Tom."

Marge and Morgan bagged the woman's body. The criminalists bagged the man. Marge went outside, stood on the front walkway, and directed the EMTs to get the bodies into the ambulance and to the coroner's office.

Andy Doring rode with the ambulance to the coroner's office so he could open the door for the EMTs.

"We're done here, JD," said Marge

"Did anyone see the woman?"

"Just Tom. He helped me bag her."

"Was she?"

"Yes."

"Before or after?"

"I think before."

Pickens felt the heat from anger flushing through his body. "What kind of sick bastard degrades a woman like that and then shoots her?"

Since Marge was used to dealing with the dead, she was able to check her emotions. "A *psychopath*. The same kind that killed the husband. And, this wasn't a random killing. It was planned."

Both thought about the serial killer that threatened Pickens and his family several years ago.

"Unfortunately, we didn't find any shells. The killer or killers were careful."

"Is there anything you can tell me?"

Marge nodded. "Probable cause for the wife was a gunshot wound. For the husband, severed carotid artery. We'll know more after the autopsies." She checked her watch. It said six-thirty. Five hours had passed since the 911 call and the attack on Jackson and Abrue. "TOD, between six and midnight yesterday."

Pickens' head snapped back. "That's hours before the 911 call. Which means they killed the Buxtons, called 911 hours later, and waited for my deputies to arrive."

"Or," said Marge, "whoever killed the Buxtons were long gone before your deputies arrived."

"Sonofabitch. If the shooters hadn't killed the Buxtons, then how did it happen? And who made the 911 call? It was a planned ambush. The shooters left here and shot up my office." A chill ran down Pickens' spine. "Why?"

Marge shook her head. "Sorry, JD, that's your bailiwick, not mine. I'll be at the morgue working until I have more answers for you." She lowered her voice so only he could hear. "And,

JD, about the pictures from the scene." Curious, he raised his eyebrows. "Are you sure you want Billy to see them, especially of the wife?"

Pickens glanced around uneasily. "No. Send them to my e-mail address at my office. I can print them on my printer. Billy doesn't need to see them." Marge nodded agreement. "Thanks, Marge. After I go to the hospital, I'm going to the office. Don't know how long I'll be there. I'll call my parents and tell them we may be working the entire weekend."

"They'll be happy to keep Sarah and Bailey."

"Yeah," said Pickens.

"Any word on Conlon?"

"Not yet. I'm sending Zeke there. He's anxious to see his partner. Thanks, Marge, and thank your team."

"I will."

Pickens and Marge stepped back while Betty-Jean sealed the front door with crime scene tape.

"We're done here," said Morgan. "Betty-Jean's going with me. She and Andy will work as long as we need them."

"Thanks, Tom," said Marge. "We'll let you know when we have something, JD."

"If there's any way you could identify the caliber of the weapon, I'd like to know as soon as possible. It might match Conlon's shooter and whoever shot up my office."

"It will have to be from a slug if we find one. I'll put Andy on it as soon as we do."

Marge left and followed the crime scene van.

"Abrue," Pickens called.

"Yes, Sheriff?"

"Go home and rest until your shift starts."

"If you don't mind, I'd prefer to start my shift now. We're down one deputy, and Conlon was my friend. I need to help my fellow deputies. I'll work without overtime pay if necessary, but

I'm not going home." Abrue raised a finger. "And, Sheriff, the shells we found in the street didn't come from the type of gun that Conlon was shot with that first time."

"You sure?"

"Absolutely. I know my weapons, and I looked at the casings. They weren't from a .38. They were from an assault rifle. Probably the same gun was used at your office."

"Shit. Call Amy and tell her. Thanks, Abrue." Pickens paused. "You prefer Lea or Abrue?"

Abrue grinned. "Definitely Abrue. Same as Conlon."

Pickens knew he had a team that was devoted to helping him but hadn't expected the newest deputy was that devoted, too.

"Thanks. We need someone here at least until Amy and I can get back to go over the scene. You be careful and don't answer a call without backup. That's an order."

"Got it."

"Zeke, you got a clean shirt in your car?"

"Yeah?'

"Change into it and get your ass to the hospital. I'll be right behind you."

Zeke didn't respond as he went to his car, grabbed the clean shirt, put it on, and was gone in a New York minute.

Abrue backed her patrol car into the driveway, and Pickens headed for the hospital.

CHAPTER 6

PICKENS PULLED INTO the hospital's visitor parking lot and noticed three vehicles. Two belonged to Dunne and Jackson. The other Pickens thought might belong to an expectant father who had delivered his wife to the maternity ward. As Pickens stepped out of his SUV, he felt the warmth from the sun that was full up. The temperature had climbed to ninety—a sign that it was going to be an unbearably hot and humid day.

The County Memorial Hospital was in a medical complex strategically located between the county's two cities. Constructed in 1949 and renovated in 2002, the hospital was in a two-story brick building and had thirty-five patient rooms.

Pickens crossed the parking lot and entered through the emergency entrance. He didn't have to ask where Conlon was. The duty nurse knew why he was there and directed him to the surgical waiting room.

As he entered, Pickens saw Dunne with her arms around Conlon's wife. Jackson was by himself, slumped over with his head in his hands. Pickens' first thought was that Conlon didn't make it through surgery, and he had lost one of his rookies.

Pickens had been reluctant to hire Conlon fresh out of the academy, but Dunne had recommended him. The reluctance wasn't because he was a rookie. It was because Conlon was a young father with a pregnant wife and two other children. Pickens had hoped for an experienced but unmarried deputy.

When Jackson looked up and saw Pickens, he immediately stood. His eyes were red and puffy from crying. It wasn't something you'd expect to see from Jackson, a rough and tumble man. Jackson shook his head.

Pickens knew his worst fear had happened. Conlon didn't make it.

"It's my fault, Sheriff," said Jackson. "I should have let him drive when he asked me. I would have been the first out of the car, and it would be me who got shot."

"Hold on, Deputy. It wasn't your fault. You were the senior deputy and should have been driving. Don't blame yourself. Blame the shooter."

Jackson ran both hands through his hair. "Yeah, but still . . ."

"Don't go there, Zeke. Let it rest."

Jackson shook his head and sat with his face in his hands.

Sergeant Dunne walked over to Pickens. As always, Dunne was meticulously dressed in her uniform with her weapon and a radio strapped to her side. She too had puffy eyes. Conlon's wife sat alone with her legs stretched out and sobbing.

"How's she taking it, Sergeant?" said Pickens.

Dunne pursed her lips and shook her head. "Really bad. Her kids are with her mother. After that last incident, she had her mother come and stay with them in case she went into labor. She called Conlon's parents, and they'll be here later. They're coming from out of town. Let me introduce you to her."

Pickens and Dunne walked toward Conlon's wife.

Pickens felt an ache in the back of his throat. He'd never lost a deputy before and hadn't had to face a grieving spouse, especially a pregnant one. Pickens had no words for such an occasion. Marge would know what he should say, but she wasn't there. It was up to him, and he wished he had the presence of mind like his dad did. He was about to say something, but Conlon's wife suddenly clutched her stomach.

"Oh, God," Conlon's wife cried out. "My water just broke. I think the baby's coming."

Jackson's mouth fell open as he stood. Pickens and Dunne rushed to the woman. Jackson ran to get a nurse.

"Stay calm, Mrs. Conlon," said Pickens.

"Easy for you to say, Sheriff. You ever have a baby?"

"Uh, no," Pickens stammered.

"Then you try to stay calm. I lost my husband, and now I'm about to give birth to his son. Ah!" she screamed. "Fuck staying calm, this baby's coming out, now," she said then howled again. "Where's Jason when I need him? Call my mom please, Sergeant Dunne."

Pickens was at a loss for words and felt useless. He wasn't in the delivery room when Sarah was born and had no idea what Marge went through during delivery. Pickens also wasn't there when her water broke. He was fishing with Leroy, and Marge gave birth shortly after he arrived at the hospital.

Dunne called Mrs. Conlon's mother and told her to come to the hospital. The baby was coming.

Two nurses rushed to Mrs. Conlon, placed her on a gurney, and wheeled her to maternity.

Pickens sat, relieved that at least for now he didn't have to offer condolences to Conlon's wife. Something he dreaded. But he'd have to face Conlon's mother-in-law and maybe his parents.

"Sheriff, if you'd like," said Dunne, "I can talk to her mother, and I can stay until Conlon's parents get here." Pickens looked up at her. "You can get started on Conlon's investigation."

Pickens' eyes narrowed. He had assumed Jackson told Dunne about the murders.

"It's not just Conlon," he said. "We found two bodies in

the house, and their deaths may not be related to the Conlon ambush."

Dunne grimaced. "Are you sure?"

"Yes. That TOD was Friday evening, and unless the shooters hung around until Zeke and Conlon showed up, there had to be another set of killers. We'll know more after the ME checks for a slug in the victims." Pickens exhaled. "But for now, that's my guess."

"Sheriff, if you'd like, I can wait here until the baby is delivered, and I can talk to her mother." Dunne glanced at Jackson. He was pacing like an expectant father. "You can take Jackson with you and start your investigations."

In his mind, Pickens wondered what he'd do when he had to confront Conlon's wife and her mother. If Dunne handled it, he'd have time to talk to Amy and Marge about how to have the conversations.

"If you don't mind, that would be a big help. I'll come back later today and speak to them."

Dunne raised her palm. "No, you go ahead. I'll also speak to Conlon's parents when they get here."

The knot in Pickens' stomach loosened. "Thanks, Sergeant Dunne." He looked at Jackson. "Let's go, Zeke."

Jackson covered his mouth with his hand. He seemed relieved to have something to do. "I'm right behind you, Sheriff."

* * *

Before Pickens left the hospital parking lot, he directed Jackson to return to the scene so he and Abrue could canvas the neighbors. They were to ask if anyone saw or heard anything Friday afternoon or evening.

As he started to leave, Pickens saw Conlon's mother-in-law and his children crossing the parking lot.

Pickens called Amy and apprised her of the situation.

"Damn, JD," said Amy, "we've never lost a deputy. Billy and the other deputies will be pissed like I am?"

"I'm pissed too. You and I will visit Conlon's wife after we finished clearing the scene. She needs time with her newborn."

When Pickens arrived at the sheriff's office, Amy had the glass from the shot-out windows cleared away, and Billy was at work on his computers. She had also updated the whiteboard. She added *8/4/18*.

"Where'd you get the plywood for the windows and entryway?" Pickens said.

Amy stepped away from the chalkboard and turned. "I woke the manager at MacLeay's Lumber Yard and got it there. He wasn't happy, but because your father had worked there, he obliged. He said anything for Mr. Pickens' son."

Pickens smiled. "He's a nice guy once you get to know him." Pickens glanced at the whiteboard. "Good start." Amy had written *Conlon Ambush* and *Buxton Murders* across the top and the date. She listed the time under Conlon and an approximate time under Buxton. Amy also started a timeline.

"Once we know more, I'll add more to the timeline." She paused for reflection. "How bad were Conlon's injuries?"

"Multiple wounds to the arms, legs, and a fatal one to the head. He might have survived the arms and legs, but the slug damaged the brain, and they couldn't save him." Pickens exhaled. "It's a shame he won't get to see his son born."

Amy shook her head. "Yeah. Maybe the baby will ease her pain some. Hopefully."

"Yeah, hopefully. We'll visit her after we finish at the scene. You ready to go?"

"Might as well get it over with. You saw it, I didn't, but I understand it wasn't pretty."

"Not by a long shot." Pickens turned. "Billy, I want you to dig deep on the Buxtons. Both of them. Phone records, financials, anything. See if they had any relatives or friends on Facebook. Check with the ME's office. Find out if they finished with ballistics and if they found a slug in the victims." He pointed an index finger. "I want something when I get back. No one's going home until we got something." He glanced around the room. "Everyone understand?" Amy, Billy, and the dispatcher nodded. "Good. Let's go, Amy."

"Wait," said Billy. "I just traced the 911 call. It didn't come from the home's landline. It was from a cell phone."

Pickens' brows hiked. "Did you trace the phone?"

Billy pursed his lips and shook his head. "It was a burner. Sorry."

"A burner?" said Amy. "Then who called 911? If it was the shooters and the Buxtons were killed sometime Friday, how did the shooters know to call 911?"

"They didn't," said Billy. "They took a chance and were probably monitoring our calls. Zeke and Conlon were setup."

Pickens slammed his fist on a desk. "Sonofabitch, why? Were they deliberately targeting Conlon?"

"I hate this," said Billy. "You want me to dig into Conlon?"

"Yes," said Pickens. "What about the camera out front? Was there anything?"

"I'll pull up the feed and check." When Billy opened the feed, everyone gathered around him and leaned over his shoulders to look.

"Fast forward to the time of the shooting," said Pickens. Billy advanced the feed. "There, freeze it." What they saw angered them. A person wearing a balaclava face mask was pointing an automatic weapon at the entrance. "Let it run." As the feed advanced, the shooter sprayed the entrance with bullets, but then the feed ended.

"He shot the camera," said Billy. "That's all we got."

"Any chance you could enhance it and get the identity of the vehicle?" said Pickens.

"I'll try." Billy enhanced the feed, but the getaway vehicle wasn't in it. "Sorry, Sheriff."

"At least you tried," said Pickens. "Amy, let's go."

Amy grabbed Pickens arm. "Wait," she said. "I can't believe I'm saying this, but maybe you should call Mitch Hubbard."

"Not a bad idea. We could use Mitch's experience." Mitch Hubbard was a retired Orlando homicide detective and had helped Pickens on the last two cases. But those cases consisted of crimes committed decades ago. This case was more like Hubbard was used to investigating. "First I have to check my e-mail."

Pickens walked into his office, opened his laptop, and brought up his e-mail. The pictures of the victims from the crime scene were there. He printed the e-mail and the photos, put them in a folder, and shut his laptop down. He then called Hubbard, advised him of the situation, the location, and asked Hubbard to meet him and Amy at the scene.

Amy then followed Pickens out the door and into his SUV.

CHAPTER 7

A T THE MORGUE, the bodies of Edward and Paula Buxton were on autopsy tables, both covered with sheets as Marge and Tom Morgan prepared to do the autopsies. Betty-Jean was processing the rape kit, the woman's underwear, and the bed coverings. Andy had started the ballistics on the shells from the shooting of Deputy Conlon.

"I'll take the wife," Marge said with a bitter tang in her mouth. "Maybe we'll get lucky, and the killer left prints on her body."

"Andy might find prints on her underwear and the shells," said Morgan. Marge flinched when he mentioned the underwear. She still felt disgusted from what the killer had done to the woman. "And DNA from the rape kit," said Morgan. "I don't expect any prints on the husband. I don't think the killer touched him."

Both switched on the magnifying lights. Marge probed the back of the woman's head, while Morgan checked the husband's forehead.

"Got a slug," said Marge as she held it under the magnifying light.

"Got one, too," said Morgan, and he did the same. "Looks like it's from a .22." He dropped it in a dish and labeled it, *husband.* "I'll get it to Andy. He can verify the caliber of the weapon."

"Mine also looks like a .22," said Marge, and dropped it in a dish and labeled it, *wife.* "Let's take pictures and send them to JD." She got a camera and added the shots of the slugs to her e-mail. Next, she used magnetic fingerprint powder to dust the body, shined the lamp over it, and carefully checked for prints. "Got latent prints on her hips and buttocks." Just saying the words angered Marge. "He wanted her to feel him touch her." She shook her head. "The bastard wanted her to know he enjoyed what he did to her. I hope JD catches him and screw bringing him to justice. Just shoot him." Marge couldn't control her anger over the killer's act of degradation. "Tom, could you take over for me? I need to step away." She had never walked away from an autopsy no matter how bad, but this one got to her.

"I'll take care of it," said Morgan. "You up to doing the husband?"

Marge felt a tenseness in her stomach and was uncertain if she could. She took a deep breath, exhaled, and regained her composure.

"I'll do it. Thanks, Tom."

They switched places, and Marge continued the autopsy on the husband. Morgan snapped pictures of the prints and sent them to Andy then completed the wife's autopsy.

"Husband's autopsy didn't reveal anything alarming," said Marge. "What about the wife's?"

"Nothing. We'll know more after the tox screens come back."

"The husband was definitely shot post mortem after his carotid artery was slit," said Marge.

"If both slugs were from the same weapon, the husband could have been stabbed by the same person that killed the wife and then shot afterward for the fun of it." Morgan shook his head. "It makes no sense."

"Nothing a *psychopath* does makes sense. It raises the possibility that there might have been one killer."

"If so," said Morgan. "then the husband saw his killer, was stabbed, then the killer went after the wife. But why?"

"Like you said, it makes no sense. We'll let JD figure it out." Marge stepped back from the table and removed her surgical gloves. "I'm done, what about you?"

Morgan exhaled. "I'm done, too. I put her TOD as between five and nine, not midnight." He took a deep breath then exhaled. "Is it too early to get drunk? Because I could use a drink."

His comment lightened the mood.

"I've got a medicinal bottle in my office. Let's have a drink."

Morgan removed his surgical gloves and followed Marge to her office. She unlocked a desk drawer, removed a bottle, two glasses and poured two drinks.

"I hate murder cases," said Morgan, and downed his drink. Marge did the same.

Marge sent an e-mail to Pickens with a one paragraph summary of their findings and the pictures of the bodies and slugs. She added that her report would be more conclusive.

CHAPTER 8

O N THE WAY to the crime scene, Amy noticed the folder on the console next to Pickens.

"What's in the folder?" she said.

"The ME's summary and photos."

"Can I see them?"

Pickens was reluctant, but eventually, she'd have to see them. "They're not pretty," he said.

"I didn't expect they would be. Let me see them." Pickens handed her the folder. Amy read the summary and cringed when she saw the photos. "Did he sodomize her before or after?"

Pickens gripped the steering wheel. "Before, according to Marge."

Amy closed the file and gave it back to him. "I've seen enough. I agree with Marge. We're dealing with a *psychopath*."

"It makes it a third time for us." Pickens turned onto Foley Circle and saw three vehicles parked in front of the Buxton house. "That's Mitch's pickup. He got here fast. I wonder why he's waiting in it." Pickens parked, and he and Amy walked over to Hubbard's truck.

Hubbard stepped out. "Bout time you got here," said Hubbard. "Your deputies made me stay in my truck."

Pickens grinned. "Just doing their job, Mitch."

Abrue and Jackson approached. "Didn't want him disturbing the crime scene, Sheriff," said Abrue.

Pickens raised his hand. "No problem, Abrue. I'd a done the same thing under the circumstances."

"How's Conlon's wife? Zeke told me what happened."

"All I know she was in maternity when I left the hospital."

Abrue shook her head. "Jason confided in me that he was happy he'd finally be there for the birth of his third child. He was in Afghanistan during the others. He and Shirley were excited." Abrue's chin trembled. "Now this."

"It's okay, Abrue. Let it out. We're all hurting." Pickens directed his attention to Hubbard.

"Good to see you, Mitch," said Pickens to Hubbard, who nodded. "Okay, deputies tell me what you learned."

Just as Abrue was about to tell Pickens about the neighborhood canvass, Jimmy Noseby, the local reporter pulled up behind Pickens.

"Just what we need," said Pickens. Noseby approached. "What do you want, Nosey?"

"It's—" said Noseby, "Never mind. I heard about the shooting. I went by the hospital, but they won't tell me anything. I stopped by your office, and they said you'd be here. Can you tell me what happened? How's your deputy?"

"That's a mouth full, Nosey. All I'll say is that Deputy Conlon didn't make it, and we're working a crime scene. If you want more, you'll have to wait until I finish my investigation." Noseby's jaw dropped and Pickens added more forcefully, "That's it. Now get, or I'll have a deputy escort you."

Noseby stomped off, got in his car, and left.

"Okay, Abrue, let's hear it."

Deputy Abrue referred to her notepad. "I talked to the neighbors on the left side of the Buxton's house. Both met after work last night at Leroy's Bar-B-Que Pit for dinner."

Leroy's was owned by Pickens high school friend, Leroy Jones.

"I probably saw them there," said Pickens. "I was there with my wife and daughter. We go there almost every Friday night.

Abrue nodded. "After dinner, they went to the Bucket & Boots Country and Western Bar for drinks and dancing. They were home by midnight, didn't notice anything, and went to bed." Abrue closed her notepad. "That's it."

"What about you, Zeke?"

Zeke referred to his notepad. "I talked to the Walshes. They went to a friend's home for cocktails at four. Stayed for dinner and were home by eight. Noticed the Buxtons lights were off and thought they had left a day early. They went to bed at ten and were asleep until the shooting started."

"That agrees with what Mr. Walsh said when I talked to him," said Pickens.

"So, they saw nothing out of the ordinary?" said Amy.

"That's what they said, Sergeant." Zeke checked his notes. "The neighbors on the right, next to them had gone to Orlando to pick up relatives. They left at five, returned at eleven and were in bed by midnight. Like the others, they noticed nothing out of the ordinary until the shooting." Zeke flipped his notepad closed. "That's it, Sheriff, no help."

Pickens shook his head and exhaled. "I was hoping for something, but it is what it is." He turned to Hubbard. "You want to go inside, Mitch?"

"Yes, but do you have any photos?"

Pickens handed him the folder. "There's a summary from the ME."

Hubbard opened the folder and began reading the summary. Next, he looked at the photos. "Okay, let's go inside."

Amy and Hubbard followed Pickens to the kitchen.

Hubbard reread the summary, then started shuffling through the photos. He kept a picture of the husband on top.

"Okay, let's see the bedroom," said Hubbard.

Pickens led the way.

The bed had already been stripped and the items removed by the crime scene unit.

Hubbard reshuffled the photos and placed the wife's on top. He looked at it and said, "Sick bastard that did this."

"Yeah," said Pickens.

"Let's go back to the kitchen," said Hubbard.

Amy led the way as Hubbard and Pickens followed.

"So, what's your assessment, Mitch?"

Hubbard reread the summary, then shuffled the photos. Next, he rubbed his chin.

"I agree with the ME. A *psychopath* did this. Also, there was only one killer."

"How can you tell?" said Amy.

"First, I noticed there was no forced entry, so the victims may have known the killer or expected him. Possibly a cab, Uber driver, friend, or relative. He surprises the husband and," Hubbard made a slicing motion with his hand, "slits his throat then goes after the wife. Surprises her and rapes her. Then he shoots her. Walks back to the kitchen and shoots the husband for the thrill. He used the same .22 revolver on both." Hubbard tilted his head. "That's my theory. You got a better one?"

Pickens scratched his head. "Sounds plausible. What do you think, Amy?"

"Fits the definition of a *psychopath*," said Amy. "It works for me, too."

Pickens started to comment but was interrupted by Jackson.

"Sheriff, there's an Uber driver here. Says she's supposed to pick up the Buxtons. What should I tell her?"

"One suspect eliminated," said Hubbard. "Let's talk to her anyway."

"Keep her there, Zeke, we're coming. We want to talk to her."

Jackson waved his hand and went to keep the driver in her car.

Amy and Hubbard followed Pickens. The Uber driver sat nervously in her car as Pickens approached.

"Is there something wrong, Sheriff?" said the driver. "I was told to pick up." She checked her phone. "The Buxtons."

Pickens waved her off. "Sorry, your passengers won't need you. But can you tell me when you got the request for pick up?"

She rechecked her phone. "Yesterday afternoon at two-thirty with pick up at noon today. I'm a little early."

"Okay, thanks," said Pickens. "You might as well go and tell your supervisor or whoever that I canceled your order."

The driver shrugged then left.

"Cross off cab and Uber driver as suspects," said Amy.

"That leaves possibly a relative or friend," said Hubbard. "Was there an appointment calendar in the house or on their phones?"

"I'll go check the kitchen and bedroom," said Amy.

"If they had phones," said Pickens, "they'd be with the bodies. I'll call the ME."

A minute later, Amy returned. "An appointment calendar in the kitchen by the wall phone, but no appointments for yesterday," said Amy. "Only the Uber for today. What about the fact that the door was ajar when Zeke and Conlon arrived?"

"That wasn't in the summary," said Hubbard. "Care to make a guess, JD?"

Pickens scratched his chin. "He wanted the bodies found, and the Uber driver would have."

"Which is in keeping with a *psychopath*," said Amy.

"Now what?" said Pickens.

"Like any homicide," said Hubbard, "we start at square one."

Pickens checked the time. "Square one has to wait," he said. "I've got to talk to Conlon's widow. Amy, so do you."

"Sheriff," said Abrue, "when you see Shirley, tell her I'll be by to see her after my shift ends."

"That'll have to be tomorrow, Abrue. Everyone is on twenty-four-hour duty, but I'll give her your message. Your job is to sit on the house and make sure the reporter doesn't come back. If he does, you have my permission to arrest him." Abrue nodded.

Amy noticed Zeke was off by himself in the driveway.

"He's been doing that since this morning," said Abrue. "And mumbling something to himself."

Amy wandered over to Jackson. "Zeke, you okay?"

He shook his head and said softly, "No. I've been trying to make sense of what happened to Conlon. There's something I missed."

Jackson was six-foot-three, weighed two hundred thirty pounds and had played offensive tackle in high school and junior college before joining law enforcement.

Amy placed her hand on his arm. "You gotta let it go, Zeke, or it will eat you up. We'll figure it out and get the shooter."

Pickens overheard the conversation and realized that Jackson had been up all night. "Zeke, go home, shower, and get some sleep. You'll feel better. Then you can go to the Warfield office. We don't need you here." Jackson was about to protest. "That's an order, Deputy."

Jackson dropped his head, then turned and left.

"What do you want me to do?" said Hubbard.

"Finish working the scene, both the murder and the ambush. You might want to talk to the next-door neighbor. He was friendly with the victims. Enough that they gave him a key to their house. I bet he knows a lot about them. And, if you can, stop by the ME's office and get whatever info they have."

"No problem. I'll see you at your office. I'll call Donna and tell her I'll be working late."

"Thanks, Mitch. Let's go, Amy."

CHAPTER 9

Late Saturday afternoon

URING THE DRIVE to the hospital, Pickens and Amy were deep in silence. Pickens's hands clenched the steering wheel. Amy tapped her fingers on her knee.

Amy finally broke the silence. "You worried about meeting with Conlon's widow?"

Pickens would have preferred the word wife instead of Conlon's widow. "I already met her. We didn't talk much because she went into labor."

"Oh, a double whammy. You know what you're going to say to her?"

Pickens exhaled. "Conlon was Dunne's deputy. She already spoke to her. But as sheriff, I must speak to her. That's why you're with me." He breathed deeply. "You've done this before, and it's your job to make sure I don't screw up."

"You won't," said Amy.

"I hope not. I wish it were to congratulate her on the birth of Conlon's child."

Amy tapped him gently on his leg. "You'll do that too. Trust me you'll do fine, and Sergeant Dunne and I will be there for you."

Pickens turned his head and grinned. "Yeah, you two are like sisters to me. Thanks."

Amy smiled. "We got your back, bro."

Pickens grinned. "I noticed you didn't say much at the house. You think Mitch is on to something?"

"I think his theory is plausible. If only he could come up with something on the Conlon shooting."

Pickens glanced at her. "Yeah. Maybe when we get back Billy will have something on it."

"Zeke blamed himself and was suffering with it. What are you going to do about him?"

Pickens' eyelids hiked. "Yeah, we'll all be feeling it when this is over. Any suggestions? I can't bury him in Warfield. He'll want to get back in the investigation, and we'll need him."

"He'd benefit from counseling."

"You offering your services?"

Amy's head shook. "No. It would be best if someone from the outside did it. Eventually, we'll all need it, but not from me. I'll recommend someone, but knowing Zeke, he'll resist."

"I'll give him the choice of counseling or a desk. Zeke will choose counseling."

Pickens turned into the hospital parking lot.

"Now that we're here, are you up to talking to Conlon's wife?"

Pickens exhaled. "No, but I'll do it. Just make sure I don't screw it up. I hope his kids and mother-in-law already left."

CHAPTER 10

As Pickens and Amy walked toward the front entrance of the hospital, a middle-aged couple and two young boys were exiting. One of the boys approached Pickens.

"Are you the sheriff?" said the young boy.

"I sure am," said Pickens.

"Are you gonna catch the man who took my daddy?"

Pickens took a deep breath. "I'm going to do everything I can to catch the person. So is my assistant, Detective Sergeant Amy Tucker."

"Are you the sergeant my dad calls Amy?" said the other boy.

"Yes, sir, and you can call me Amy, too."

"Okay, Jason, that's enough. We have to go home now," said the woman. "Grampa needs a nap."

Pickens looked at her and the man. There was a slight resemblance between Deputy Conlon and the man.

"Mr. and Mrs. Conlon, I'm Sheriff Pickens, and I'm sorry for your loss." He extended his hand, but neither Mr. or Mrs. Conlon took it. "Your son was one of my best deputies."

"Thank you," said Conlon's mother. "We'll be making arrangements for our son."

"My office will arrange for full honors."

"That won't be necessary," said Conlon's mother. "I'm sorry, but we have to get the boys home. Let's go boys."

The two boys slumped their shoulders.

"Do we have to?" said Jason.

"Yes," said Conlon's father. "Don't argue with your grandmother. Let's go."

"Bye, Sheriff Pickens and Amy," said Jason as the boys left, followed by their grandparents.

"That was cold," said Pickens.

"Maybe," said Amy. "They're grieving, and I guess they just want to get away from the hospital."

Pickens tilted his head. "If you say so. Let's go visit Conlon's wife."

When Pickens and Amy entered the hospital, they went right to the information desk. They didn't have to ask for Mrs. Conlon's room. Apparently, as the wife of a fallen deputy and mother of his newborn daughter, Shirley Conlon had become a celebrity, and everyone wanted to assist her. The information desk sent them to one of the two private rooms the hospital had for VIPs.

Upon arriving at Conlon's room, Pickens and Amy were met by Sergeant Dunne.

"Sheriff," said Dunne, "you just missed Conlon's parents." Dunne and Amy made eye contact. Their way of acknowledging each other.

"We met them at the entrance," said Pickens. "They didn't seem to want to talk about their son."

"Mrs. Conlon is having a hard time dealing with his death," said Dunne.

"I'm sure she is," said Pickens.

"She said when Conlon enlisted, she didn't want him to deploy and worried the whole time he was serving. She hoped after he got out of the service, he'd go back to college, get a degree, and go into a safe profession."

"What's a safe profession, today?" said Pickens.

"I almost said that, but under the circumstances, I didn't. Conlon's parents paid their respects to his wife, saw the newborn, then didn't want to be in the hospital. That's why they took the grandchildren home." Dunne shook her head. "I don't blame them."

"How's Conlon's wife holding up?" said Amy.

"Hard to tell. Shirley has the baby, and her mother is with her. The hospital staff has been a blessing to her. But I'm sure it will soon hit her about her husband."

"Probably after her mother leaves," said Pickens. "Will she see us?"

"She's been asking for you."

Pickens' eyes narrowed.

"I think she wants to apologize for the way she reacted when she went into labor."

Pickens grinned. "She doesn't have to. Under the circumstances, she had a right to."

"Any leads yet?" said Dunne.

Pickens shook his head. "We're considering the possibility that Conlon might have been targeted. After all, that was the second time he'd been shot at. It's just a hunch. Is there anything you know about Conlon that might help?"

"Not that I know of. Deputy Abrue might. She and Conlon were tight since they went through the academy together, and she and Conlon's wife were close. I'll ask her if you'd like me to."

"Couldn't hurt," said Pickens. "She's at the scene. Mitch Hubbard is working it. She said she'd be by to see Shirley when she gets a chance. Might be a while."

"If you don't need me here, I could go there. Or I could call her."

Pickens scratched his chin. "I know it's below your paygrade, but I'd rather you stayed here as a precaution."

"Do you think Shirley is in danger?" asked Dunne.

Pickens shrugged. "Just a precaution. Amy and I are going to the scene. I'll send Abrue here to relieve you." He paused. "I sent Zeke home to be with his family and then report to your office. He's having a hard time dealing with Conlon's death and needs a shoulder."

Dunne grinned.

"You want me to give him some mothering. Not my usual hardass?"

Pickens smiled. "Something like that."

Dunne smiled.

Just then Deputy Conlon's mother-in-law approached. Pickens wondered if she would treat him like Conlon's mother did.

"Sheriff Pickens," said Conlon's mother-in-law, "I'm Corina Ashley, Shirley's mother." Mrs. Ashley extended a hand. Pickens shook it. "Did you get to talk to Jason's parents?"

Mrs. Ashley was a short woman in her late forties or early-fifties and had brown hair with streaks of gray.

"We met at the entrance. They said they were making arrangements for their son. I offered full honors, but Conlon's mother declined."

Mrs. Ashley shook her head.

"That's not going to happen," she said. "Shirley will want full honors for Jason, and he would have too. The Conlons weren't happy with Jason's choice of professions, and they weren't pleased that he married Shirley. That's why they eloped." Mrs. Ashley smiled. "Six months later Jason enlisted. He missed the birth of both his sons. Today was supposed to be a memorable occasion for them as he'd be here for his daughter. Then this happened." Her voice cracked.

Pickens gave her a moment. "How's she holding up?"

Mrs. Ashley patted her eyes with the back of her hands. "Sorry," she said.

Pickens raised his palm.

Mrs. Ashley continued. "Shirley is tougher than she looks. She knows what it's like to be a single mother. My husband passed away when Shirley and her brother, Buddy, were in high school." Mrs. Ashley smiled. "I raised them by myself. Buddy enlisted at the same time Jason did. He's still in the army. I called him, and Buddy got to talk to his sister. He'll be home for the funeral and will be a pallbearer. If any of your deputies want to, Shirley would be pleased."

"I'll make it happen," said Pickens. "Can we see her now?"

"Yes, please."

Pickens and Amy entered the room. Conlon's wife was cradling her newborn. She smiled when she saw Pickens and Amy.

"Sheriff Pickens come meet Ainsley Conlon. Isn't she the cutest?"

Pickens smiled, as did Amy. Pickens approached the bed.

"She certainly is," he said. "She looks like her mommy." The baby cooed. "And she sounds like her daddy."

Pickens realized his mistake, but Conlon's wife dismissed his comment.

"She cries like Jason did, too." Mrs. Conlon smiled. "Did you meet Jason's parents?"

"Yes. We chatted briefly. They were in a hurry to get your boys home."

"Jason turned those two into little devils, but Ainsley will give them a handful." She studied both Pickens' and Amy's faces. "Is there something you want to ask me, Sheriff?"

Pickens glanced at Amy and tilted his head, signaling for Amy to ask.

"Yes," answered Amy. "We're wondering if your husband had any enemies that might have targeted him." Amy exhaled. "I have to ask, were there any problems?"

"Absolutely not," snapped Shirley. "Our marriage was solid. And as far as I know, Jason had no enemies."

"We had to ask," said Pickens. "It's standard procedure. I'm sorry."

"I'm sorry, too. I've got a lot on my plate right now."

"If there's anything you need, you call me. Everyone is at your disposal."

"Thank you. Jason had a life insurance policy that should help temporarily. He had enough saved when he got out of the army to make a large down payment on the house. But with three mouths to feed, I'll need his survivor's benefits. I'll get them, won't I?"

"I'll make sure you do. Don't you worry."

"Thank you. If you don't mind, I need to feed Ainsley."

Pickens smiled. "We'll leave you to your privacy. Take care of that little one."

Shirley smiled.

Pickens and Amy left the room.

"Will she get survivor's benefits?" said Amy. "Conlon wasn't with us long enough."

"She'll get them if I have anything to say about it. Conlon died in the line of duty. If that's not enough, then I'll resign and the hell with the job."

Amy touched his arm. "I'll resign, too and I bet every deputy will." She whispered in his ear, "Fuck the job."

Pickens grinned and turned to Dunne.

"Sergeant Dunne, we're leaving. I'll send Abrue here. And thanks for keeping watch over Conlon's wife."

Dunne saluted and said, "Goes with the job."

*   *   *

As Pickens and Amy walked out of the hospital and stepped off the curb into the parking lot, Pickens noticed a rapidly approaching car. When he saw a gun stick out from the passenger side window, he shoved Amy to the ground and covered her with his body as bullets flew around them.

When the shooting ended, Pickens and Amy drew their weapons and knelt in the shooting position but didn't fire for fear of hitting an innocent bystander. Besides, they didn't have a clear shot. The car was speeding behind a row of parked vehicles.

The car exited the hospital parking lot just as Jimmy Noseby, the reporter, entered. He pulled his car near where Pickens and Amy stood and got out of it. Amy was on her radio, calling in the incident.

"I saw the whole thing," said the reporter. "I got it on my phone. Even got a shot of the driver." The reporter hesitated and pointed at Pickens' head and arm. "Sheriff, you're bleeding."

Amy turned just as Pickens' knees buckled.

Amy dropped to the ground. "Noseby, go get help," she shouted. "Go."

The reporter ran toward the hospital entrance, entered, and shouted for help.

Amy cradled Pickens in her lap. She ignored the blood on his head and arm.

"Dammit, don't you die on me." She rocked him in her arms. "Stay with me, please."

A woman who was in her car and had witnessed the incident got out and ran to Pickens and Amy.

"I'm a doctor," she said. "Let me help."

"No," shouted Amy. "Don't you touch him."

The woman noticed the stripes on Amy's sleeve.

"Sergeant," she said, "I'm a doctor. Please let me look at his wounds. It's vital I do."

Pickens opened his eyes and mumbled. "Let her, Amy."

The doctor first checked his head wound. It was bleeding profusely.

"You were lucky, JD. It could have been worse. You're going to need stitches and an overnight stay in the hospital for observation." The doctor reached into her medical bag and took out bandages and covered the wounds. "These will work until we get you to emergency. Were you hit anywhere else?"

Pickens managed to point to his rear.

"Okay, roll him onto his side, Sergeant. I'll take a look," said the doctor.

Amy rolled him onto his right side.

"Probably a flesh wound, but you'll need stitches." The doctor smiled. "I'll take care of them."

"I bet you will, Elaine," said Pickens.

The doctor grinned.

Two orderlies wheeling a gurney along with a nurse had arrived. Behind them were Sergeant Dunne and the reporter.

"Get him up and to emergency," said the doctor. "I'll be right behind you."

The orderlies picked up Pickens and placed him on the gurney. Pickens grunted when they did.

"I'll see you soon, JD," said the doctor.

"Whatever," said Pickens as the orderlies wheeled him away.

"Wait," said Amy, "am I missing something? Do you two know each other?"

The doctor smiled. "We dated in high school and college." She winked and walked away.

"Is he going to be okay?" said Dunne.

Amy shook her head. "Yeah. He has to spend the night in the hospital for observation. He scared the hell out of me."

"He'll be in goods with Dr. Elaine Smathers. She's good."

"I'll bet she is." Amy's eyes narrowed. "It would serve him right if he got an ass burn from lying on the hot pavement."

"What should I do with the video of the shooting?" said the reporter.

Amy's brows hiked. She'd forgotten about it.

"Email it to Billy Thompson."

"Who gets to call his wife?" said Dunne.

"Would you like to?"

"Oh no, not on your life. You're the detective. You get to." Dunne grinned.

"Thanks," said Amy, then dialed the ME's office.

CHAPTER 11

A T THE BUXTON crime scene, Hubbard was thoroughly going through the house. He had talked to the next-door neighbor, Orville Walsh, and learned nothing more than Pickens did. But Walsh's comment about other couples intrigued Hubbard.

Hubbard checked the closets and dressers for any evidence that might provide clues. He was in the master bedroom, attempting to get a feel of what the killer had been thinking when something in the air-conditioning vent caught his eye. Hubbard stood on the bed to get a closer look. It looked like it might be a camera. He got off the bed, got a chair from the guest bedroom, and went to the front entrance.

"Deputy Abrue," he called out, "can you come into the master bedroom, please?

Abrue followed Hubbard.

"Look at that vent." Hubbard pointed. "Do you see anything?"

Abrue was much shorter than Hubbard and had difficulty seeing what Hubbard saw, but eventually, she saw something.

"What do you think it is, Mr. Hubbard?"

"I think it's a remote video camera. You're my witness that I'm gonna remove the vent and take whatever it is out."

Hubbard climbed onto the chair, took out his Swiss army

knife, and unscrewed the vent. He already had on latex gloves, so he wasn't concerned with leaving prints.

"You think the victims filmed their murder?"

"If they did, we just got lucky. We'll have to find the camera's source. I already checked the closets in each bedroom, so it's not there."

Suddenly, Abrue's radio beeped. She stepped into the hall to listen to the radio call from Amy.

"I gotta go, Mr. Hubbard," Abrue called out. "There's been another shooting."

Hubbard's brows hiked.

"Where?"

"At the hospital." Abrue's voice trembled. "Sheriff Pickens was shot, and the shooters were last seen heading east on Cumberland Highway. That's not far from here. I might be able to catch up with them before they make it to the next county. Sorry, I got to go."

"Go," said Hubbard. "I'll finish here and lock up. Then I'll go to the hospital." Hubbard paused. "And Deputy—"

Abrue froze.

"Be careful out there," said Hubbard.

"Copy that," replied Abrue and left the bedroom. She got in her patrol car, radioed that she was in pursuit, and took off with lights flashing.

After Abrue left, Hubbard started his search for whatever was storing the data from the camera. He stood in the center of the room and surveyed it. He glanced at the mirror on the wall over the dresser. Something about it seemed off.

"No," he said, "it can't be." Hubbard saw a remote on the nightstand, picked it up, and looked at it.

The remote was one he'd never seen before. He pressed on, and a tiny blue dot appeared on the jewelry chest below the mirror. He pressed record, and the dot turned red. When he pressed play, the mirror lit up revealing the bed and him. It wasn't just a mirror; it was also a flat screen TV. Next, Hubbard pressed rewind and stop after a few seconds. Then he pressed play and saw a video of him by the bed. Curious, Hubbard pushed rewind then pressed play. What he saw disturbed him.

"Son of a bitch," said Hubbard. "Mrs. Buxton wasn't a stranger to anal sex and was a willing participant. Good thing Abrue's not here." Hubbard checked the time stamp. It wasn't Friday but two weeks ago. "Damn, it's possible the Buxtons knew their killer or killers and invited them into their home."

Hubbard reversed the feed until it came to another video three weeks earlier. The Buxtons were in bed with another couple participating in various forms of group sex.

"That's enough," said Hubbard and pressed off. "It's not only homicide but what the killer did to Mrs. Buxton could be considered a *sex crime*. And I'd bet there were two killers. I wouldn't be surprised if they're in a video session." He took a deep breath. "JD has to see this and get it into evidence." Hubbard decided to return the camera to the air conditioning vent.

Hubbard walked out of the bedroom, locked up the house, and headed for the hospital.

CHAPTER 12

MARGE AND MORGAN had finished the autopsy on the Buxtons, and she was about to go pick up Sarah when she got Amy's call.

"How did this happen, Amy?" Marge snapped. "You were supposed to look out for him like he does for you."

Amy held the phone away as Marge launched into a tirade. When it ended, Amy responded.

"We were both shot at," said Amy. "JD saved me from getting shot."

"He took a bullet for you?"

"Yes," said Amy. "If it weren't for his quick reaction, we'd both be dead. He saved my life."

"I'm sorry I snapped. I'll be there shortly."

Amy ignored her outburst. As a grief counselor, she knew Marge was expressing her concern for her husband.

"How bad is it?"

Amy relayed what the doctor had said and that Pickens would spend the night at the hospital for observation.

"Who's his doctor?"

"Dr. Elaine Smathers. I heard she's excellent."

"Yeah," said Marge, "and one of his old girlfriends. I'd better hurry."

Amy breathed a sigh of relief after Marge ended the call.

Next, Amy called Hubbard to brief him on the situation.

"I heard," said Hubbard. "I'm on my way there now. How bad was it?"

Amy told him about Pickens' wounds. She heard him laugh when she mentioned Pickens' butt wound.

"Marge is on her way here. It's going to be chaos when she gets here. Maybe you should wait until tomorrow morning to visit JD."

"I get the picture. I can wait, and I'm sure JD will be glad I did, what with Marge."

"You're right. Are you done with the crime scene?"

"Yeah," answered Hubbard. "I found something interesting." He told her about the video equipment but not the content. "Can you spare Deputy Thompson?"

"Why?"

"If you send him to the house, I'll go there and show him the equipment, and he can disassemble it and take it to the office." Hubbard paused. "But Detective, I don't want him to do anything with it until JD gets to see it."

"Is there something you're not telling me, Hubbard?"

There was an ominous silence as Hubbard pondered an answer.

"Yeah, there is," answered Hubbard.

"As bad as the crime scene pictures?" said Amy.

"Worse."

"Okay, I'll tell Billy to box the equipment, mark it *confidential* and for the sheriff's eyes only. How's that?"

"Thanks, Detective." Hubbard paused. "And, Detective, these shootings aren't about Deputy Conlon. They're about all of you. Tell JD to put everyone on alert."

"Yeah. Copy that, Hubbard."

After the call ended, Amy called Billy and gave him his instructions and told him about the reporter emailing him a video from the attack on her and Pickens. Then she told Billy to have every deputy be on alert and use caution at all times.

Dunne had waited to hear about Amy's call to Marge.

"How did it go, Detective?"

Amy cleared her throat and shook her head.

"It went," she said. "I'd never want to piss Marge off."

"I agree," said Dunne, "and JD is going to get a mouth full from her."

"Tell me about it."

"How about you, Detective? How are you doing?"

Up until then, everyone had been concerned about Pickens and had seemed to have forgotten about Amy. She had been running on adrenaline to stay focused.

"I'm . . ." Amy's voice cracked.

Dunne broke protocol and instinctively wrapped her arms around Amy and hugged her close. Amy welcomed Dunne's comfort and pressed her head against Dunne's shoulder. When the hug ended, Amy wiped her eyes with the back of her hands.

"I know how you're feeling," said Dunne and put her hand on Amy's arm. "I've been there."

Amy shook her head.

"Yeah. Sometimes I forget your military record." Amy covered Dunne's hand with her own. "I won't anymore."

Dunne lightly squeezed Amy's arm.

"Thanks for the hug, Sergeant . . ."

"It's okay to call me Mia, Amy."

"Thanks, Mia."

Both grinned. The last time they bonded was at Pickens' home after a serial killer had threatened Pickens and his family.

"I guess we should go see the boss," said Amy.

Dunne pointed at Amy.

"First you should change your shirt. I've got an extra one in my car. I'll get it, and you could change there."

Amy hadn't realized her shirt had Pickens' blood on it. When she looked at it, she suddenly realized how close she had come to getting shot and possibly killed or ending up in the hospital like Pickens. The reality caused an ache in the back of her throat.

"I guess I should," Amy said as her hands trembled.

They glanced around, then warily walked to Dunne's patrol car. Dunne got the shirt from the rear of the vehicle and eyeballed Amy.

"This should fit. If not, who cares." She handed Amy the shirt.

Amy removed her bloodied shirt.

"What if someone sees me in my bra and says something?"

"We'll arrest them for voyeurism," said Dunne.

Both grinned.

Amy changed shirts, and then they headed to the hospital entrance to see Pickens.

Noseby, the reporter was standing at the door.

"Were you watching me, Nosey?" said Amy.

The reporter grinned.

"Did you like what you saw?" said Amy. "Say yes, and I'll cuff you."

"No, no, no," said the reporter. "I didn't see a thing. I swear." Amy glared at him. "I was just waiting to find out how the sheriff was."

"He's fine," snapped Amy, "and don't ask for a storyline. You can write about what you saw but don't mention the sheriff was shot and in the hospital. He doesn't need everyone in town visiting him. Especially the football team. Do I make myself clear?"

The reporter raised his hands. "Clear," he said. "But I'm going to add that a deputy was shot and died." Before Amy could say anything, the reporter added, "I got my sources, and I know his wife just gave birth. I promise I'll be discreet."

"You better be," said Dunne. "Now get away from here before we arrest you."

The reporter left, and Amy and Dunne entered the hospital.

*   *   *

When Marge arrived at the hospital and parked, she called Pickens' parents and told them he was in the hospital for an overnight stay. She downplayed the seriousness of his wounds so as not to alarm them and asked them to keep Sarah and Bailey overnight. Pickens' parents were relieved and agreed.

Marge then went into the hospital and was directed to Pickens' room. Marge was well-known at the hospital but not as a celebrity, but because she was the ME.

Pickens was in the other VIP room next to the one where Shirley Conlon was. Like her, Pickens was considered a celebrity.

As Marge approached Pickens' room, two young female volunteers were fawning over him. They were high school cheerleaders. When they saw Marge, they bolted from the room.

Amy and Dunne returned from getting coffee and approached Marge.

"We're so sorry, Dr. Davids," said Dunne.

Marge held a hand up. "I know you both are. But please call me Marge. And Amy, once again I'm sorry for snapping at you."

"No problem," replied Amy.

Marge glanced into the room. "He looks like he's asleep, but he's not. Two volunteers just left, and I bet he enjoyed their company."

"Uh," said Amy, "we're gonna go enjoy our coffee. Let's go, Mia."

Amy lightly elbowed Dunne, and they left.

Marge entered the room.

"Okay, Sheriff," she said. "I'm going to change the bandage on your rear end. Would you please raise it so I can?"

Pickens opened his eyes. "Oh no, you're not."

Marge grinned.

"Damn, Marge, you woke me."

"And those girls didn't?"

"You saw them?"

"Yes, and they won't be checking on you again." Marge scowled. "Dammit, JD, what the hell happened?"

"I was shot."

"I know that, but why you and why in the hospital parking lot?"

Pickens rubbed his chin. "I don't know, but Amy said Mitch told her it's not about Deputy Conlon but all of us." He shook his head. "I agree, and Amy put all my deputies on alert. Marge . . ."

"What?"

"Where's Sarah?"

"Still at your parents."

"Thank goodness." He pointed his finger at her. "I want you to stay here tonight." Marge's eyes narrowed, and he added, "Don't argue with me. I'm concerned for our safety." Pickens glanced around the room. "Besides, this room is like a hotel suite. There's plenty of space for the two of us." He tilted his head. "Or, you could sleep with me." Pickens grinned.

"Now's not the time for joking, JD. Get serious, and I'm not sleeping with you. You were shot. Remember?"

"I know, but it's just a flesh wound."

"Dammit, JD, it's not just a flesh wound. That's why you're hooked up to that monitor and staying overnight for observation. It's serious, JD, except for your butt wound."

"Dr. Davids is correct," said Dr. Smathers who had entered the room. "You're lucky you're not dead. Your wounds were serious, and you passed out, JD, after you got shot. Which means there could be something serious going on and we won't know until tomorrow. If it happens again, we'll do an MRI to see if the bullet caused damage."

"Thank you, Dr. Smathers," said Marge. "He's thick-headed and won't listen to me."

"He didn't want to listen to me in the parking lot. He's always been a thick-headed son of . . ."

"Hey wait a minute," said Pickens. "I'm here and can hear you."

"Yes, but you're not listening," said Marge. "Did you hear what Dr. Smathers said? You could have died, JD."

Pickens held his palms up. "Okay, already. I surrender. But, Marge, you have to stay here tonight."

"I can arrange for a small bed if you'd like, Dr. Davids," said Dr. Smathers.

Marge glanced around the room. "Thank you, but I'll be fine in that recliner bed. All I need is a pillow, and I'll be comfortable."

"I'll arrange for one, and I'll arrange for meals for both of you." Dr. Smathers grinned. "But yours will be better than hospital food, Dr. Davids." She smiled. "Sleep tight tonight, JD."

"Yeah, thanks," said Pickens.

As Dr. Smathers walked out, Marge turned to Pickens. "I have to call your parents and explain what happened."

"Wait," said Pickens, "don't tell my mom. She'll get upset.

Tell my dad it's just a flesh wound and they're keeping me overnight as a precaution. You're staying because you love me. He'll understand."

Later that afternoon, Conlon's wife brought the baby to see Pickens. Her mother pushed her in a wheelchair.

"I hope we're not intruding," said Shirley. "I thought maybe a visit from Ainsley might cheer you up."

Pickens smiled. "You're not intruding, and Ainsley is welcome as are you. Meet my wife Dr. Marge Davids, the county..."

"The county medical examiner," said Shirley. "Jason mentioned you several times. It's a pleasure to meet you."

"It's a pleasure to meet you, too," said Marge.

"You're lucky your husband wasn't..." Shirley's voice cracked and tears came to her eyes.

"Yes, I am," said Marge and approached Shirley. "But you have your daughter, and that's not only lucky but something special. Our daughter, Sarah, was special to us."

Marge realized how lucky she was that Pickens survived and how, unfortunately, Mrs. Conlon's husband hadn't. If the roles were reversed, how would she react to Pickens death?

The baby cooed.

"Shirley, we've stayed long enough," said Mrs. Ashley. "Ainsley needs to nap."

"Yes, mother," said Shirley and her mother wheeled her out of the room.

Marge walked over beside Pickens, leaned over and kissed him.

"Thank God, you're alive, JD."

*　*　*

While Marge was with Pickens, Amy and Dunne used the time alone in the visitor's waiting room to strategize. Since Conlon was under Dunne's command, she would work that case. As the only actual detective, Amy would handle the Buxton homicide.

First order of business for Dunne was to sit down with Jackson and get him to talk about the shooting to see if they could get a description of the vehicle and possibly the shooter. Next, she'd keep him at the Warfield office for light work until he went for counseling, which Amy would arrange for Monday.

Amy decided she'd see what Hubbard discovered at the Buxton house. Since Hubbard was acting as a consultant, she'd overrule him and look at the video.

"We've got our marching orders," said Amy. "now let's execute them"

"Let's not bother JD with our plans. He needs to rest," said Dunne. "We'll just say goodbye and leave him in Marge's hands. I'll radio Abrue and tell her the hospital is her assignment. She can check in on Conlon's wife."

Amy nodded her head. "Solid plan."

They went to Pickens' room, said they were leaving and that Abrue would be there soon.

As they walked to the parking lot, Dunne contacted Deputy Abrue, she was on Cumberland Highway in pursuit of the suspect vehicle. Deputy Ritchie Ortiz was a half-mile behind her.

"Any sign of the vehicle yet?" said Dunne.

"No," said Abrue, "and if I don't see them soon, they'll be in the next county. Ortiz is now behind me. We're both in pursuit. Should we keep going, Sergeant?"

"How far until the county line?"

"About two miles."

"Go another mile, then turn around if you don't see them. Then come to the hospital. Your assignment will be to relieve me and guard the sheriff and Conlon's wife. It will give you a chance to visit her."

"Got it," said Abrue. "Thanks, Sergeant Dunne, for the chance to visit with her."

When Dunne ended the call, Amy said, "Why don't you go to Warfield? I'll wait for Abrue. You've been here long enough."

"Thanks," said Dunne.

CHAPTER 13

SUNDAY, AFTER CHURCH, Mitch Hubbard and his wife, Donna, arrived at the hospital to find Pickens and Marge enjoying brunch. Pickens' bed was raised in the sitting position, and a table was in front of him.

"Look who's up and eating," said Hubbard.

"Mitch," said Pickens. "I'm glad you're here. They won't let me go home. Can you help me escape?"

"If he does," said Mrs. Hubbard, "he'll spend the night in a room down the hall."

Hubbard hunched his shoulders. "Sorry, JD, I hate hospital food."

"But I'm not having . . ." Pickens trailed off at Marge's glare. "Well, I am, but Marge isn't.

"Keep it up, Pickens," said Marge, "and you'll get to know the surgeon, too."

The Hubbards chuckled. Pickens frowned.

"Can he at least tell me if he found anything at the Buxton house?"

"If he does," said Mrs. Hubbard, "he'll need one of those surgeons. We're here to visit you, not talk shop."

Hubbard hunched his shoulders. "Sorry, JD, Donna's right. You'll have to wait until you get out of here."

"Can you at least meet with Amy and go over what you found at the Buxton house?"

"That I can do," said Hubbard.

"Excuse me while I talk with my patient in private," said Dr. Smathers who had entered.

"We were just leaving," said Mrs. Hubbard. "Take care, JD."

Pickens waved.

"Okay, Doc, give it to us."

"I'm keeping you in bed for observation at least a week."

Pickens jaw dropped.

"If it is wasn't for that thick skull of yours, we might have had to do brain surgery. You were lucky, JD."

Marge listened intently.

"We still can't rule out a concussion. And the bandage stays on at least a week."

Pickens touched the bandage and took a quick breath.

"Your shoulder wound was a through and through, but you won't be throwing any footballs for a while. Again, you were lucky with that one." Smathers smiled. "Now the other wound, that's different. It will be a while before you can drive and sit. You'll need a cushion."

Marge interrupted. "He was lucky because he's thick-headed." Smathers grinned. "And, you're saying he has to use a whoopee cushion, is that right?"

"Whoopee cushion works, Dr. Davids."

Marge and Smathers winked.

"Hold on," said Pickens. "What's with the whoopee cushion?"

"It's either that or you stand all day," said Smathers. "If you stay in the hospital, you won't need the cushion. Am I right, Dr. Davids?"

"Definitely, Dr. Smathers. Your choice, JD."

"Shit," said Pickens. "I'll stay here but can I communicate with my office by phone?"

"I think we can arrange that. What do you think, Dr. Davids?"

Marge grinned. "I agree as long as he waits until Wednesday. He's had enough excitement. Any argument. JD?"

Pickens exhaled. "I give up. I'll wait until Wednesday."

"Now that that's all set, I'll leave you two alone. Thank you, Dr. Davids."

Marge winked as did Dr. Smathers.

"JD," said Marge. "I'm going home to change clothes. I'll get Sarah and bring her here. She'll want to see her daddy."

*   *   *

Amy and Billy were in the office working on the cases, when Amy cornered Billy.

"I know Hubbard found something at the Buxton house."

Billy ignored her and continued looking at a website.

"Billy," Amy raised her voice. "I'm in charge now. Tell me what he found."

"But . . ."

"Don't but me. Tell me before I bust you down to private."

"You told me to mark it for sheriff's eyes only."

"I know what I told you. Now tell me what Hubbard found."

Billy exhaled. "It's video equipment. It uses Wi-Fi. Everything it recorded is on a chip."

"Show me. In JD's office. Now."

"Okay, take my laptop, and I'll get the box."

They went into Pickens' office, and Billy inserted the chip from the data source taken from the Buxton home into his laptop.

"You sure you want to do this, Amy?"

"Just do it," she snapped.

Billy opened the video file and handed the remote to Amy.

She pressed on, and the screen on Billy's laptop revealed the last session that Hubbard saw. Next, she pressed play.

They didn't expect what they saw. The Buxtons were in bed with another couple. The men were enjoying anal sex with the women while the women made love to each other.

"I've seen enough." Amy shook her head. "Nobody knows about this except us. I'll tell JD what's on the video."

"But, Amy . . ."

"What?" she snapped.

"What if the killer is in the video?"

Amy bit her lip. "It's up to JD if he wants to look, but he'll probably want you to run facial recognition. That's up to him. I'll ask."

"Detective Tucker, what are you doing?" said Hubbard who had arrived. "I thought we agreed no one would look at the video until JD had a chance to?"

Amy crossed her arms. "We did, but I'm in charge while JD is in the hospital. You should have told me what was on the video, Hubbard."

"I wanted to spare you . . ."

Amy glared at him. "From what? I'm a big girl and a seasoned law enforcement officer. I can handle ugliness. I did in the past." She was referring to the serial killer that threatened Pickens and his family, the Wilson murder, and the Groves murders. "You had no right to hide this from me, Hubbard."

Hubbard winced. "I'm sorry. I was cautious. I meant no offense, and you're right you're in charge. JD asked me to work with you." Hubbard extended a hand. "Can we forget it, Detective?"

"Amy," said Billy, "he apologized. What's more important, the cases or your ego?"

"The case," Amy said while avoiding eye contact with Hubbard. "So, what's your take on the video?"

"I believe the Buxton's knew their killers and invited them into their home for sex based on what I saw in the video. I also believe a male and female. They're probably in the video."

"I agree," said Amy. "Should Billy run the video and do facial recognition?"

"Might as well. There's no sense waiting for JD." He turned to Billy. "Did you send a copy of the hospital shooting to Sergeant Dunne?"

"Yes. She called and asked me to."

"Sergeant Dunne will talk to Deputy Jackson and ask if he recognizes the vehicle," said Amy and told Hubbard about their plan.

"Good plan, Detective. I would have done the same."

Amy half-heartedly grinned.

While Amy and Hubbard were talking, Billy was on his computer viewing the bodycam feeds from both instances when Conlon was shot, and the video shot by the reporter. He had all three on the monitor.

"Amy," said Billy, "you need to look at this."

Amy and Hubbard joined Billy at his desk.

"At what?" said Amy.

Billy pointed to the monitor.

"I brought up the feeds from the Conlon shootings and the video from the hospital." He pointed to the first shooting. "The vehicle and the license plate match the one from the hospital shooting." Billy didn't want to say Pickens' shooting. It pained him to think about it.

Amy and Hubbard leaned in closer.

"And the vehicles are the same," said Billy. "A Mercury Cougar. And the license plates are a match, too."

"We already knew the license plate was bogus," said Amy. "Can you determine who the vehicles' owner is?"

"I'll try, but it's going to be difficult."

"How about the driver?" said Amy.

"If you look closely at the video, the driver looks like a female. I'll run facial recognition on her, and I'll make a composite and send it to Sergeant Dunne. She can show it to Zeke. Anything else you want me to do?"

Amy looked at Hubbard. He nodded.

"Yes," she said. "Go through the Buxton feed and run facial recognition on the Buxtons' . . ." She wasn't sure what to call the other couples.

"Their sex partners," said Hubbard.

"On them," said Amy, and nodded.

"How far back should I go?" said Billy.

"As far back as the feed goes but not more than four months," said Hubbard. "If we need more, you can do it later."

"You've got your marching orders, Billy," said Amy, "but no one, and I mean no one sees that feed. Regardless of what's on it, we need to protect the privacy of the dead. Understood, Corporal?"

"Understood, Detective."

"Since it will take some time to do the recognition," said Hubbard, "let's go back to the house. There's something I want to check."

"Like what?" said Amy.

"Won't know till we get there."

As they were about to leave, Amy's phone beeped.

"It's JD," she said and answered the call. "Why aren't you resting?"

"Resting? You call stuck in a hospital bed resting?"

He couldn't see Amy shake her head.

"I want to know what's happening," said Pickens. "I asked Mitch Hubbard to work with you."

"He's here now."

"Now tell me what's going on. And make it quick. I haven't got much time."

She told him about her and Dunne's plan.

"We're reviewing evidence from the Buxton's house."

"What evidence?"

"A video feed," she replied and glanced at Hubbard.

"Don't tell him what we saw," mouthed Hubbard.

"What's on the video?"

"I'm not going to tell you over the phone, JD. You can watch when you're back on duty."

"I'm on duty, Detective. Just because I'm in the hospital doesn't mean I can't know what's happening." She couldn't see his eyes narrow. "Tell me what's on the video."

"No," Amy snapped. "I'm in charge, and I say no. If you want me to resign and turn in my badge, I will."

"Forget it. What else is happening?"

She explained Hubbard's hypothesis but still refused to describe the sex tape.

"I agree with Mitch. Tell Billy to view the feed and do facial recognition. Also, do the same with Nosey's video."

"You remember that?"

"I remember he said he caught the driver on film. Have Billy send a composite to Sergeant Dunne so Zeke can look at it." Pickens paused. "In my desk, there's a phone book with numbers for police chiefs and sheriffs from the surrounding counties. Call and alert them and ask if they could provide backup. We're down a man, one's posted at the hospital, and Zeke is on desk duty. We need all the help we can get."

"On it," said Amy.

"Since Mitch is there, ask him to call any contacts he has at state for help. Might not be a bad idea to contact Ellison. He has contacts. Maybe we can get the highway patrol to provide backup."

"Done," said Amy, then told him about her conversation with the reporter.

"Good work. Anything else?"

Hubbard scribbled, *ask about the autopsy results.*

"Yes," she said. "I'll need to speak with Marge or Tom Morgan about the Buxton autopsies."

"I can't talk to Marge. She doesn't know I'm calling. I'm supposed to wait until Wednesday. You're on your own. And don't tell her I called. Is that all, Detective?"

"When are they sending you home?"

"Not for a week and I can't sit." She couldn't see him squirm in the bed. "Still hurts back there." He couldn't see her smile. "I'll need someone to get my vehicle. It's in the hospital parking lot."

"Um, about that," said Amy. "I got your keys and I . . ."

"You what?"

"I needed a ride to the office, so I took your vehicle. You didn't expect me to call a taxi or grab a ride with Noseby, did you? And I took your weapon and badge."

"I don't suppose you moved into my office, too."

"We needed someplace private to review the video feed."

"I'll buy that." He paused. "And, Detective, I got full confidence in your ability. But remember I'm still the sheriff."

"Copy that," she said and ended the call.

"I take it Marge wasn't there," said Hubbard.

"No, and she doesn't know he called." She related Pickens' instructions to Hubbard.

"Not my place to tell Marge." He smiled. "I still got contacts, but Ellison has more."

"I know. We used him in the past. Would you call him for me? Last time I called him, he conned me into lunch."

Hubbard nodded.

"I'll call Sergeant Dunne and relay JD's instructions."

"Let me call Ellison first and tell him to expect a call from Sergeant Dunne. That way she's taking charge."

"Good idea."

Hubbard called Ellison and told him of their plan. Ellison agreed to help.

Amy called Dunne and relayed Pickens' instructions and for her to call Ellison and that he was expecting her call. Also, not to tell Marge that Pickens had called her.

CHAPTER 14

AMY WATCHED AS Hubbard walked through the Buxtons' kitchen and the bedroom. His interest was on the waterfall kitchen island and the bedroom dressers.

"If you tell me what you're looking for," said Amy, "maybe I could help you."

"I'm not sure what I'm looking for. It's a gut feeling I have." He went back into the kitchen, bent over and glanced over the top surface of the island.

Amy did the same and saw it.

"That looks like dust or a powdery substance," she said and straightened. "Cocaine residual?"

"Could be," said Hubbard. "If the Buxtons invited their killers for sex, they might've wanted to get high to enjoy it. We'll need a criminalist to take a sample and verify the substance."

"We can ask Marge tomorrow. I'll call her first thing in the morning." Amy leaned back, shook her head, then exhaled. "It's not good to speak ill of the dead, but those people disgust me. Why would a man and woman engage in such acts? And how could a husband enjoy watching his wife sodomized by another man? And how could she watch her husband sodomize another man's wife or girlfriend?"

"We thought the killers were psychopaths, but it's looking more like the victims were, too," said Hubbard.

"No, they're sadistic sociopaths."

Hubbard shook his head.

"Last time I was here, I didn't see a purse, a wallet, a set of keys, or phone book. I wonder if the criminalists bagged them."

"We'll see," said Amy.

Hubbard took a step toward the bedrooms, then turned and looked around the kitchen as if examining the room.

"Something bothering you, Hubbard?" Amy asked.

He tilted his head. "Yeah. We got sex and drugs. Where did the drugs come from? Did the Buxtons have them or did the killers bring them?"

"Good question. If the Buxtons had the drugs, where'd they get them? And how long had they been using?"

Hubbard rubbed his chin. "Maybe we should take another look in the bedroom. We might find their hidey-hole."

Amy followed Hubbard into the master bedroom.

"Now where would they hide their stash?" said Hubbard.

"Behind one of the dressers?" said Amy.

"Too easy, but worth a look."

Hubbard moved the large dresser under the mirror. Amy removed the man's chest.

"Anything?"

"No," said Amy. "You?"

"No . . . wait," said Hubbard, "think I found something."

Amy pushed the man's dresser back in place and joined Hubbard.

Hubbard bent over and reached for something.

"Forget it," he said, "I thought I found the stash. Keep looking."

Hubbard replaced the dresser in its original location.

"Maybe they didn't have a stash," said Amy.

Hubbard rubbed his chin. "If they didn't, then the killers

had one." He shook his head. "They may have, but I have a feeling the Buxtons also did. Keep looking."

Amy continued looking in the bedroom, including tapping on the wall for a possible hiding place.

Hubbard stood by the bed, surveying the room.

"Ah shit," said Hubbard, "it can't be."

"Can't be what?"

Hubbard pointed. "The mirror. It's also a flat screen TV."

"Too easy," said Amy.

"You ever owned a wall mount TV? They swing out so you can angle them." Hubbard stood by the flat screen, grabbed a corner and swung it to the left. The right side came away from the wall facing the window sitting area.

"Told you it was too easy," said Hubbard and removed a small package attached to the back. He opened the package and removed a small packet. He counted the number of packets in the package.

"Only three," he said. "Maybe they were running low." Hubbard held the package in his hand. "It's possible the killers were the Buxtons' suppliers, and this was sex and a deal that went wrong."

"Sex for drugs?"

"Then why kill a customer? No, something went wrong. Maybe the cocaine they took was laced with something. We'll ask the ME to analyze the package."

"Anything else we need to do here?"

"No, we're done."

"When I talk to Marge," said Amy, "I'll ask if she did a tox screen."

CHAPTER 15

Monday, August 13

AMY AND HUBBARD watched Billy run facial recognition on the Buxtons' sex partners. Billy was at three-months and was having difficulty with the ones he found.

Amy stepped away and decided to call Marge at her cell phone number.

"Good morning, Amy, how can I help you?"

"How's the patient?"

"Antsy to get back to work and a royal pain in the ass."

Amy smiled, but Marge couldn't see it.

"We'd like to talk with you about the Buxton's case. We found some evidence at the house that you weren't aware of."

"Such as?" said Marge.

"I'd rather not explain over the phone. It's sensitive."

"I saw the wife's body, Amy, and took pictures. Nothing's more sensitive."

Amy cringed. "Can we come to your office, please?"

Amy couldn't see Marge's eyebrows draw together.

"I'm at the hospital, but I'll meet you there," Marge said brusquely. "Dr. Morgan will join us."

"Mitch Hubbard will be with me," said Amy.

Hubbard waited to hear what Marge said.

"So?" he said.

"She's not happy," Amy told him about the conversation. She tapped Billy on the shoulder. "You're on your own and remember what I said about the video feed."

Billy turned his back to her. "You don't have to remind me again, Detective, I'm not deaf."

*   *   *

In Warfield, Sergeant Dunne was at the offices of Ellison Investigations, Bobby Ellison's private investigating practice. Dunne didn't know what to expect as she'd never met Ellison.

But it was the same for Ellison as he'd never met Dunne. He only knew what Hubbard had said about her—spit and polished, no-nonsense, and no first names.

When Dunne entered the office, Ellison's assistant greeted her.

"Good morning," said Lu, "you must be Sergeant Dunne, Bobby's expecting you. I'm Lu, his assistant."

"Do you have a last name?"

"I do, but everyone calls me Lu."

"I prefer to address you by your last name."

"Sorry, not gonna happen. It's either Lu or hey you. It's how I prefer it."

Dunne exhaled. "Very well. Is Mr. Ellison in?"

"Hey, Bobby," yelled Lu, "your appointment's here."

The office door opened and Ellison stepped out.

"Geez, Lu, I'm not deaf. Can't you use the telecom?"

"I would, but we don't have one. You're appointment's here. Meet Sergeant Dunne."

Ellison took one look at Dunne and knew she was everything Hubbard said she was. Dunne's uniform was starched, and her shoes spit-shined. To Ellison, she resembled a hard ass drill sergeant.

"Good Morning, Sergeant Dunne. It's a pleasure to meet you."

Dunne nodded and didn't offer her hand.

"Would you like a cup of coffee," said Ellison.

"I'm fine, thank you. Can we get on with our business?"

Ellison glanced at Lu. She raised her eyebrows.

"Sure, let's do it in my office."

Dunne followed Ellison and sat in front of his desk. She handed him the file with the composite.

"There's a composite of the driver and pictures of the vehicle in question. Corporal Thompson started facial recognition on the woman."

Ellison opened the file.

"Thompson's good," said Ellison. "But Lu's better and faster. Hey, Lu," he shouted.

Dunne cringed.

"What?" shouted Lu.

"Come in here. I got a job for you."

Lu entered, and Ellison handed her the file.

"Run facial recognition on the woman and run a search for owners of Cougars. Let me know if you need my contacts."

Lu smiled, took the file, and left the office.

"Shouldn't take her long. You want to wait or should I call you when we got something, Sergeant Dunne?"

"Call me. I'll be in my office." She took out a business card and placed it on the desk. "I lost a deputy, Mr. Ellison, and his wife just had a baby. I'd appreciate fast service."

"Excuse me, Sergeant Dunne, but I was asked to work with you. I'm good at what I do. Ask JD and Hubbard. You'll get fast service and much more as long as we work together. I already called my contacts at the State."

Dunne's eyebrows hiked.

"I'm not only a PI, but a retired homicide detective. I have a lot of contacts. FHP is assigning three highway patrol officers to provide backup for the sheriff's office. They'll be at your disposal or Sergeant Tucker's. Whoever wants them."

Dunne wasn't expecting Ellison's quick response. Hubbard had said Ellison would help but getting the highway patrol involved, wasn't something she expected.

"I'm sorry if I seemed curt," said Dunne. "It was a long weekend, and I want to catch the SOB who shot my deputy."

"Believe me, so do I. I'm on your side, Sergeant. I'll call as soon as Lu gets something."

"Thanks, Mr. Ellison."

Lu stood in the doorway.

"There were many Mercury Cougars registered in Florida but only seven of the 2001 model and color used in the shootings," said Lu, "and none in this county. There were eight, but that one expired."

"Told you she was fast, Sergeant Dunne."

Dunne's eyes widened.

"Find out who the owners are," said Ellison. "If we need to, see if you can find out who the expired registration belonged to."

"Got it," said Lu and she went back to her desk.

"Want to wait around while she does her search?" said Ellison.

"No, you have my number, call when you have something. I'll see my way out." When Dunne walked past Lu's desk, she said, "You're good, Lu."

Lu smiled.

After Dunne left, Lu stood in the entrance to Ellison's office.

"She's a hardass, Bobby, so don't try charming her. It won't work. Act professional."

"I always act professional, but that one scares me. How's it going?"

"I'm chasing Cougars. Just like you did for that last client who let a con man beat her at her own game and took off with a fortune."

Ellison smiled. "Yeah, but I caught him. Say, Lu, when are you gonna have dinner with me?"

Lu shook her head. "Not until you get over Irene." Irene Noristan was the woman who was killed by a deranged woman with a shotgun.

Ellison rubbed his chin. "Irene was a good woman. I wonder what happened to her killer's partner?"

"Why," said Lu, "is JD looking for her?"

"No, and neither am I. Good luck Cougar hunting."

Lu shook her head.

CHAPTER 16

MARGE AND TOM Morgan were waiting in her office when Amy and Hubbard arrived. Morgan had placed three chairs in front of Marge's desk.

After Amy and Hubbard were seated, Marge said, "So, you think you found something at the crime scene that we missed. Was it the substance on the island?"

Amy and Hubbard did a double take.

"We're processing it and will determine if it's the same substance we found in the victims' noses. Hopefully, we'll have an answer this afternoon."

"We also took samples of the victims' blood for a tox screen," said Morgan. "We should have the results soon."

"And," said Marge, "we sent samples to a lab in Pittsburgh for a rush on DNA."

Amy and Hubbard's eyes widened.

"We did it as a precaution," said Marge. "The preliminary report didn't disclose that we did those things. JD asked for a quick summary and the crime scene photos—which he received." Marge paused to let her comments sink in. "Now tell me what you found that we weren't aware of."

Amy turned to Hubbard for guidance.

"We found a video," said Hubbard.

"A video?" said Marge. "Was it of the murder?"

"No," said Hubbard, "It was . . ." Hubbard hesitated.

"Was what, Hubbard? Don't play games with me." Marge slammed her hands on the desk. "Dammit, tell me. I'm over twenty-one, Hubbard, in case you hadn't noticed. And I'm married to the Sheriff."

Hubbard exhaled. "It was a sex video."

"A what?" said Morgan. "What are you trying to say? That the victims were . . ."

"Weren't what we thought they were?" said Marge. "Especially the woman?"

"Something like that," said Amy.

"How bad was the video?" said Marge.

"It didn't portray the victims in a good way," said Hubbard. "And we found this behind the mirror." Hubbard set the bag with the package of packets on Marge's desk. "We found it behind the mirror, or should I say flat screen TV?"

Marge handed the bag to Morgan.

"I'll get those analyzed along with the substance," said Morgan.

"What's your hypothesis on this, Hubbard?" said Marge.

"We think there were two perpetrators," answered Hubbard, "male and a female." He told her about his theory that the incident was about sex and drugs that went wrong.

Before he could continue, Marge interrupted him. "Are you saying the suspect didn't rape Mrs. Buxton. They had consensual sex?"

"I'm saying I believe the victims invited the perpetrators into their home to party and the perps provided the substance, and the substance was bad."

"Possible," said Marge, "but maybe the victims didn't know much about their guests. It might have been a first for them.

And once we analyze the substance found at the scene and what you provided us, we'll know if the drugs were bad."

"If the substance was bad," said Morgan, "whatever was in it caused a psychotic reaction and the horrific results. Molly would do that."

"Have you considered if it was a first-time event for the victims and perpetrators, they might not be in the video?" said Marge.

"Shit," said Hubbard, "no, I didn't."

Marge smiled. "Would you two like me to do your investigative work for you?"

Amy frowned. "No thanks, you've got enough on your plate."

"And we've got more work to do," said Hubbard, also frowning.

"Anyway," said Marge, "ballistics came back on the shells from the three shootings. They were all .223 caliber, probably fired from the same assault rifle. It's probably not registered, but that's something for Billy. It's in the report. I'll email the report to Billy."

"At least that's something," said Amy. "Send the report to Sergeant Dunne. She's handling that matter with Bobby Ellison. We're splitting responsibilities."

"Ah, Bobby Ellison," said Marge smiling. "If anyone can keep him in check, Sergeant Dunne can."

Amy grinned.

"I don't want you talking to JD about this until Wednesday. He needs his rest."

"We'll wait until Wednesday," said Amy.

"Good. You're in charge, Detective. You and Sergeant Dunne do what you do best. Besides, he'd just get in your way."

Amy grinned. "You're right. It can wait. I got Hubbard, and

Sergeant Dunne has Bobby Ellison working with her. We don't want JD mucking things up."

Marge smiled. "Thanks. We'll call you as soon as we have the results of the tox screen and substance analysis."

"Hold on," said Morgan and placed a box in front of them. "Victims' personal effects. You'll want to go through them."

He and Marge couldn't resist smiling.

"And," said Marge, "here's the latest autopsy report. Since you're in charge, Detective, you might as well have it." Marge narrowed her eyes. "You'll see that my team worked the entire weekend while I was in the hospital with my husband, the sheriff."

Amy winced, then she and Hubbard left.

Once outside, Hubbard said, "I sensed a bit of hostility in there."

"That's probably because we initially came across as implying they weren't thorough in their job." Amy shook her head. "That's something JD would do. Damn, he's rubbing off on us."

"Yeah," said Hubbard.

"Good thing we didn't tell her about JD's call."

"At least he won't be interfering."

*   *   *

Later that day, Ellison called Dunne and said Lu had something and did she want him to tell her over the phone.

"No," said Dunne. "I'm on my way to your office. I've got something for you. I'll be there in ten minutes."

Ellison and Lu waited for Dunne to arrive. Lu had a yellow pad with the names of the registered owners of a 2001 Cougar and the results of her calls to the owners. Ellison was eager to share the information.

When Dunne arrived, she had a folder in her hand.

"Is what's in that folder for me?" said Ellison and grinned. "Who shares first, you or me?"

"Me," said Dunne. "I've got the ballistics report on the shells from the shootings and images of them." She glanced at Lu. "The ME sent the shells to a ballistics expert. It's in the report. Can you find something, Lu?"

Lu smiled. "Maybe. If the weapon's registered or if the shells are similar to ones used in a previous crime. I'll give it my best."

"Thanks," said Dunne and handed Lu the folder. "Your turn, Ellison."

He smiled. "Actually, it's Lu's turn." Ellison turned. "Have at it, Lu."

Lu glanced at the yellow pad.

"I managed to contact the owners of 2001 Cougars in Florida. Four were women. The others were men. One of the women was in her eighties and had her car in the garage. She hasn't driven it in years. She's holding on to it until it's a classic. The other two women live in North Florida and rarely drive their Cougars. They inherited them from their parents." Lu held up a palm. "Honestly, they're keeping them as a remembrance of their parents."

"What about the fourth one?" said Dunne.

"In her sixties and lives in Bartow. Keeps hers in the garage. It belonged to her deceased husband. She's keeping it for her grandson when he's old enough to drive."

"And the men?"

"Jacksonville, Tallahassee, and Live Oak. All three belong to a classic car group and only drive theirs once a month to show off. And, no one but no one drives their Cougar."

"We can scratch them off," said Ellison. "Lu is trying to get the name of the expired registration."

"It will take time, but I'll get it," said Lu. "And I'll work on the ballistics."

"I've got a contact that can help," said Ellison.

Dunne grinned. "Thanks, Lu. Keep me posted, Ellison."

Ellison's jaw dropped. "Don't I at least get 'a nice work, Ellison?'"

Dunne grinned. "Keep me posted, Ellison."

CHAPTER 17

L U HAD NO luck finding out who was the owner of the expired registration. Ellison had better luck with the ballistics. He had Lu send them to his contact at FDLE. The shell casings matched ones from a five-year-old shooting at a convenience store in Ocala. The Ocala police department reported that there were no suspects, and as best they could determine the weapon was unregistered. It remained an unsolved case.

"Where does that leave us, Bobby?"

"Up a shit's creek, Lu. I'll call Sergeant Dunne. Any luck on the driver?"

"The image was too grainy for facial rec, but it looks like a woman. You have any theories?"

Ellison rubbed his chin. "Remember when I asked when you'd have dinner with me?"

"Yeah, and I told you when you got over Noristan."

Ellison pointed a finger. "This is gonna sound crazy, but what if Price, the woman who was the serial killer, had friends and they're getting revenge for her?"

Lu shook her head. "It does sound crazy. This is about shooting cops and has nothing to do with Price. You're not going to tell Sergeant Dunne that, are you?"

"Why not? It's only a theory. But what else have we got?"

"What's only a theory, Ellison?" said Dunne, as she entered Ellison's office.

"Couldn't you call first, Sergeant Dunne? Did you have to barge right in?"

"I'm in charge of this investigation, Ellison. I do whatever I want. Now, what's this theory?"

Ellison told her his theory.

"You're right," said Dunne, "it does sound crazy. Liz Price was a psychopath, and the only friends she had were sorority sisters. Only one of them was close to Price, and she gave up Price. If you want to pursue that theory, you're on your own. Just remember you work for me, and I'm not going down that road."

Ellison scowled. "I don't work for you, Sergeant Dunne, I'm helping you, remember. And my theory was a suggestion. You got a better one?"

Lu got between them. "Back off both of you," she said. "Arguing won't help. Sergeant Dunne, Bobby was making a supposition because we're not having any luck."

Lu then told Dunne about the ballistics finding and the lack of her ability to determine who was the owner of the expired registration.

Both Dunne and Ellison raised their hands.

"I'll keep digging," said Lu, "and I'll find something. Both Bobby and I consider Pickens a friend even though Bobby is a pain in the ass to Pickens. And, we want to help you."

Dunne frowned. "Sorry. This case is getting to me."

"It's getting to all of us," said Ellison. "I've still got more contacts, and I'll come up with something."

"Thanks, Ellison, and thanks, Lu. Keep me posted, Ellison."

CHAPTER 18

WEDNESDAY, PICKENS CALLED Amy and had her set up a conference call between her, Hubbard, Dunne, and Ellison. Dunne and Ellison were in Ellison's office.

When all four were on the line, Pickens said, "Before anyone asks, I'm fine and convalescing, so don't ask questions. I'll do the asking. Starting with, what's the latest? You first, Amy."

Amy mentioned Hubbard's theory but didn't elaborate on the contents of the video because Dunne and Ellison were on the line.

"You don't believe the Buxton woman was raped based on the video evidence, is that what you're saying?"

"Yes," said Amy, "and we also discovered cocaine. The ME is examining it to see if it was laced. The tox screens showed there was cocaine in the victims' blood and something else. The ME sent samples to the state crime lab for further analysis. She's waiting for DNA results, too. Billy was able to pull five facials off the video."

"And," said Pickens.

"Two were the victims. The other three were females. There were other men and women, but Billy wasn't able to get their faces clearly. He's running recognition as we speak. This one's a bitch, JD."

"Yeah. Wish I could be there, but Marge and the doctor got me confined to bed."

They couldn't see him squirm. He couldn't see them grin.

"Your turn, Sergeant Dunne."

"We're not having better luck," said Dunne. "Ellison sent the shell casings to his contact, and they matched an incident in Ocala."

Dunne told him the rest of the story.

"Ellison's assistant wasn't able to identify the driver, so I gave the video to Alexia Norbin, the graphics designer who helped ID Jessie Groves. I should have something today or tomorrow."

Pickens was about to respond, but Ellison interrupted and told Pickens his theory about friends of Liz Price.

"You have to ask," said Ellison, "who would want to kill you all? Seems like a revenge thing to me. And if the Price woman had any friends as violent as her, maybe they'd come seeking revenge for her."

Dunne was furious and interrupted Ellison.

"It's a dumb theory. Price was a psychopath, and her only friends were sorority sisters. And we all know how they felt about her, especially Allyson Healey."

"Hey," said Ellison, "it's a theory. Does anyone have a better one? If not, then I got a business to run, and I need to work my own cases."

They couldn't see Pickens shake his head.

"Sorry, Bobby, I agree with Sergeant Dunne."

Pickens couldn't see Dunne exhale and Ellison frown. But he sensed there was friction between Dunne and Ellison.

"Bobby, I know you're upset, but this case is personal to Sergeant Dunne and me as well as my team. I need your help, and I would appreciate it as a favor to me. Sergeant Dunne needs your help, too, and she'd appreciate you staying on the case." Pickens paused. "Right, Sergeant Dunne?"

Everyone waited for Dunne's answer.

"I'm sorry, Ellison. Like the sheriff said, the case is personal to me and I'm a little frustrated. I need your help."

No one could see Dunne and Ellison shake hands.

"Since that's settled, I'll check in again Saturday unless you need me. Oh, Conlon's wife called. His funeral is on Wednesday at the Episcopalian Church in Warfield. Full dress uniform for everyone."

"Got it," said Amy.

After lunch, the high school head football coach and the offensive backfield visited Pickens. Six cheerleaders accompanied them. The word was out about Pickens' shooting, and he wouldn't be coaching for some time. The team wanted to be sure he was okay.

During the afternoon, several of Pickens' old girlfriends paid a visit. They timed their visits for when they knew Marge was at her office, and Pickens basked in the joy of their company.

*   *   *

Friday afternoon, Pickens went home. His head was bandaged, his right arm in a sling, and he needed a cushion to sit on. Dr. Smathers prescribed mild pain medication in the event he needed it.

Marge drove Pickens home. Sarah, Bailey, and Pickens' parents waited to greet him. As soon as he got out of Marge's car, Sarah and Bailey rushed him. Sarah put her arms around him, and Bailey licked his left hand.

Pickens' mother gasped when she saw the bandages and the sling. His father nodded.

"I'm okay, Mom, it's nothing serious. I can't hug you, but you can kiss me. Dad, I can shake your left hand."

Pickens' mother kissed him and touched his cheek. His father smiled.

"What's for dinner? I haven't had real food since last Friday."

"I ordered pizza," said his mother, "it will be easier for you and everybody."

That night, Pickens enjoyed pizza at home with his whole family.

CHAPTER 19

ONDAY, MARGE RECEIVED the Buxtons' DNA results and their blood analysis. She had sent the DNA to Dr. Vadigal's lab in Pittsburgh and requested a quick turnaround. The blood samples went to the state's crime lab.

First, she opened the DNA report and gasped as she read it.

"Tom, look at this. Is this possible?"

She handed Morgan the report.

His jaw dropped.

"If it is, it sheds new light on the victims. Are you going to tell JD?"

"Not yet. First, I want to talk to Billy Thompson." Marge reached for her phone and pressed the numbers.

"Deputy Thompson. Mrs. Davids, how can I help you?"

"Billy, have you completed your research on the Buxtons?"

"Yes, ma'am, and I found something weird. They were both . . ."

She interrupted him. "Don't tell me. I think I know what you found. Have you told anyone yet?"

"No, ma'am. I was going to tell Amy and let her tell the Sheriff."

Marge exhaled. "Please don't. Wait until Thursday or Friday when the funeral is over. They don't need any distractions. Please, Billy."

At his desk, Billy's brow wrinkled. "But . . ."

"Billy, JD just got out of the hospital, and he planned Deputy Conlon's funeral. Please, don't get him worried about the Buxtons. And Amy doesn't need to know yet. I know you feel a sense of duty to them but waiting won't hurt the case. And what I discovered is more important than what you did. Which is why I'm asking you to hold off."

Marge couldn't see Billy glance around the office looking for someone to help him. He was apprehensive. He'd withheld information from Amy before, but that was at the request of Pickens. And Billy never withheld information from Pickens except for the contents of the video.

"Are you sure this is the right thing to do? The Sheriff is my boss, and I report to Amy."

"Trust me, Billy, it is. Don't forget the Sheriff is my husband, and I think I know what's best for him."

She heard Billy breath a worried sigh.

"Okay. I'll hold off until you talk to the Sheriff. But I'm worried."

"Thanks, Billy. Believe me; it's for the best."

After she ended the call, Morgan waited.

"Think he'll hold off?" he said.

"I hope so." Marge exhaled. "Let's see what other surprise is in the state's report."

She opened the envelope and read the report, then gave it to Morgan.

"Not surprising that they had traces of PCB in their blood." Morgan shook his head. "But we didn't expect they'd find ceftriaxone and azithromycin. They're for . . ."

Marge clenched her jaw. "Treating gonorrhea. And it goes to motive. This was a revenge killing."

"You're going to put it in the final report, right?"

"Yes, but JD isn't getting it until Friday."

"Are sure you're doing the right thing?"

Marge breathed a heavy sigh. "Yes."

"What about the killer's DNA? Was it in the report from Vadigal's lab?"

Marge rubbed her chest. "I was so concerned about the Buxtons I forgot to check."

She went back to the envelope and took out that report.

"They didn't get a match."

"Did they try CODIS?"

"No. JD can have Billy do it." She took a deep breath. "After I finish the report, you can check it to be sure I got everything right."

CHAPTER 20

TUESDAY, DR. SMATHERS removed the bandage wrapped around Pickens' head and replaced it with one that wasn't as noticeable and that he could cover with his hat. His right arm stayed in the sling, but he was free to discard the cushion when he sat. But he still needed a driver since he was right-handed. Amy chauffeured him.

The first thing Pickens did after leaving Smathers' office was have Amy take him to the sheriff's office for an update.

Amy and Hubbard asked to talk to him in private. Pickens frowned and went to his office.

"Okay, let's have it. Start with the video." Pickens waited. "Tell me about it, Mitch."

Hubbard explained the contents of the video and their theory about sex and drugs and Mrs. Buxton not having been raped.

Pickens held a hand up.

"I don't need to hear anymore. Let's talk to Billy."

Amy and Hubbard were relieved.

Billy evaded the issue of the Buxtons' research and talked about the three female facials he pulled off the video.

"It was difficult," said Billy, "because they weren't actually looking at the camera. They were . . ."

"I get it, Billy," said Pickens. "They were having sex."

Billy exhaled. "Yes, but I got enough shots to produce composites. It won't be easy. I don't have the right software. I'm still running them."

"Good work. I'll talk to Sergeant Dunne and Ellison on Friday."

Amy, Hubbard, and Billy's brows hiked. They were surprised he didn't want more and would wait until Friday to talk to Dunne. Billy was especially pleased since he was off the hook about the Buxton research findings.

CHAPTER 21

Wednesday, August 22

PICKENS AND AMY were getting ready to go to Warfield for Conlon's funeral. They had dressed in full uniform. Suddenly Pickens' phone chirped.

"Dammit, not him."

"Not who?" said Amy.

Pickens answered the call. "What the hell do you want, Bo? I'm busy. I've got a funeral to go to."

"That's why I'm calling, JD."

Pickens interest piqued. "What about it?"

"I saw that car that was in the newspaper picture."

"When? Where?"

"This morning. I was on my way home from the lake when it flew past me."

Amy listened with curiosity.

"How do you know it was the same car?"

Pickens heard Tatum's exhale.

"Because I had one just like it. It was a gift from a recruiter. I gave it to my daughter, and her husband had sort of an accident. He kinda demolished it, and what was left went to the salvage yard. They canceled the insurance and let the registration lapse. Anyway, the Cougar flew past me. I think it headed to Warfield or away from it."

Pickens mouthed, "He saw the Cougar," to Amy. "Did you see the driver?"

"Yeah, I sure did, and she weren't wearing a mask like in the picture."

Pickens brows hiked. "She? It was a woman driving?"

"Yeah. I swear. And there was a passenger, but I couldn't see if it was a male or female. If they were your shooters, you best be careful, JD, they may still be around."

"Don't worry, we will be. Thanks, Bo."

As soon as Pickens ended the call, Amy said, "Tatum saw the Cougar and a woman was driving? Do you think it was our shooters?"

"Not sure, but we're not taking any chances. We'll alert everyone with a BOLO." He checked his watch. "Let's go. We don't want to be late."

They left in Pickens' SUV, and Amy drove.

Pickens had arranged with the surrounding law enforcement agencies for a motorcade to Lake City, Conlon's home town and final resting place. Since Conlon served under Sergeant Dunne, and Deputy Abrue was a close friend of the Conlons, both would go with it.

Pickens was surprised when they arrived in Warfield. People had started to line up along the sidewalks to honor Deputy Conlon. As the elementary and middle school principal, Dunne's husband gave the students the morning off to support Conlon's children and honor their father. Even the mayor and other dignitaries would be there.

Billy's drone club provided eyes in the sky. Marge gave Betty-jean and Andy time off to participate as members of the club.

Other law enforcement agencies helped patrol the surrounding streets and roads in the event the Cougar showed.

After the ceremony, they'd join the motorcade. When it crossed into other counties, their law enforcement personnel would join the motorcade. It would be the same to Lake City.

Ellison had set up a command center in the satellite office, and all communications were on the same frequency. Pickens and Amy were fitted with earpieces so they could monitor the conversations and any chatter about the Cougar.

Every member of Pickens' staff wore their dress uniform reserved for special occasions. Pickens and Amy sat with Dunne and Abrue.

Conlon's parents, his aunt, his uncle and two cousins sat in the front row. Across the aisle, sat Conlon's wife, his children, mother-in-law, and his brother-in-law dressed in his military parade uniform.

The small church was packed with Pickens' deputies, dignitaries from the city and county, other law enforcement officers, and several of Conlon's former unit dressed in their military parade uniforms.

At the request of his wife, Conlon's brother-in-law delivered the eulogy. When the service concluded, a bagpiper played taps, and Conlon's brother-in-law, Deputies Abrue, Jackson, Ortiz, and two ex-army buddies of Conlon carried the casket out of the church.

Pickens extended his condolences to Conlon's family.

Pickens' deputies and members of other law enforcement agencies lined the walkway, stood at attention and saluted.

Jimmy Noseby, the reporter, captured the entire scene for his front-page article.

Once the casket was in the hearse, the motorcade proceeded through town enroute to its final destination.

The people who lined the streets had a hand over their heart as a tribute to the fallen deputy.

Billy's drone club radioed the patrol cars that there was no sign of the Cougar. They did the same as the motorcade left town and headed for Lake City. Other law enforcement personnel were on alert as the motorcade traveled north.

The Cougar was never sighted.

CHAPTER 22

FRIDAY, WHEN PICKENS left the house, Marge told him he'd have her report by ten o'clock. After Pickens and Amy arrived at the sheriff's office, he had Amy arrange a meeting with her, Billy, Hubbard, Dunne, and Ellison in the conference room. He didn't tell her, but he wanted to see for himself how they were holding up under pressure.

Pickens was surprised to see Marge when she delivered the ME's final report.

"I didn't expect to see you. I thought . . ." said Pickens.

"The report's too sensitive to be e-mailed or faxed," said Marge. Pickens brow furrowed. "You'll see when you read it."

Pickens glanced at the report and stiffened.

"You sure about this?"

"Yes." Marge nodded. "The lab also did a nationwide vital records search. It's in the report. You'll understand when you read it that it's stuff that makes nightmares. I have to go. How's your head?"

Pickens exhaled. "The head's fine." He lowered his head. "It's the damn shoulder and this sling."

"Deal with it. You need to come to grips with the fact that you were shot and almost killed and you're Amy's hero."

He rubbed his chin with his left hand.

"Yeah, there's that."

"It's more than that," she snapped. "You mandated counseling for your deputies. Damnit, now mandate it for yourself."

Marge turned to leave but stopped.

"One more thing. I love you, JD Pickens."

He grinned. "I love you, too, Marge Davids."

After Marge left, Pickens picked up the report and was about to read it when his office phone rang.

"Sheriff Pickens," he said.

"Pickens, I'm the Chief of Police in Eustis. We had an incident last night that you might be interested in."

"What kind of incident?"

"Two officers responded to a call about a possible home invasion. When they arrived at the scene, they were cautious because of your BOLO. They approached the house with weapons drawn, and one of the officers noticed a vehicle start up and approach. The occupants opened fire on the officers, but they were alert enough and fired back. They weren't hurt, but they were sure it was that Cougar in the BOLO."

"I'm glad they weren't hurt. Could they ID the occupants?"

"Nah, they gave pursuit but the Cougar outran them, and they lost it. And the license plate was different than the one in the BOLO. What's your thought, Pickens?"

"I think they decided to go after someone else. We thought it was about us, but it looks like it's about all law enforcement."

"They got a grudge against law enforcement for something that happened to them or someone they know?"

"Yeah. If it happens again, we'll know for sure that it's all law enforcement. Thanks, Chief."

"Anytime. Well, not anytime like this. Hell, you know what I mean. I had two officers at that deputy's funeral. Hope I don't have to do it again."

"Me, too. Hold on, Chief. You might want to be extra vigilant this weekend. They came after us four times. Be prepared."

"We are. All nighttime calls require two patrol cars. And if anything looks suspicious, they call for backup immediately."

"Good thinking."

After the call, Pickens went back to the ME's report and read it twice to be sure he understood what was in it, but he had a hard time believing what he learned about the Buxtons. He grabbed the report and went to the conference room and closed the door behind him.

On one side of the conference table sat Amy and Hubbard. Across from them sat Dunne and Ellison. Billy sat at the opposite end from Pickens. All had a pad and pencil in front of them.

"Thanks for being here and for your participation at Deputy Conlon's funeral." Everyone nodded. "Let's start with the Cougar case." He purposely avoided calling it the Conlon case. "Anything new?"

"We haven't had any luck yet on the driver," said Dunne. "We're waiting for the graphic artist to get back to us. She's been busy but promised something soon. We'll get it to Lu, and she can run with it."

"We're hoping my contact can get prints off the shell casings," said Ellison, "but they're busy, too, and we don't have priority. Lu is still trying to track down the expired registration owner."

Pickens was pleased that Dunne and Ellison used we and not I. It meant they were working as a team.

"Forget about that Cougar."

Dunne and Ellison's eyebrows raised. Both were curious.

Pickens told them about Bo Tatum's call Wednesday and how the Cougar was headed north.

"I have something else," said Pickens. "I got a call from Eustis." He proceeded to explain the call.

"If it's about all law enforcement," said Dunne, "then I agree, the shooters are seeking revenge."

"But for who?" said Ellison.

"I expect you two to find out," replied Pickens. "Have Lu check for old crimes in the central Florida area. Maybe there's one that stands out."

"We'll have her get right on it," said Dunne. "Right, Ellison?"

Ellison was checking his phone and scribbling on the pad.

"Are we interrupting you, Bobby?" said Pickens.

Ellison put the pencil down.

"No. I was making some notes. When I first got here, I noticed your board."

"What about it?"

"I saw a pattern." Ellison pointed a finger. "The first ambush was Saturday, July 21. The second was August 4, and the Eustis one was last night, August 16."

Dunne wrote the dates on her pad.

"Each was two weeks apart," said Ellison. "And except for last night, on weekends. If the Cougar's gonna strike again, it will probably be this weekend or in two weeks. Probably in Eustis. Hopefully, not here."

"I see it," said Dunne. "What happens in-between ambushes?"

"Could be anything," said Ellison. "We still have the services of those three state troopers. I suggest you pair them up with your deputies, JD, and do like the Eustis police are doing. Only answer calls with two patrol cars and call for backup if something looks suspicious." Ellison paused. "Hell, I got a carry permit, and I'll make myself available in Warfield if necessary. Sergeant Dunne can coordinate everything."

"I'll do the same," said Hubbard.

Pickens had already mulled it over, but it had to be Dunne's decision.

"Sounds like a plan. What do you think, Sergeant Dunne?"

All eyes pointed at Dunne.

"I think it's a good plan," said Dunne. "But I don't like the idea of using two armed citizens."

"JD can deputize Mitch and me," said Ellison. "I'll sign something that says so, and I'll only charge a dollar a night if you use my services. How about you, Mitch?"

"I'm already a consultant," said Hubbard. "JD deputized me once before. I'll sign something, and my fee's the same."

"What say you, Sergeant Dunne?" said Pickens.

"Works for me."

"Hubbard and Ellison," said Pickens, "raise your right hand." Pickens shook his head. "No, your other right hand. That's better. You swear to obey the rules of a sheriff's deputy and not fire your weapon unless absolutely necessary?"

"I swear," said Hubbard and Ellison.

"Sergeant Dunne, you have two new deputies at your disposal. But don't pair them together."

"Don't worry. I won't."

"Billy and I can pair up if necessary," said Amy.

"That's two more. I'd pair with someone," said Pickens and pointed to his right arm, "but I'm handicapped. I'll stay in touch with my radio on."

"We'll change the radio frequency," said Dunne, "as a precaution."

"Since that's taken care of let's talk about the Buxton case. Anything new? How about those facials, Billy?"

"Do you need Ellison and me for this?" asked Dunne.

Dunne didn't know much about the Buxton case, and Pickens preferred not to share the contents of the ME report with her and Ellison. Maybe he would at a later date when he felt it appropriate.

"You've got enough on your plate, Sergeant Dunne," said Pickens. "We can handle this. How's Jackson doing?"

"He finished his counseling and is back on regular duty."

"Guess your talk with him helped," said Pickens.

Dunne glanced at Amy. "A little motherly love helped."

Amy nodded as did Dunne.

"You want him here or in Warfield?" said Dunne.

"Keep him in Warfield. He'll be close to his family." Pickens again pointed to his right arm. "With me out of commission and Conlon gone, we're gonna have to juggle the schedules."

Dunne nodded, then she and Ellison left the room.

"Okay, Billy, how about those facials?"

Billy breathed a sigh of relief. He was relieved Pickens hadn't asked about the background searches on the Buxtons.

"Couldn't get any matches. I'm trying different angles hoping to get better ones. Then I'll run them through DMV again. I said it would be difficult."

"Keep trying. What about the background on the Buxtons?"

Billy glanced at the ME report in front of Pickens. He cleared his throat, hoping Pickens would read it first.

"Something bothering you, Billy?"

Billy coughed. "No."

"Then, let's have it."

"Both Mr. and Mrs. Buxton had the same birthdate," he said with a shaky voice, "and there was no record of a marriage. At least not in Florida. I couldn't get a maiden name for Mrs. Buxton, either." He exhaled. "It's weird."

Pickens opened the ME report.

"It's because she doesn't have one."

Billy's jaw dropped. Amy and Hubbard straightened in their seats.

"The Buxtons' DNA was a familial match."

"They're related to each other?" said Amy. "Like brother and sister?"

"Apparently," said Pickens. "According to a nationwide vital records search, they had the same parents. Both parents are deceased, and there were no other siblings. Their blood samples showed in addition to cocaine, traces of PCB." Pickens nervously rubbed his chin. "The worst part is the husband had ceftriaxone and azithromycin in his."

"You sure, JD?" said Hubbard.

Pickens tapped the report. "The ME was positive."

"But those are drugs for an STD treatment," said Hubbard.

"Gonorrhea, according to the report."

Amy grabbed Hubbard's arm. "Are you kidding me? He infected other women and maybe his sister?" She shook her head. "What a sick bastard."

"Sick is putting it mildly," said Hubbard. "Goes to motive. He infected the wife or girlfriend of the killer, and he got revenge for it by not only degrading Buxton's wife but killing her."

"And the killer's wife or girlfriend got satisfaction by slitting Buxton's throat," said Pickens and looked at Amy. "Are you okay?"

"No," she replied, "I feel sick to my stomach. Excuse me. I'll be right back." She rushed out of the room.

Pickens watched her leave and worried why the results had upset her. It wasn't like her to let a case bother her.

"She's taking the case personally," said Hubbard. "Don't blame her. It's got to me, too."

"Me, too," said Billy.

Pickens took a deep breath. "Both cases are getting to all of us." He lifted his right arm slightly. "Especially me. We'll wait for Amy to compose herself then continue. Anyone want coffee? There's a pot in the break room."

"I'm fine," said Billy and grabbed his water bottle. "I'll wait here."

Pickens left the room. Hubbard followed.

"Might as well use the time to update the board," said Hubbard.

He erased Conlon but left ambush then wrote *8/14/18 – #2.* Then *8/16/18 – Eustis # 3.* Under Buxtons, he wrote *Victims B/S* then *Motive – STD Revenge.*

"I bet Sergeant Dunne has a board like this one," said Hubbard.

"I'm sure she does. Let's get some coffee."

*   *   *

Amy returned to the room after composing herself and sat.

"Sorry," she said.

"Don't apologize," said Pickens. "I felt sick when I first read the report."

"Same here when I first saw the video," said Hubbard.

"Yeah, but I'm trained to . . ."

"You're human like us," said Pickens.

Billy sat silently and absorbed the conversation. He was already unnerved and didn't want to let on that he was.

"Billy," said Pickens, "any chance you could get into CODIS and see if they have anything on the killer's DNA? Mitch might have a contact."

"I have one," said Hubbard. "I also have one at CDC. Maybe the female is in their STD database."

"Coordinate it with Amy. Maybe we'll get lucky."

"We need more than luck on this one," said Amy.

"Before we break up," said Pickens, "was there anything worthwhile in the box the ME gave you?"

Amy slapped her hand on the table. "Damn, what with you getting out of the hospital, the funeral, and me chauffeuring you. I forgot about it."

Pickens picked up the pencil with his left hand, started to write something, but the point broke. He tapped the pencil on the pad and took a deep breath.

Amy braced herself for the firestorm of criticism that was sure to come.

"An honest mistake," said Pickens.

Amy did a double take. When she glanced at Billy, he looked surprised too. Hubbard was scribbling something on his pad and seemed disinterested.

"Get to it first chance you get," said Pickens. "It's not like we're going to solve the case overnight, and we got the weekend to worry about."

Amy was still shocked.

"Now that I'm back, I'll stay on the sideline and act as the coach. You're still in charge of this case, Amy, but if I see a need to step in I will. Same goes for Sergeant Dunne's case." Pickens paused. "The good thing is no one from the county commission has bothered me. But that won't last long." He stood, and the meeting adjourned.

Pickens went to his office.

Billy went back to his desk to try and get into CODIS and the CDC. He was relieved he didn't have to listen to anything else about the Buxtons.

Amy and Hubbard joined Billy at his desk.

Hubbard called his contacts and got access for CODIS but not the CDC. They wanted a subpoena.

"Sorry, Billy, I tried. At least we got CODIS."

"Maybe CODIS will give us something, but it will take some time. Might not know until Monday. I'll let you know what I learn."

"That's fine. We got other business to take care of. Let's hope you don't have to."

CHAPTER 23

SUNDAY MORNING, PICKENS was having breakfast with his wife and daughter when his phone chirped. It was the dispatcher.

The first thing Pickens thought was that the Cougar had been sighted Friday or Saturday night. If it had, why hadn't he heard about it on his radio? And why hadn't Amy or Dunne contacted him?

"Pickens here," he said into the phone, "what's up?"

"Sheriff," said the dispatcher, "I have the chief of police from Eustis holding. Should I have him call you?"

"Yeah, give him my cell number."

"Something wrong, JD?" said Marge.

He hunched his shoulders. "Something must have happened in Eustis."

Pickens phone chirped.

"Chief, everything okay?"

"No. Dammit. That damn Cougar hit us again last night."

Pickens rolled his eyes. "Anyone hurt?"

"No. Thank goodness I listened to you. But they got away. My officers managed to get a look at them. There were two of them, both Caucasian females."

Pickens bit his lip. "Two Caucasian females? You sure?"

"Sure as hell. Think they'll try again?"

Pickens explained Ellison's theory and that it might be two weeks before they hit again somewhere.

"So, I got two weeks to prepare for them?" snapped the chief.

Pickens felt as angry as the chief.

"Maybe, maybe not, but I wouldn't take any chances. You should do like I did and alert the nearby counties."

"Will do. Sonofabitch, what's with the Cougar?"

"Good question," said Pickens and ended the call.

"Sounds like something happened in Eustis," said Marge. "Was it that Cougar again?"

Pickens exhaled. "Yeah, but no one was hurt." He shook his head. "There were two females in the Cougar."

Marge's eyes narrowed.

"Yeah, two females, according to the Eustis police." He gave her a summary of the chief's call. "I gotta call Sergeant Dunne and get her on this."

Pickens hesitated before he called Dunne and mulled the situation over in his head. Why were two females suddenly on a rampage against law enforcement on weekends? What did they do in between the ambushes? Did they plot their next ambush or did they do something else during that time? Was it revenge for a wrong against them or someone close to them? All good questions he'd posit to Dunne, and maybe between her and Ellison they'd get answers.

He called Dunne.

"Sheriff Pickens, I was about to call you," said Dunne.

Dunne had skipped the greeting, so Pickens did.

"I got a call from the Eustis police chief." Pickens told her about the call and the two Caucasian females.

"Caucasian? At least we have a better description than we had, although not much better. So, we're good for another two weeks?"

"Yeah," said Pickens, then laid out his questions. "Maybe

you and Ellison should check for anything involving law enforcement and citizens this time of year."

"Ellison already has Lu doing that."

Pickens was surprised. "He has? Based on what?"

"Based on his revenge theory about Price. It's not about her, but he believes the attacks had to do with revenge for something. We'll find out. You can bet on it."

"I'd take that bet. Good work. I'm gonna add detective to your title Sergeant Dunne."

"Does it come with an increase in pay?"

"Unfortunately, no, just more responsibility."

"I can handle the responsibility. As for the increase in pay, if I weren't happy with my job and my boss, I'd complain, JD."

Dunne couldn't see Pickens smile when she addressed him as JD and not Sheriff as she always did.

"After this is over, I'll see what I can do about the money, but you just got a pay increase."

"Doesn't hurt to ask for more, does it?"

"No, it doesn't, Detective Sergeant Dunne."

He couldn't see Dunne smile.

After the call with Dunne ended, Pickens' home phone rang. Marge answered it.

"He's fine," she said, "and is in the kitchen. We just finished breakfast. Sure, you can speak to him."

She handed the phone to Pickens and mouthed, "The county chairperson."

Pickens frowned.

"Hello, Connie. I wondered how long it would take before you called. I'm surprised you didn't visit me while I was in the hospital." He winked at Marge.

"I did, JD. You were asleep, and I didn't want to disturb you."

"You did?" said Pickens. "You should have."

"Anyway, I'm glad you're okay. Sorry about your deputy. We'll do everything we can for his wife."

"Thanks. She'll appreciate it."

"Any suspects in both cases?"

"We're working on a number of good leads. It's too soon to speculate."

"Yeah, that's what you always say. Keep me informed, JD."

"I will, Connie. Say, while I have you on the phone, I'm gonna need to replace Deputy Conlon, and I could use another deputy. Can you give me some help on it? Please."

He couldn't see her smile.

"Please? That's a first for you. I'll see what I can do. Take care, JD."

"You, too, Connie."

"So?" said Marge. "Will she help you?"

"She said she'd see what she can do."

"At least she didn't say no."

"Yeah, at least."

Pickens stood and refilled his coffee cup.

"Marge, you're a doctor, right?"

Marge's eyes narrowed. "Last I checked I was, and it still says MD on my license plate. Why?"

"How long do I need to . . . ," He raised his elbow. "Wear this damn sling?"

He bit his lip and winced as a bolt of pain shot his shoulder.

"That's your answer, as long as it takes for your shoulder to heal. Damnit, JD, the wound could have been worse, and you'd be in a body cast to prevent you from using your arm. You have to be patient. Ask Dr. Smathers if you can start physical therapy to avoid atrophy." She shook her head. "Don't try to be a hero. Be a coach. You have two deputies that are capable of handling matters. I'm sorry if you don't like my answer, but it's what's right."

Pickens took a deep breath.

"I don't like being on the sidelines and watching."

"Deal with it, JD, or you'll end up back in the hospital and maybe lose the use of your right arm." She glared at him. "I'm serious."

Pickens sat and shook his head.

"Okay. I'll deal with it, but it won't be easy."

"Nothing in life is easy, JD."

CHAPTER 24

MONDAY, WHEN PICKENS arrived at the office, Billy was with Amy, and he walked over to Billy's desk. Billy was still having difficulty with facial recognition, and Pickens sensed his frustration.

"Still, no luck?" said Pickens.

Billy exhaled. "No. I said I didn't have the right software. Maybe the state's crime lab does. I'm starting to give up trying."

"Maybe you should go back farther," said Amy. "How far back did you go?"

"Four months like you told me. But actually, it was eight months because the video stopped recording four months ago."

"Wait," said Hubbard, who had just joined them. "You mean the Buxtons stopped having sex parties four months ago?"

"Or, they stopped taping them," said Billy.

"Billy has a point," said Pickens. "What made them stop?"

"The STD?" said Hubbard.

"The STD?" said Amy. "You think others caught it, and the group might have disbanded?"

Hubbard rubbed his chin. "Could be, and if it was the reason, then maybe Buxton wasn't the host and someone else infected him?" Hubbard shook his head. "Which means the killers either thought Buxton did or maybe they're going after other members of the group."

"Because they have a vendetta against the whole group," said Amy. "If that's the case, we can expect more murders. Hopefully not in our county."

Pickens enjoyed watching his detectives sort through the issues.

"Have Billy check if there were any similar homicides in the past four months," said Pickens. "You two handle it. I have to make a phone call."

Pickens went into his office.

"As if I haven't got enough on my plate, now he wants me to check the state's homicide records?" said Billy.

Hubbard put his hand on Billy's shoulder.

"Ease up, Billy," said Hubbard. "You work on the facials. I'll call my contact at the state and ask them to search the homicide records."

"Thanks, Hubbard."

"While you two do that, I'll go through the Buxton's personal effects," said Amy. "Maybe I'll find something."

Pickens made his call then received one.

"Sheriff Pickens," he said.

"DJ, it's Frank Rinaldo. You remember me?"

Frank Rinaldo was a retired Broward County homicide detective. He'd helped Pickens in the past on the Liz Price case.

"Yeah, I remember you. What can I do for you, Compdaddy?"

"First off, your Spanish still sucks."

"Your English sucks, Rinaldo." Pickens grinned. "My name is JD, not DJ. I listen to records, I don't play them."

Pickens heard Rinaldo's laugh. It sounded like a donkey braying.

"You got me, *amigo*. I need a favor."

"I hope it's an easy one because I'm up to my ass here with a double homicide and I lost a deputy in an ambush."

"Oh, *amigo*, sorry about your deputy."

"Thanks. What's your favor?"

"It's about your double homicide."

Pickens went rigid. "What about it?"

"Broward has one, too."

Pickens leaned forward in his chair.

"So, what's theirs have to do with mine?"

Pickens waited for Rinaldo to answer.

"Does STD sound familiar?"

Pickens almost dropped the phone.

"Hey, you still there, *amigo*?"

"Yeah, I'm here. How did you know my case had to do with STD?"

"I'm retired, not dead, Pickens, and I still have contacts. You interested?"

"I'm interested."

"The detective in charge of the case is a friend of mine. We play poker twice a month. He asked me to call you."

Pickens exhaled. "Why didn't he call me?"

"What difference does it make? He asked me to call you. He wants to talk to you. You want his number or not?"

Pickens considered calling Amy and Hubbard into his office but didn't. He was getting bored with being on the sideline and sitting out the action.

"I do, but I got a situation here," said Pickens, then told Rinaldo about the ambush at the hospital.

"*Ay, caramba*, Pickens. You not up to your ass, you're up to your elbows. Tell you what, Pickens, why don't I have the detective call you."

"That would help," said Pickens.

"His name is Don Everly like in the *Everly Brothers*. You remember them, don't you?"

"Frank, I'm not as old as you."

"Right. Anyway, I'll give him your number, and he'll call you."

"Uh, Frank, I got another situation. I'm scheduled to have physical therapy at two o'clock. Can you have him call me before one or else tomorrow?"

"I can do better than that. Everly is waiting for my call. He'll call you in fifteen minutes. I'll butt out and you two can cooperate."

"I think you mean collaborate."

"Whatever. Maybe we'll talk again, DJ."

Pickens shook his head.

"It's JD . . . Ah the hell with it."

Pickens heard Rinaldo bray.

He didn't have to wait fifteen minutes. His phone rang after seven.

Pickens recognized the area code.

"Sheriff Pickens."

"Pickens, this is Don Everly. Our mutual friend Frank Rinaldo told me to call you."

"Rinaldo's more of a friend to you than me. He said you're working a homicide that involves STD and you think it might be related to mine. First off, how did you learn about my case?"

"From your crime report. A Detective Sergeant Tucker filed it. I had my people flag any case that had similarities to ours. Yours does."

Pickens again considered calling Amy and Hubbard into his office, but he was curious.

"Such as?"

"The STD and how the victims were killed. Both of mine

were shot in the back of the head and the husband had his throat slit. Is that similar to yours?"

"Close enough. Was the female . . . ?" Pickens had difficulty saying sodomized.

"Yes, then she was shot in the back of her head."

"Which victim had the STD?"

"Both. What about your victims?"

"Only the male."

"You got any ideas, Pickens?"

Yeah," said Pickens then told Everly about the video.

"Group sex?" said Everly. "Maybe I should go back to the scene and check the television and the AC vent."

"Any chance you could send me a headshot of the female? We're having difficulty getting a facial off the video. We might be able to make a comparison to one of the females in the video."

"I can fax one. But how does it help?"

"If she's in the video, we'll have the names of four in the group. We could see if they were in contact with each other. If they were, maybe we'll get lucky and get more names off their phones."

"Good idea. Based on your revenge theory, we got a pair of serial killers, and there will be more murders somewhere in Florida."

"There's that," said Pickens, then realized he had to step back onto the sidelines.

"When you send the fax, put your name and phone number on it. I got two detectives working the case, and they'll contact you. I've got other business to take care of."

"Frank told me about your arm. Good luck with PT. I went through it when I got shot in the arm. What're your detectives' names?"

"Detective Sergeant Amy Tucker and Mitch Hubbard."

"Mitch Hubbard? I thought he retired and took up quail hunting somewhere in Central Florida."

"He did. Hubbard's acting as a consultant. It's not the first time he did."

"A consultant, huh? Like Rinaldo does for me."

"How do you know Hubbard?"

"We crossed paths when I worked in Orlando vice. I left Orlando after Broward offered me a chance to work homicide. Maybe if I stayed in Orlando until Hubbard retired, I might have got his job. But, hell, that's in the past. I'm happy where I am."

"I hear ya. I'm happy here. Just wish I didn't have the damn arm to deal with."

"Patience, Pickens, you'll be throwing a ball around pretty quick."

"As long as it's a football," said Pickens. "Do me a favor, Everly, when you talk to Tucker and Hubbard, act like I didn't tell you everything. I'm supposed to be on the sidelines. Let them fill you in." Pickens reconsidered his decision. "Better yet, you call Detective Tucker. Tell her you were referred to me by Rinaldo—which you were—and say when you mentioned STD, I told you to call her since she's in charge of the case."

"Got it. You're a good guy, Pickens."

"That's what my wife tells me." Pickens smiled. "Now, I'm gonna make a lunch date. Good talking to you, Everly."

After talking to Everly, Pickens called Marge.

"Sheriff Pickens," said Marge, "to what do I owe this call?"

Pickens smiled. "I need a lunch date, and you were on my mind. Actually, you're always on my mind."

"Have you been drinking on the job, Pickens?"

He laughed. "No, I'm serious. I was thinking of you for lunch. Can we make it a date?"

He heard her giggle.

"Okay, but no funny stuff or you'll need a sling for your left arm."

"Ha, ha—speaking of arms, I got an appointment at the hospital with a physical therapist. I was hoping you'd drop me there after lunch. I'll call you when my appointment's over, and you could take me home." Pickens grinned. "Sound like a plan?"

"Sounds like you got something else on your mind. I'll clear my schedule and wait at the hospital for you. What time should I swing by?"

Pickens checked his watch. "It's almost noon. How about now?"

"I'll be there in half an hour. I have some paperwork to finish."

"Oh, and, Marge, I love you."

"You, too, JD."

While Pickens talked to Marge, Everly called Amy. Pickens wasn't privy to the conversation because he waited in his office until it was time for Marge to arrive. He waved as he left his office and walked out the door, leaving everyone stunned by his quick exit.

*   *   *

Marge waited for Pickens to finish his physical therapy. When he walked into the waiting room, he was smiling and held his sling in his right hand.

Pickens bent his right forearm.

"Happy day, Marge, I don't need this damn thing anymore unless I feel I need it."

Marge clapped her hands. "That's great, JD, but you're not going to start coaching yet, are you?"

"Not yet, but as soon as I can raise my arm high above my head, I will. The therapist said it might be in a week. He had me start with lower arm movement and some full arm movement. I got exercises for both." He rubbed his right shoulder. "Damn if it didn't hurt when he made me raise my arm. I'll still need a driver for another week." Pickens grinned. "Then I'll be independent again."

Marge shook her head. "You've always been independent. You just want to be a kid again."

He wiggled his head. "Yeah. It will be great being a kid again and a coach on the field again. My appointments are at nine. Will you take me?"

"Of course, I will. I'll take you to your office and pick you up when you're ready to go home. I'll arrange my schedule."

"Thanks. Let's go home."

CHAPTER 25

TUESDAY, WHEN PICKENS strolled into the office, Amy and Hubbard were huddled around Billy's desk. Pickens walked over to the board and read the latest entries. Amy and Hubbard had posted what they learned from Everly, including the names of the victims. They added a note to check the Buxtons' phone contacts and the headshot from Broward's female victim.

"Impressive," said Pickens. "You two were busy yesterday."

Amy, Billy, and Hubbard were surprised to see Pickens wasn't wearing the sling.

"Where's the sling, JD?" said Amy.

"Don't need it." He grinned. "I started PT yesterday." He raised his forearm. "I go every morning. Marge takes me. Another week and I'll have full use of the arm and can drive. You want to fill me in, or I can call Sergeant Dunne and get an update from her."

"The detective you referred to us was real helpful," said Amy. "Billy's doing a comparison of the victim's driver license to the video." Amy nodded Billy's way.

"I got the license photo off DMV," said Billy. "They're not a perfect match but better than fifty percent. It looks like one of our women is Tanya Zeller, the Broward victim. Take a look."

Pickens thought using the driver's license photo was better than his idea of the headshot.

Billy turned in his seat so Pickens could lean in and get a closer look.

Pickens tilted his head left then right.

"Close enough. Good job, Billy."

"We went through the Buxtons' phones and made a list of contacts," said Hubbard. "Everly sent a list to compare it to."

"Any luck?" said Pickens.

"So far, seven numbers match," said Amy. "We'll get names and addresses before we call any. Mitch is working on how we approach the people. We have to be careful because they might not have been part of the group."

"Let me know if you need my help." Pickens tilted his head toward his office. "I'm gonna check in with Sergeant Dunne."

Amy, Hubbard, and Billy's jaws dropped. They expected Pickens to take control of the case.

Amy followed Pickens into his office and closed the door.

"You okay, JD?"

Pickens smirked. "Yeah. I don't want to step on your toes. It's your case, Amy. You handle it the way you want. Just keep me informed."

Amy did a double take. "But . . ."

"But what, Detective? As I said, it's your case so deal with it." He flicked his hand. "Now go. I'm gonna call Sergeant Dunne."

Amy shook her head and left.

"Is he okay?" said Hubbard.

Amy hunched her shoulders. "He said he was and didn't want to interfere."

"Then do your job, Detective," said Billy. "The Sheriff has faith in you and Hubbard."

"Billy's right, Detective," said Hubbard. "JD is doing what a good leader does. Delegate and get out of the way. Let's do our jobs."

"Yeah," said Amy with determination.

* * *

After Amy left his office, Pickens called Dunne. She was at Ellison's office when she answered.

"Sheriff Pickens, how's the arm?"

"Better. I'm going through PT and no more sling as of yesterday. How's the case going?"

"Lu discovered thirty-seven incidents of robbery to investigate."

"What's Ellison doing?"

"He's culling through the reports with me to narrow down the incidents, so we don't waste our time. He's also checking the names of the investigators to see if he knows any of them. He'll make the calls since he has more experience at it then I do. I'll listen in on the conversation."

"You're doing a superb job, Detective Dunne. Keep me informed. Like you, the case is personal to me, and I want Conlon's killers brought to justice as quickly as possible."

"Don't you want to get involved with the investigation?"

"Nope. It's your case. I'd just get in the way. You and Ellison seem to be doing a good job working together."

"We have our disagreements, but Ellison has more experience, so I lean on him. Lu is our intermediary."

"I bet she keeps him in place. Take care, Detective Dunne."

Dunne hesitated. "Um, Sheriff, isn't it about time you started calling me Mia when it's the two of us speaking."

"I'll call you Mia if you call me JD."

"Got it, JD."

"Got it, Mia." Pickens grinned and ended the call.

CHAPTER 26

WEDNESDAY, AFTER PHYSICAL therapy, Pickens went right to the board and saw the additions Amy and Hubbard had added. Two names had *CNA* for *called no answer* next to them. The other two had *WCB* for *waiting for a callback*. Next to each name was a driver's license photo.

Amy and Hubbard had made progress. Pickens' confidence level escalated. He knew he made the right decision to stay on the sideline and let his detectives do their jobs. Of course, Amy and Dunne had Hubbard and Ellison to assist them. Homicide wasn't an everyday occurrence for Amy and Dunne.

"Good progress," said Pickens. "You two have been busy."

"We're slowly getting there," said Amy. "Hubbard and I divided the names between us, and we're making calls."

"And I just got two more names," said Billy. "It's interesting the calls stopped over three months ago."

"Maybe someone got the STD and notified everyone," said Hubbard. "And that was why the group disbanded."

"Either the killers started notifying, or got notified," said Amy. "I'd bet they got notified."

Pickens wanted to wade in on the conversation, but as the coach who had delegated to his assistants, he had to standby and listen. Nevertheless, if he did wade in, he'd side with Amy.

"And I'd bet that the killers' phone number is on the list," said Hubbard. "If it's not, then they might have been guests of someone in the group."

"If only they all used the same doctor for the STD prescription," said Amy, "we'd be able to track down the host carrier."

Hubbard shook his head. "Wouldn't make a difference. The answer would be *patient confidentiality*."

"So, where does that leave us?"

Hubbard went to the board and pointed. "Right where we are now," he said. "Telephoning like mass marketers."

"I wonder if Detective Everly had any luck. Let's call him."

Billy watched the expression on Pickens' face and knew he was enjoying the conversation. Billy grinned, and Pickens winked.

"I can see I'm of no use here," said Pickens. "The high school football team needs me, so I'll be at the school after PT for the rest of the week. If you need me, you have my number. I'll come in Saturday for a briefing. Billy, could you drop me at the high school?"

Billy glanced at Amy and Hubbard. They were on the phone with Everly.

"They don't need me right now, so I can take you."

Pickens and Billy left.

When Billy returned, Amy and Hubbard stood in front of the board. Hubbard put check marks next to the names they hadn't made contact with yet.

"Unless someone calls us back," said Hubbard, "the case is going nowhere."

"And Everly's not having any luck either. As far as I'm concerned there's nothing we can do. Hopefully Sergeant Dunne and Ellison are having better luck."

"Hopefully. Amy, I'm going to take the rest of the day off.

Tomorrow, too. If anyone calls or if Everly calls, you got my cell number. I've got things to do at home that Donna's been nagging me about. I can be here in a heartbeat. But I'll come in Friday regardless."

"I'd take the day off if I could, but unfortunately I'm not a consultant. And Billy still has to get names and addresses to go with the numbers on the list." She waved. "Say hello to Donna."

Hubbard smiled, waved to Billy and left.

CHAPTER 27

FRIDAY, PICKENS CONVINCED Marge to let him drive to physical therapy, and then drop him off at the high school. He'd bum a ride home.

Hubbard arrived later than usual and went right to Billy's desk. Amy hovered over him.

"I miss anything?" Hubbard asked.

Amy looked up, startled. "Billy got two names and addresses. Unfortunately, they belong to the Buxtons and Zellers. He's got a possible on two more."

"But I probably won't have them until tomorrow," said Billy. "It's not easy getting them without help from the phone company, but I have a way."

"At least you're getting them," said Hubbard. "Anyone return our calls?"

"No," said Amy, "and Everly's not getting any call backs either. We're at a standstill."

"Solving homicides always has standstills," said Hubbard. "That's why they take time."

"I hate waiting," said Amy. "Any ideas what we do in the meantime?"

Hubbard grinned. "Sit around and bullshit. That's what we did when I worked homicide. I'd bet Ellison did the same.

Speaking of him, have he and Sergeant Dunne had any luck yet?"

Amy shrugged. "Beats me. Maybe we'll find out tomorrow when JD comes in."

"I'll hang around until noon. If nothing happens, I'll go home. Donna wants me to go shopping with her." He shook his head. "I'd rather something broke on the case. Then I'd get out of shopping. I hate it, especially with Donna. She likes to touch everything, and it takes hours. It's worse than being stuck in a subway."

"How do you know what that's like? There aren't any subways in Orlando."

"There are in New York City, and we got stuck several times when we visited. Never again."

"Got another name," shouted Billy. "But it's on Everly's list of phone numbers. Want me to call him or do you want to, Amy?"

"Give me the info. I'll text it to him."

Other than Billy getting the names and addresses, nothing happened on the case. Hubbard went home after lunch. Amy and Billy busied themselves with office matters.

CHAPTER 28

IT WAS AFTER dark, when Pickens and his family were in his pickup truck on their way home from dinner at Pickens' parents' house. Sarah was in the back seat. Bailey lay next to her with his head against her leg.

Suddenly the dog stood and barked.

Pickens glanced in the rearview mirror and saw an approaching vehicle with its brights lit. Marge saw the lights in the side mirror.

"Must be teenagers who don't recognize your truck," said Marge.

Bailey barked again.

Pickens extended his right arm. "Just in case," he said.

Marge opened the glove compartment, took out Pickens' Beretta, and handed it to him.

Pickens set the weapon in his lap just as the oncoming vehicle bumped his truck.

"Sarah, get down next to Bailey," said Pickens. "You get down, too, Marge."

Marge slid in her seat, and the vehicle rammed Pickens' truck again.

Pickens rolled the window down, grabbed the warning light off the dashboard, turned it on, and put it on the roof. He reached for his weapon when the vehicle swerved and slammed into the driver's side.

Pickens saw the gun protruding from the vehicle's passenger window and started to raise his weapon when he was hit three times in the head. He lost control of the truck as it went off the road and flipped upside down.

Marge opened her eyes and saw Pickens' lifeless body. She heard Bailey whimper and a soft moan from Sarah. She attempted to get out of the truck to save her daughter. She climbed out the window and cut herself on broken glass but was safely out of the truck.

She heard the sound of sirens and panicked. Marge had to get Sarah. She stood and was trying to open the rear door when a fireman grabbed her and pulled her away.

"No," screamed Marge. "I have to save my daughter."

But it was too late. The truck burst into flames.

Marge watched as her family perished in the blaze, then fainted.

CHAPTER 29

"WAKE UP, SWEETHEART," said Pickens, "you're having a nightmare."

Marge screamed, "No, God, no."

Pickens shook her gently.

"Wake up, dammit. You're having a bad dream."

Marge opened her eyes and nearly fainted when she saw he was alive and not burned to ashes.

"It's okay, Marge, you were dreaming."

"Is Sarah okay?"

"Yes, she's in bed with Bailey. Everybody's fine. So are you."

Marge's eyes teared.

"Hold me and don't let go." She buried her head in his chest. "I love you, JD Pickens."

Pickens held her tight. "I love you, too."

After Marge showered and dressed, she went to the kitchen. She smiled when she saw her family. Pickens and Sarah were tossing small pieces of Shredded Wheat at each other. Bailey caught the misses. Usually, she'd yell, "Stop that." But seeing her family alive and enjoying themselves brought happy tears.

Pickens, dressed in his uniform, stopped when he saw her.

"Hey, you're awake. I made coffee." He held up a palm. "No, you sit. I'll get you a cup."

Marge sat.

"Morning, Mommy," said Sarah.

"Good morning, Sweetheart." Marge extended her arms. "Give me a hug."

Sarah pranced over and hugged and kissed her mother.

Pickens set her coffee next to her.

"JD, can you stay home today? We can do something with Sarah and Bailey."

Pickens had convinced Marge to let him start driving himself to his physical therapy session as the therapist gave him the okay to start driving as long it was only around town and not long trips.

"Please," said Marge.

The way she looked when she said please was always sexy and irresistible.

He smiled. "Okay. I'll call and get an update. Don't forget tonight we're having dinner at my parents' house."

Marge tensed. "Can we do it some other time? I'd rather not do it this weekend."

Pickens' brow wrinkled. "Does this have anything to do with your nightmare?"

She rubbed her wrists. "Yes."

Pickens reached out and stroked her arm. "I'll call my mom. She'll understand."

*   *   *

Pickens called Amy and had her set up a conference call with Dunne. Fortunately, both Hubbard and Ellison were available. Hubbard was with Amy, and Ellison with Dunne.

"Sorry, I can't be there," said Pickens. "I've got a pressing matter at home." He heard whispering and sensed concern. "Don't worry. It's nothing I can't handle. So, who wants to go first?"

"We will," said Dunne. "We made a list of robbery incidents. We excluded home invasions and narrowed it to those where the suspects were captured, and we felt relatives might be seeking revenge. Of those, we selected nine to contact the investigator handling them."

"With five of those," said Ellison, "I know the detectives. Sergeant Dunne suggested we call them first."

Pickens was pleased that Ellison had deferred to Dunne.

"If I know those guys, and I believe I do," said Ellison, "they're off for the weekend."

"We'll call them on Monday," said Dunne.

"Anything else?" said Pickens.

"No," said Dunne. "I wish we had more."

"Maybe on Monday you will. Good job, Detectives Dunne and Ellison. Amy, you're up."

"We're not doing much better. We've got some names and addresses off the list but haven't made contacts yet. Neither has Everly. Two of the names are already dead."

"We're at a stalemate, JD," said Hubbard, "which isn't unusual when working homicide."

"Tell me about it," chimed in Ellison.

"Then my coaching football hadn't hurt. You didn't need me." Pickens smiled. "Maybe I'll take a couple of weeks off." He heard several exclamations of 'What?' "Just kidding. I'll see you on Monday. Take the rest of the weekend off." Pickens grinned and hung up.

"Was he kidding?" said Amy.

"Beats me," said Dunne. "Ellison and I are taking his advice. Have a great weekend." Dunne hung up.

"Might as well do the same thing," said Hubbard. "See you two Monday."

Amy and Billy shrugged.

"So?" said Billy. "What do we do?"

"Have a nice weekend, Corporal." Amy winked and left.

Billy sat dumbfounded, but eventually, he too went home.

CHAPTER 30

Sunday, September 2

VINNIE AND THERESA Palmera had returned from a two-week vacation in Costa Rica. The Palmeras were both in their mid-forties and owned a string of fitness centers in Gainesville, Florida. Vinnie managed the centers, and Theresa was a fitness instructor. They both owned cell phones but rarely gave out the numbers except to employees for emergency purposes. Business calls went to the office phone. They also had a landline at home, but only used it for special purposes.

After settling in, Vinnie noticed the flashing light on the answering machine. He pressed play, and the machine said there were seven messages. Vinnie listened to them and then called to his wife.

"Hey, Babe, I wonder why we got four messages from a Detective Everly from Broward County."

"Did he say what he was calling about?"

"No, just to return his call it was important."

"What's so important in Broward County?"

"How the hell do I know?" Vinnie was losing his patience.

"Call him back tomorrow or whenever."

Vinnie was sitting in his favorite chair with a cup of coffee and reading the Sunday newspaper when an article caught his attention.

"Hey, Babe, check this out."

Theresa was sitting across from him, also with a cup of coffee but reading the home section of the paper.

"What now? You know I don't care about sports—except women's."

Vinnie folded the paper. "It's not about sports, it's about a murder in Tampa Palms, and I think we know the victims."

He got her attention. "What are you talking about? We don't know anyone in Tampa Palms."

"Yeah, we do. They were at a get-together."

"Are you sure?"

"I think they were that young couple who only came once. Remember?"

"Oh yeah, now I remember. She was shy and hesitated to participate until she got high. Did you do her?"

Vinnie smiled. "I was her first before she let others have her."

"Was she any good?"

"As good as could be expected considering she was spaced out. How about him, did he do you?"

"Once and he wasn't that good."

Vinnie scratched his chin. "Think he infected you?"

She contemplated it. "Who knows."

"Anyway, read the article."

He handed her the paper, and she studied the article.

"Definitely not that young couple. It says the victims were in their late forties." She covered her mouth and gasped. "Geez, what a horrible way to die. Both shot in the head and the man had his throat cut."

"Maybe we should call that detective in Broward County. Whaddaya think?"

"You call him but not today. I wish I knew who gave me the damn STD."

"Me too. You think it was someone in the group?"

"Maybe. It's a good thing we told the others and dropped out of the group."

"I'm curious, did you have sex with anyone outside the group?"

Theresa slapped her husband. "I can't believe you said that. No, have you?"

Vinnie put his hand on his burning cheek. "Of course not."

"You had better not have and gave this damn thing to me. I swear I'll kill you if you did."

Vinnie took her in his arms. "Babe, I'd never do that. Remember I wasn't the last one to have sex with you, so it wasn't me. If you hadn't gone to the doctor, you would have infected me."

Theresa wiped her tears. "Well, some sonofabitch gave it to me." She gazed into his eyes. "Would you kill the sonofabitch that did?"

He ran his fingers across his throat. "I'd slit him from ear to ear."

"I love you."

"I love you, too." He offered her a sly look. "I know it's early, but want to go to bed?"

She grinned. "Will you wear a condom?"

"Absolutely."

"You know what? Forget the damn condom. Use the toy, and I'll give you head."

CHAPTER 31

ONDAY, PICKENS DROVE his SUV by himself to physical therapy then drove to the office. When he arrived, Amy was on the phone. Ellison had arrived ahead of Pickens and was listening to the tail end of Amy's conversation.

"Scratch another name off the list," said Amy.

Pickens and Hubbard narrowed their eyes.

"That was a detective from the Tampa Police." Amy told them about the homicide the Tampa police discovered Saturday in Tampa Palms.

"How did they get your name?" said Pickens.

"I left several messages to call me. Tampa got my name off the answering machine and called to ask why I called. I told them about the two homicides and that we had numbers but not names, and their victims' number was on my list. The detective said she'll fax the crime report. If they get any prints or DNA, she'll let us know."

Hubbard walked over to the board, put a blank next to the phone number, and wrote *deceased*.

"That makes the body count now six," he said. "How many more can we expect?"

Amy shook her head. "We've still got, what, a hand full of numbers yet—so does Everly."

"Who knows how many more we should expect," said Hubbard, "but there will be more."

Pickens phone chirped.

"Speaking of Everly," said Pickens, "it's him calling."

Amy's eyes narrowed. She wondered why Everly called Pickens and not her.

"Everly," said Pickens, "what's up?"

"I tried to call Detective Tucker," said Everly, "but she's been on her phone."

"Hold on, she's right here. I'll put you on speaker."

"What's up, Everly?" said Amy.

"I got a call from a Vinnie Palmera. He and his wife Theresa live in Gainesville." Everly went on to tell them about the Palmeras being on vacation in Costa Rica, coming home, the messages from Everly, and seeing the article about the homicide in Tampa Palms.

"We know about Tampa Palms," said Amy.

"Then you know more than I do. Anyway, when I explained why I called him, Palmera opened up about the get-togethers they attended. After I described our two homicides and that video you saw, he came clean about them. He said ten couples participated in, I guess you could call it swinging. They met once a month at a different location. About four couples at a time depending on who could make it."

Everly paused, and they heard him exhale.

"Palmera also said that one time someone invited a younger couple to attend. He didn't know their names and never saw them again. I can't believe what they did at those get-togethers. The Palmeras stopped attending after someone gave his wife gonorrhea."

The phone suddenly went silent as if they were disconnected or Everly hung up for some unknown reason.

"Sorry about that. I needed a breather. Anyway, Palmera is

e-mailing me a list of the names, phone numbers, and addresses of the ten couples. When I get it, I'll fax it to you, Detective Tucker. I'll keep making calls if you want me to, but I gotta tell you it bothered me listening to Palmera."

"It bothered me, too," said Hubbard.

Amy and Hubbard quickly conferred.

"Tell you what, Detective Everly," said Amy, "you work your case in Broward. I'll give your list to the Tampa detective, and she can make calls. If you turn up anything, let us know."

"Thanks, Detective Tucker. Good luck. I hope someone catches those killers, and they get what they deserve."

"Same here," said Pickens, and ended the call.

"Sonofabitch," said Amy, "we gotta catch these killers."

Pickens noticed that lately, with the case, Amy's vocabulary had become distasteful. But who was he to judge? When he got angry, there was no limit to his choice of words.

"Yeah," said Pickens.

Amy went to the board and added the latest victims' names as well as the Palmeras. She left space for the names that were in the fax.

"We've got three homicides so far," said Amy. "How many more can we expect?"

"No more than seven," said Hubbard. "While you're updating the board, you might as well add a question mark and circle it. It represents those unknown guests. The circle is for when we find a connection to them."

Amy did as Hubbard suggested.

"What do we do now?" said Amy.

"I have a suggestion," said Billy. "It's something one of my teachers taught me."

"What the hell does a teacher have to do with the case?" shouted Amy and kicked a nearby wastebasket.

"Hold on, Detective," said Pickens. "I know you're feeling frustrated, but Billy was offering help."

"How the hell do you know what I'm feeling? I've been working my ass off while you've been playing football with a bunch of high school kids."

Pickens' jaw tightened.

"In my office, Detective. NOW!"

Amy followed Pickens into his office, and he slammed the door behind her.

"What the hell was that about? You think I enjoyed getting shot, spending a week in the hospital, my arm in a sling, and having you and Marge chauffer me?" Pickens raised his hand. "Don't bother to apologize. You wanted the case, Detective, and I gave it to you. Including the responsibility that goes with it and the willingness to accept help when offered. Billy offered it, and you belittled him." Pickens glared at her. "Don't you think Billy has worked his ass off on the case? He's here before you. Leaves after you're long gone and comes in on weekends on his own time. Today is Labor Day, and he didn't take the day off. And what about Mitch Hubbard? He's here and isn't even getting paid for his services. Damnit, it's not all about you, Detective. NOW, go out there and apologize to Billy."

Pickens opened the door and walked behind Amy.

"Where's Billy?" said Pickens.

"He went to lunch," said Hubbard, "and said he might not be back."

Pickens placed his hands on his hips as did Hubbard.

"Go find Billy, Amy, and you had better bring him back. DO YOU UNDERSTAND?"

Amy turned and stormed out of the office.

"Whew, that was some tongue lashing you gave her, JD. My ears are still burning."

"It's not the first time, and she deserved it. If she knows

what's good for her, she'll get over it. I'm not sure who I need more her or Billy."

"You need both, JD."

"Maybe."

"You know what we need, JD? A ride into the country for a sausage dog and a beer. What say ya?" Hubbard grinned.

"I could use a dog and a beer. You're on." Pickens hesitated. "But someone has to be here to collect Everly's fax."

Hubbard turned and pointed toward the entrance. "How about Abrue? She's familiar with the case, and just arrived."

"Not a bad idea. Abrue," yelled Pickens.

"Yes, Sheriff."

"We're expecting a fax from a Detective Everly in Broward County. When it gets here, put it on my . . ." Hubbard shook his head. "Put it on Amy's desk." Hubbard grinned. "Mitch and I are going to lunch, and we won't be back."

"Got it, Sheriff. Can I ask you a question?"

"Ask away, Abrue."

"Is Sergeant Dunne any closer to capturing Jason's killer?"

"It's killers, Abrue, and Sergeant Dunne is working diligently to catch the women. We all are."

Abrue's brows hiked. "Did you say women?"

"Yes, Abrue, two women."

"When they catch the bitches, can I be there?"

Pickens grinned. "We'd all like to be there, Abrue. Let's go, Mitch."

Outside of the office, Hubbard said, "Good thinking letting Amy and Billy spend the rest of the day together. They'll work out their differences."

"And I'll eventually work out mine. Let's take two cars. After lunch I'm going to the high school," Pickens smiled, "for football practice. What about you?"

"I'm gonna call Tatum and see if he wants to go fishing."

Later, Pickens called Abrue. She said the fax came in and she'd put it on Amy's desk, and Amy and Billy had returned from lunch.

"Tell them I won't be in tomorrow. I'm going to Warfield to speak with Sergeant Dunne and Bobby Ellison. I'll see them when I see them."

CHAPTER 32

WHEN PICKENS ARRIVED at the Warfield office on Tuesday, Dunne wasn't there, but Deputy Zeke Jackson was. Jackson looked different from the last time Pickens saw him. His shoes and holster were spit-shined, and his uniform neatly pressed. His air of confidence had returned, and he looked menacing—like he did as an offensive lineman in high school.

"Deputy Jackson, it's good to see you."

"Good to see you, Sheriff. How's the arm?"

"Much better. I can't throw a football yet, but I can drive."

"I heard you had a couple of chauffeurs. How was it?"

"Have you ever been a passenger with a female driver?" Jackson grinned. "You press a brake pedal that isn't there, you brace yourself against the dashboard when she comes to a sudden stop, and you grab onto the 'Oh shit bar' when she makes a quick turn." Pickens shook his head. "It's worse than bumper cars."

Jackson and Pickens both laughed.

"So, Zeke, how ya doing?"

"I'm doing good, Sheriff. Sergeant Dunne took good care of me." He ran his hands down his uniform. "Look at my uniform. She's wearing off on me."

"I see that."

"Any chance I can stay in Warfield? I like being under her command."

"I'll arrange it. By the way, where is Sergeant Dunne?"

"She's with Bobby Ellison at his office. Want me to call and tell her you're here?"

"No, I'll go there. Say, Zeke. You remember anything from that night?"

"Not the shooting," said Jackson. "Everything was in my report and on the bodycams. But I remember something from when I entered the kitchen."

Pickens narrowed his eyes. "What?"

"Vanilla," said Jackson.

Pickens brows hiked in confusion. "Vanilla? As in cooking vanilla?"

"No. As in perfume."

"Perfume? Zeke, you're not making any sense."

"Last week was my wife's birthday, and I bought her perfume and something else." Jackson smiled, and Pickens had an idea that something else meant it was personal. "She had the perfume on this morning. That's why I remembered. It was Bare Vanilla by Victoria Secret. When I entered the kitchen, I caught a whiff of vanilla."

"You sure, Zeke?"

"Absolutely. Like I said, my wife reminded me of it."

"I'll pass it on to Amy and Hubbard. Good work, Zeke, and stay safe."

* * *

The last time Pickens was in the neighborhood of Ellison Investigations was when he interviewed Barbara Hobbs as a suspect in the twenty-year-old murder case of Anne Wilson. He'd ruled her out but discovered the murder weapon—a tennis trophy—which led to the conviction of Wilson's husband and business partner.

Ellison Investigations' neighborhood consisted of offices, shops, a restaurant, and a bar. The bar was where Ellison liked to go after lunch and for happy hour. It's also where Amy met Hobbs' husband. Wilson's ENT practice no longer existed. It was now owned by another doctor.

Pickens tucked his SUV next to Dunne's patrol car. Just as he entered Ellison's office, his phone chirped.

He checked caller ID and frowned.

"Shit, just what I need," he said and answered. "Connie, what can I do for you? I'm busy right now."

"And good morning to you, JD. I hear you're back on the sidelines and driving. How's the arm?"

"It's fine, but why are you calling?"

"Do I need a reason to call you? I am the chairperson of the commission—which means I can call you when I feel like it."

"Get on with it, Connie. I know you've got a reason."

"The commissioners want an update. It's been what, almost two months since your deputy was first shot and over a month since you were. Give me something, JD."

Pickens glanced at Lu and held a finger up. Lu raised her eyebrows.

"Tell the commissioners we're working two homicide cases, and they don't get solved overnight." He winked at Lu. "We're checking some good leads and got a few suspects, but that's all I can say. And speaking of my deputy, when will his widow get his benefits?"

"We're working on it."

"Work faster," said Pickens. "She needs those benefits and deserves them. While you're at it, I added the title of detective to Sergeant Dunne and promised her a pay raise. It doesn't have to be big, just something."

"I thought you already had three detectives. Why do you need another one?"

"Two of those are unpaid consultants, that's why. And since I lost Deputy Conlon, I'm shorthanded. I need two replacements and quick."

"More money and more deputies. What do you think I am, JD?"

Pickens grinned. "You're a woman who can move mountains when she wants to. Do your best, Connie."

"I'll try. Anything else?"

"Want to go on a date?"

"A date? Will Marge be with us?"

Pickens smiled. "Yes, and Sarah too."

"Okay, when and where?"

"Friday, seven o'clock at Leroy's Bar-B-Que Pit."

"Isn't there a game on Friday?"

"Shit, I forgot. Make it Saturday, same time and place."

"Should I dress sexy?"

Pickens shook his head. "You always dress and look sexy."

"See you Saturday night."

After Pickens hung up, Lu had a grin that stretched from ear to ear.

"A date with one of your old girlfriends?" said Lu. "Not too smart."

Pickens's eyes narrowed. "She's married, and her husband will be there." He grinned. "It's a double date."

"If you say so."

Pickens shook his head. "Is Bobby in?"

"Hey, Bobby," Lu shouted. "Sheriff Pickens is here."

Ellison stepped out of the conference room.

"Geez, Lu, we're not deaf," said Ellison.

Lu nodded at Pickens.

"Hey, JD, come on back. Wait until you see what we've done."

Pickens followed Ellison. Dunne had her back turned and was writing on a board.

"A murder board," said Pickens. "I'm impressed."

"It was Sergeant Dunne's idea. We culled the list of robberies down to five."

Dunne turned around. "We prioritized them by order of probability," said Dunne. "One being the most likely. Ellison was able to get portions of the case files from the investigators."

"I still got contacts," said Ellison.

Pickens studied the board and pointed. "What's number three about?"

"Why number three?" asked Ellison.

Pickens hunched his shoulders. "Don't know. Something about it caught my eye."

Dunne picked up a stack of files and pulled one out. Pickens was impressed not only with her ingenuity but her organization skills.

"Attempted bank robbery of a Wells Fargo bank branch that ended with one suspect killed and the other in Raiford," said Dunne. "Both white males from Bartow."

"Did you say Bartow?" exclaimed Lu.

"Yeah," Ellison replied. "Why?"

"That list of Cougar registrations I put together for you. Hold on." Lu grabbed a stack of files and went through them until she found the one she wanted. "Here it is. Agatha Brackett, a grandmother who had a Cougar in her garage and saved it for her grandson until he learned to drive."

"So?" said Ellison.

"What if the grandson was the son of one of the bank robbers?" replied Lu.

Pickens rubbed his chin. "Did either of the suspects have a family?"

Dunne checked the incident report.

"The one was killed," said Dunne, "He was married and had two daughters. The other was single."

"Just because he was single doesn't mean he didn't have children," said Lu. "I'll check for birth certificates, just to be sure."

While Lu searched vital records, Pickens told Dunne of his phone call with the chairwoman of the county commissioners, and Jackson's request to stay under her command.

"I'd be happy to have him," said Dunne.

"I knew you would, which was why I'm recommending it."

"Got it," called Lu. "Unfortunately, his last name's not Brackett. It's Goodloe."

"Maybe that grandmother was married more than once," said Ellison. "Was the birth mother's first name Agatha?"

"Yes," said Lu. "Oh, I get it, check marriage certificates."

Lu didn't wait for a response, she went right to her computer.

"Got it," Lu yelled. "Two certificates. One with Brackett, and the other with Goodloe. She's his mother."

"Bingo," exclaimed Ellison. "We got them."

"Got who?" Said Dunne.

"The shooters. Two women. Well, I'll be damned."

"Two women?" said Dunne. "Out for revenge of what happened to their men?"

"Looks like it. You got a better idea, Sergeant Dunne?"

Dunne looked at Pickens. He nodded.

"Nope, works for me," she said. "Now, what do we do?"

"Got any suggestions, JD?" said Ellison.

Pickens was tempted to give his input, but he wanted Dunne and Ellison to work the case without him.

"You're the experienced homicide detective, Ellison, you decide."

"We'll decide," said Ellison. "Won't we, Sergeant Dunne?"

"After lunch," said Dunne. "Care to join us, Sheriff?"

"I'd like to, but I want to go to the high school and have lunch with the coaches, strategize, then practice. Mind if I come back tomorrow?"

"Please do," said Dunne.

"How about you, Bobby, you okay with it?"

"Works for me, too."

"Good, but I'll be here later as I have an appointment with my therapist," said Pickens.

He didn't say which therapist as he had agreed to Marge's request that he see someone once a week for five weeks to talk about the shooting. He had three more sessions left and didn't want anyone to know about them.

CHAPTER 33

B EFORE LEAVING ELLISON's office, Pickens texted Billy.
Billy, need to speak to you privately. Call me.
Just as he stepped into the hot sun, Pickens' phone chirped.

"Thanks for calling, Billy. How are you doing?"

"Okay. Amy and I patched things up."

Pickens felt relieved that they had.

"How's Amy doing?"

He heard Billy exhale.

"She's struggling without you or Mr. Hubbard."

"Mitch isn't there?"

"No. When are you coming in?"

Pickens was concerned that Hubbard might have decided not to help Amy unless Pickens was present.

"Not until Thursday. I'm helping Sergeant Dunne and Ellison. And I've got an appointment tomorrow."

"How's their case going?"

Pickens didn't want to tell Billy how much progress Sergeant Dunne had made.

"They've narrowed down some suspects," Pickens said. "Lu, Ellison's assistant, is helping. She's not as good as you, but she's the best they got."

Pickens knew that Billy would appreciate the compliment.

"If she needs any help, have her call me."

"Thanks, Billy. I'll call Hubbard and see if I can get him to go in. And, Billy, we didn't have this conversation."

"Okay, Mom, I'll call you again soon."

Pickens smiled and ended the call. Next, he dialed Hubbard.

"Hey, JD, what's up?"

"Where are you?"

"Having lunch with Donna. Care to join us?"

"At the Senior Centre?"

"No, across the street. I'd wave to you, but I can't see you."

Pickens looked across the street to look into the restaurant window, but a truck blocked his view.

"No thanks. I'm having lunch with the coaches at the high school." Pickens paused. "Mitch, I need a favor."

"Ask away."

"Can you go into the office?" Pickens hoped Hubbard would say yes.

"Not today. I have to finish a honey-do-list Donna gave me. How are things on the home front?"

Pickens told Hubbard about his conversation with Billy.

"How about tomorrow?" said Pickens.

"Will you be there?"

"No. I'm helping Sergeant Dunne and Ellison with their case."

"How's it going?"

"They've narrowed down a few suspects." He didn't want to tell Hubbard they were further along than he and Amy.

"Good for them."

"Mitch, Amy needs your help."

"Hold on. Let me talk to Donna." Pickens heard muffled voices then Hubbard spoke. "Donna said she prefers me out of the house during the day. Something about high-maintenance and a pain-in-the-ass."

Pickens laughed. "Tell Donna I sympathize with her and agree with her." Pickens paused. "And, Mitch, we didn't have this conversation."

"Okay, Mom, I'll call you soon."

Pickens grinned and was about to put the phone in his pocket when an elderly woman shook her finger at him for not looking where he was going while talking on the phone. Pickens smiled and put the phone in his pocket.

Just then, someone shouted, "Gun."

The bullet struck Pickens, knocking him backward.

Within seconds, Dunne and Ellison were out on the sidewalk. Ellison kneeled beside him.

"You okay, JD?" asked Ellison.

Pickens put his hand over his heart. "Yeah, but I think my phone is dead."

Dunne and Ellison couldn't help but grin.

"Did you see who did it?" asked Ellison.

"No."

Seeing the commotion, Hubbard bolted from the restaurant and charged across the street and shoved his way through the crowd that had gathered.

"JD, what the hell happened?" said Hubbard.

"I got shot. That's what happened," said Pickens. "Luckily, for me, my phone took the bullet."

"Who did it?" asked Hubbard.

"He doesn't know," said Ellison.

"You don't think it was the Cougar, do you?" asked Dunne.

"Why would they take a chance in broad daylight at noontime?" said Pickens. "And would somebody help me up, please?"

Ellison and Hubbard each grabbed an arm and lifted Pickens to his feet.

Dunne surveyed the crowd.

"Did anyone see what happened?" asked Dunne.

Several in the crowd bowed their heads. Others turned and walked away.

The elderly woman who had scolded Pickens waved her hand.

"I did," she said and stepped forward.

"Were the driver and the passenger by any chance women?" asked Dunne.

"No. It was those Brantley brothers out joyriding as usual. They belong in school, not taking shots at the sheriff." The woman crossed her arms.

"The Brantley brothers?" said Ellison. "I know their parents. Mrs. Brantley works as a waitress across the street. Are you sure?"

"Yes, I'm, sure," she replied and scowled. "You think I'm blind and didn't see what I saw?" Ellison raised a palm. "If you know the parents, then you know they can't handle those boys. Never could. Their daddy drives a rig and is out of town a lot."

While the woman talked, Dunne took notes.

"What were they driving?" asked Dunne.

"What else," replied the woman, "a black pickup. I'd recognize that truck anywhere, what with those flames on the front. Their daddy never shoulda gave it to them."

"I'll need to take your statement," said Dunne.

"Sure. Do you have a phone with a microphone?" said the woman.

"Mine does," said Lu.

"Then, here's my statement." She gave her name, address, telephone number, and proceeded to recite everything she previously told them. "You print it, and I'll come by in the morning after breakfast and sign it. I eat breakfast across the street in the restaurant. You call them and say you're ready for me."

"Thank you, ma'am," said Ellison.

"It's miss. I'm not as old as you think I am, young man," said the woman and winked at Ellison, then sashayed off.

Lu patted Ellison on the shoulder.

"You still got it with the women, Bobby," said Lu.

Pickens, Dunne, and Lu laughed.

"Ha, ha," said Ellison.

"Call Jackson, Sergeant Dunne," said Pickens. "Maybe he can catch up with those kids."

Dunne dialed Jackson but got no answer.

"Try again," said Pickens.

Dunne was about to call when her phone chimed.

"Sorry, Sergeant," said Jackson, "I was indisposed."

Dunne ignored his comment and told Jackson about the incident and had him try to locate the pickup and the teenagers.

Hubbard and Ellison were still holding Pickens' arms.

"Thanks, guys, but I can stand on my own," said Pickens. "I gotta get to the high school."

"You sure you're okay to drive? I'm concerned about where you were shot." said Dunne.

"Yes, Sergeant. Let me know how Jackson makes out." He reached for his phone. "Never mind, I'll call you after I get a new phone. This one has to go to the ME for ballistics on the slug."

"I can give you one of my extra ones," said Ellison. "You can return it after you get a new one."

"Thanks, Bobby, I appreciate it. You might as well get me a bag to put my phone in."

Ellison hurried into his office and returned with a flip phone and a bag and gave them to Pickens.

"Keep it as long as you need it," said Ellison.

Pickens looked at the phone. "It reminds me of the one

I had before Marge made me get an iPhone." Ellison grinned. "Add this incident to your board, Sergeant Dunne. I'll see you tomorrow." Pickens put the phone in his other pocket and rubbed his chest.

"Maybe it's not a good idea that you drive just yet," said Hubbard.

Pickens took a wobbly step and stopped.

"Yeah, maybe I shouldn't. I'll call the head coach and tell him I'll see him Thursday. Guess you got me for the afternoon, Sergeant Dunne. But you'll have to buy me a sandwich. I'll eat in Bobby's office."

"I'll get the sandwiches, and we can have lunch together," said Lu. "And while we're eating, I'll check your chest." Pickens' brow furrowed. "Don't worry. I've had to check Bobby's wounds a number of times. Some of his clients' enemies weren't always friendly."

"I'll think about it," said Pickens. "Now, can everybody go about their business. I'm fine."

The crowd dispersed, and Hubbard went back to the restaurant. Dunne and Ellison followed him. Pickens and Lu went into Ellison's office, and Lu ordered sandwiches from the restaurant.

While Dunne and Ellison were at lunch, Lu insisted that Pickens let her check his chest to see if there was serious bruising or a broken rib. Pickens was reluctant at first, but Lu refused to give him his sandwich if he didn't.

"Oh, come on, Sheriff, it's not like I haven't seen a man's bare chest before and you're just another man as far as I'm concerned. Don't be a sissy. I won't bite." Lu winked.

"But," said Pickens.

"But hell. I want to see your chest, not your ass. Now open up before I do it myself."

Pickens relented and unbuttoned his shirt. Lu pressed her hand against his rib cage near his heart.

"Ouch," shouted Pickens.

"Ouch because a rib's broken or because you're sore?"

"Sore. Are we done now?"

Lu grinned. "If you want to or I can check some more."

"Damn, Lu, are you trying to seduce me?"

Lu smiled. "Now would I do such a thing? Sheriff, you're a married man, and I'm, oh, never mind, button up. There are no broken ribs, just bruising. It's gonna hurt. I can put a bandage around you if you want."

Pickens wondered what Lu meant by I'm.

He raised a palm. "No, I've had enough of bandages. I'll manage without one. Thanks, Lu."

Pickens buttoned his shirt just in time because Dunne and Ellison returned from lunch. Lu handed Pickens his sandwich and bit into hers.

"How's the patient?" said Ellison.

"He's fine," said Lu. "No broken ribs, but a huge bruise."

"How will you explain it to Marge?" asked Dunne.

"Shit," said Pickens. "I don't know. How would you tell her I got shot again?"

"You could not tell her and keep it a secret," said Ellison. "But be prepared if she hugs you, you'll have to wince and bear it."

"I believe in the honesty policy," said Dunne. "Tell her and get it over with. If you hide it, she'll eventually see it, and it will be harder to explain why you didn't tell her."

"Or that," said Ellison.

"Damnit," said Pickens. "I'll tell her tonight." He felt a knot in his stomach, thinking about it. "But if I don't show up tomorrow, check the obituary section in the newspaper."

They all laughed.

"I'm glad you think it's funny, but I'm serious."

"Speaking of seriousness," said Dunne. "Ellison and I have a strategy."

Pickens brows hiked. "You came up with a strategy over lunch? This I gotta hear."

"Ellison suggested we go to Bartow and talk to Agatha Brackett. We'll act like we're talking to people who own Cougars and ask if we could see hers."

"That's it?" said Pickens. "That's your strategy? Infringing on someone's jurisdiction?"

"You have a better idea, Sheriff?" asked Dunne.

"I do. You could call the Bartow Police Department and tell whoever is in charge that you want to talk to a resident of theirs who might be a suspect in the killing of an officer. He or she might know Brackett because of her son."

"And we'd be following protocol," said Dunne.

"You would, and protocol, says that I make the call," said Pickens.

Dunne looked at Ellison. He shrugged.

"I like that idea better," said Dunne.

"And I should go with you?" said Pickens. "After all, the case is very personal for me."

Dunne looked at Ellison, and he nodded.

"It's personal for me, too," said Dunne. "We'll both go with Ellison.

"Lu," instructed Ellison, "look up Bartow on *Wikipedia* and print three copies."

Seconds later, Lu yelled, "Got it. Bartow population is larger than our whole county and has a police department that's much larger than your office, Sheriff, with a police chief. Here you are." Lu gave them each a copy of the printout.

"Thanks, Lu," said Pickens. "Now all we need is the name

of their chief. This doesn't show it, but it has the department's phone number. I'll call and ask to speak with the chief."

Dunne's phone chimed. "It's Jackson." She answered the call. "Uh, huh. Yes, he's here. Hold on." She put the phone on speaker. "Okay, Deputy, repeat what you told me."

"I caught up with the pickup, but they wouldn't pull over. They tried to outrun me, but unfortunately, the driver lost control when an oncoming truck caused him to swerve. The pickup went off the road and slammed into a highway sign."

"Were they hurt?" asked Pickens.

"They're both in the hospital. The driver is in surgery. I'm at the hospital now." They heard Jackson take a breath. "The passenger was okay, but he's confined to a bed. What should I do about them, Sheriff?"

Pickens mulled it over. He was shot, but luckily, he survived. One of his attackers might not survive.

"Cuff the passenger and read him his rights. Let him call his mother. We'll deal with the other boy after he gets out of surgery. I'll be there as soon as I can." Pickens hung up the phone.

"You sure you want to do that?" asked Dunne.

"Yes, I'm sure," Pickens snapped. "It's the second time I was shot, and I've only got two experienced deputies. I need them both. See if you can get in touch with Abrue and have her relieve Jackson. I need him available, not in the hospital."

Dunne knew better than to argue with Pickens when he was in a bad mood. She called Abrue—who was off duty—and had her go to the hospital, relieve Jackson and send him back to the office.

"Okay, now I'm going to call the Bartow police chief," said Pickens and dialed the number on the *Wikipedia* printout.

"Sheriff Pickens," said a woman who barged into Ellison's office. "What the hell do you think you're doing?"

Pickens turned when he heard his name called and froze. The others were stunned.

"I beg your pardon, ma'am," said Pickens.

"I'm Eva Brantley. You sent a deputy after my sons. Now they're in the hospital and you had the youngest arrested. What the hell were you thinking? All they did was joyride through town."

Pickens grimaced. "Is that what your son told you?"

Mrs. Brantley's nostrils flared. "You calling my boy a liar?"

Pickens' body tensed from his anger. He unbuttoned his shirt and exposed his chest.

"See that bruise," he snapped, then placed his hand on his shirt pocket. "If it weren't for the phone in my pocket, I'd be in the hospital or dead." Pickens' face turned red from anger, and he took a step forward. "Your boys took a shot at me." He took another step, and Mrs. Brantley retreated a step. Pickens wanted to say, "If you were a man, I'd get up in your face," but didn't. Instead, he thrust a finger at her and said, "I don't call that joy riding. You better get your boys an attorney because as soon as they're out of the hospital, I'll have them locked up in jail. Then I'll charge them for attempted homicide of a law enforcement officer. And," Pickens glared, "they'll spend the rest of their young years in prison. You'll never see them graduate high school." Pickens thrust his finger again. "You understand me?"

Mrs. Brantley retreated farther, turned, and hurried out of Ellison's office, slamming the door behind her. It rattled the window.

Everyone was silent. Then Ellison spoke.

"Lu, remind me to replace that window with bricks like the rest of the front."

No one laughed, especially Dunne.

Pickens buttoned his shirt and took several deep breaths.

"Let's get this over with," said Pickens, then clutched his chest.

"Are you okay, Sheriff?" asked Dunne.

Pickens exhaled. "Maybe I should sit."

Ellison grabbed a chair and Pickens sat.

"If you're gonna go to the hospital," said Lu, "maybe you should have a doctor look at your chest. I might have been wrong, and you cracked a rib."

Pickens thought about it. If he saw a doctor at the hospital, word would get to Marge. The situation had gotten out of hand, but what choice did he have.

"Thanks, Lu, I will." He exhaled. "Okay, let's try it again." Pickens dialed the number for the Bartow Police Department.

After asking to speak with the Chief of Police, Pickens was told he was on vacation and directed to the Chief of Detectives. He was told that although Agatha Goodloe had a Bartow mailing address, her residence was in Polk County, and he should call the Polk County Sheriff's Office.

Pickens then dialed the Polk County Sheriff's Office and was referred to Captain Leslie Winslow in charge of criminal investigations.

"Captain Winslow speaking. How may I help you, Sheriff Pickens? Is this about that Cougar that's wreaking havoc?"

"You know about it?" asked Pickens.

"Yes, we've got all our deputies on alert since you posted it. So, how can I help?"

"If you don't mind, I'd like to put you on speaker. I have two detectives with me who are working the case."

"Go ahead."

Pickens pressed speaker. "Captain Winslow, let me introduce you to Detective Sergeant Dunne and Detective

Ellison." Winslow acknowledged them. "They believe they have a person of interest who lives in Polk County. Her name is Agatha Goodloe, and she owns a Cougar."

"I know Goodloe," said Winslow. "She's the mother of one of Polk County's infamous hometown heroes, Jake Brackett, who's incarcerated at the state prison." Winslow went on to tell Pickens what he already knew about Brackett and his partner Bobby Teeks. "Agatha was married to Jake's father, Earl Brackett. He was a mean drunkard and beat Agatha and the boy until he died of cirrhosis. Agatha later married Vern Goodloe. He also drank but not like Brackett. Goodloe had a good job, owned his own home, and took care of Agatha and the boy until Jake turned twenty-one. Then he kicked him out of the house. Best thing he coulda done. Jake was in trouble with the law since he was a teenager. Spent time in juvie along with Teeks. So, you think Agatha knows something about the shootings?"

Pickens thought he'd never get a chance to speak.

"She owns a Cougar," said Dunne.

"So," said Winslow. "I'm sure other people own one."

"She claims it's in her garage until her grandson is old enough to drive it," said Dunne, "and that grandson would be Jake Brackett's son. She said the Cougar belonged to her late husband."

"I still don't follow you, Detective."

"We'd like to question her about it," said Pickens, "and we'd like your help."

Pickens waited for Winslow to respond.

"I'd like to help," said Winslow, "but are you sure this isn't just a fishing expedition?"

"We don't think it is," said Ellison, who could no longer remain silent. Ellison wanted to say, that it had been his idea to make the trip, and he'd be damned if they didn't get to interview Goodloe. But he bit his lip and waited for Winslow's answer.

Pickens, Dunne, and Ellison gritted their teeth as they waited for Winslow.

"We'd rather not do it without your help," said Pickens, who was losing his patience.

"I'd rather you didn't, either," said Winslow. "As much as I think it's a waste of time, I'll go with you, but not today."

"That's okay," said Pickens. "How about tomorrow? We want to get it over with as soon as possible. If Goodloe owns the Cougar that's involved in the shootings, we can prevent any more from occurring."

Pickens felt his comment would tip the scale in his favor.

"Okay, tomorrow, but after lunch," said Winslow. "I have meetings in the morning."

"Works for us," said Pickens. "We'll be there at one. Thanks, Captain Winslow."

"You're welcome, Sheriff. I should make you come earlier and make you buy me lunch."

"Works for me," replied Pickens and smiled. "What time?"

"Twelve, and don't be late. I'm a time freak and always eat lunch at twelve sharp."

"We'll be there at eleven-forty-five."

Pickens ended the call before Winslow could change her mind.

"What do you think?" asked Pickens.

"Methinks the captain protests too much in favor of Goodloe," said Ellison.

"I agree," said Dunne.

"So do I," added Pickens.

"Or, she agreed to lunch to assess us and determine if we're on," said Dunne and made the quote sign with her fingers, "a fishing expedition."

"Or that," said Pickens.

"Won't be the first time someone sized me up before agreeing to help," said Ellison.

"We'll find out tomorrow," said Pickens.

"Eleven-forty-five is cutting it close, JD. What about your therapy appointment?"

"I'll push it to earlier. You two meet me at my office, and we'll take my SUV." Pickens remembered that he'd told Billy he wouldn't be in until Thursday. "Wait for me in the parking lot. I don't want to have to explain to Amy what we're doing. Understood?"

Dunne and Ellison both frowned. They were confused about why he didn't want to tell Amy what they were doing, but Pickens made it clear when he said understood that they were to follow his order.

"Understood," said Dunne and Ellison.

"Good, I'll see you tomorrow. Now I have to go to the hospital."

Pickens left before Dunne or Ellison could ask any questions.

CHAPTER 34

WHEN HE ARRIVED at the hospital, Pickens checked on the status of the Brantley brothers with Deputy Abrue who had replaced Jackson. She assured him that both were doing fine. The one who had surgery had survived. Their mother visited both.

"Mrs. Brantley didn't have kind words for me, Sheriff," said Abrue.

Pickens clenched his jaw. "She didn't have kind words for me when I first met her. Don't take it personally."

"All in the line of duty," said Abrue. "Should I cuff the one who had surgery?"

Pickens would have liked to but didn't feel there was a need.

"No, he's not going anywhere. Stay vigilant. I have to see a doctor about my chest." Pickens placed his hand over his pocket. "Those boys shot me there."

"I heard. Zeke told me. You okay?"

Pickens was certain that if Jackson told Abrue, she probably told Deputy Ortiz and word was out that he got shot again.

"I'm fine. While I'm here, I want a doctor to be sure I didn't crack a rib." Pickens pointed. "Stay vigilant, Abrue." Pickens walked down the hallway to Dr. Smathers' office.

"Oh, hell," said Dr. Smathers fanning herself, "did hell freeze over? What brings you here, JD?"

Pickens' grin stretched from ear to ear. "I sorta got a problem."

"Sorta? What does that mean? You do or don't?"

Pickens scratched his chin. It was a tell sign.

"You have one," said Smathers. "What happened?" He kept grinning. "Come on, JD, out with it. In case you didn't know, this is a hospital, and I'm a doctor. I'm sorta busy."

"Oh hell, I got shot again."

Smathers stood and rushed to him.

"Where and when?"

"Here," Pickens unbuttoned his shirt and exposed his chest. "In Warfield. I'm okay, but my phone is dead."

Smathers pressed her hand to his chest and rubbed it.

"Ouch. Damnit, Elaine, I was shot. Now's not the time to manhandle me."

"You wish, JD. I'm checking for a cracked rib, but you don't have one. It's just a bruised rib."

"Don't you have to take an x-ray?"

Smathers shook her head. "Are you playing doctor now? No, I know what I'm doing."

"You're not gonna bandage me again, are you?"

Smathers smiled. "I sure am. It's just a precaution. I'll remove it Monday, or you could have Marge do it."

"I know you'd like to, but I'll have Marge do it."

Pickens knew she'd love to rip off the bandage

Smathers smiled. "Your choice. Take your shirt off and don't be bashful. I've seen it all before, remember?"

Pickens smirked and reluctantly removed his shirt.

Smathers wrapped Pickens' chest, then patted his rear.

"All set, honey, you can go home now. But don't do anything strenuous." She winked. "You know what I mean."

"Funny, Elaine. Now I have to explain to Marge."

"Oh, I'd love to be there." She smiled. "Good luck, JD. Hold on. You might want to lose the uniform. It's made you a target."

"I'll think about it," said Pickens. As he left Dr. Smathers office, he heard her humming a song from his high school years when they dated.

*   *   *

Pickens hoped that Marge would still be at the office when he got home, but she wasn't. Her car was in the driveway. He parked next to it and sat awhile to come up with how to tell her that he got shot again.

"Oh hell, what's the use?" he said. "No matter what I say, she's gonna yell. Take your lumps, Pickens, and get it over with."

He got out of the SUV and went into the house and expected Marge would be waiting with an angry look that would melt a polar cap.

Marge, Sarah, and Bailey were anxiously waiting for him.

"JD," said Marge, "I heard what happened. Dr. Smathers called me."

Pickens forgot that Smathers and Marge knew each other and occasionally spoke.

Marge put her arms around him.

Pickens flinched. "Careful, honey, I'm still sore, and my phone's dead. I'm gonna need a new one." He handed her the bag with his phone in it. "Here this is for you to run ballistics."

Marge stepped back. "I'm so sorry. Can I get you anything?"

He decided it was the perfect time to play the sympathy card and lowered his head like a kid.

"Could I have ice cream, please?"

"Daddy needs ice cream," said Sarah. "Bailey and I will keep him company."

Pickens loved it. Sarah and Bailey were on his side.

"But you'll spoil your dinner, JD."

Stay with it, JD, Pickens said to himself, *Play the card to the end.*

"I'm not that hungry. I had lunch, but it didn't agree with me."

"I'm so sorry, JD."

She's buying it, Pickens said to himself.

"I'll get the ice cream, and the three of you can enjoy it."

Sarah winked, and Bailey barked. He hadn't fooled them.

Pickens felt like shouting, *Touchdown,* but refrained.

Later, in bed, Pickens told Marge what happened.

"Are you really going to send those boys to prison?"

"Of course, I am. They shot me and my phone's dead. Their mother still thinks they were joyriding. Someone needs to teach them a lesson."

Marge knew it was best not to disagree with him when he was angry.

"If you say so."

"I do," he said. "I need a favor."

She gave him a coy look. "Sexual or business?"

If his chest weren't sore, he'd wrap his arms around her and make love to her. But, Dr. Smathers said he shouldn't.

"Personal. I need tomorrow's appointment pushed up an hour. Can you help me out?"

"Oh," said Marge, "I can do it. I'll call first thing in the morning. And I agree with Dr. Smathers. You should lose the uniform."

"I'll consider it. I sure wish I wasn't sore. There's something else. I made a date with Connie Dupree and her husband for Saturday at Leroy's. I told her Sarah would be with us. You okay with it?"

"Will it be business or social?"

"Both. I need two new deputies and need her to rush a request."

"Should I dress sexy?"

"You always do. So does Connie."

"Sexy it is. Now, let's get a good night's sleep."

CHAPTER 35

MARGE WAS ABLE to push Pickens' Wednesday morning's therapy session to an hour earlier, and he made it to his office in time to meet Dunne and Ellison. Both waited in Ellison's vehicle so Dunne wouldn't have to explain why her patrol car was there.

Ellison had parked far enough from the sheriff's office so his car would go unnoticed. Pickens tucked his SUV next to Ellison's car and rolled the window down.

When Ellison and Dunne were out of the car, Pickens said, "Sorry, Bobby, regulations require that Sergeant Dunne sit up front with me." He pointed his thumb. "You get the backseat."

Ellison peered in the back window.

"At least it is cleaner than my car," said Ellison.

Dunne and Ellison got in, and Pickens headed for Bartow and Polk County.

Dunne tapped her chest. "How's the bruise today?"

"It's tight. Fortunately, it's only a bruise. I stopped at the hospital yesterday and had it bandaged." Pickens didn't mention the reaction he got from Marge and Sarah and hoped Dunne wouldn't ask.

"How did Marge react when she found out you got shot again?" Unfortunately, Ellison asked.

"She gave me ice cream to make me feel better."

Dunne and Ellison laughed.

"Is that your uniform for the day, JD?" asked Ellison.

Pickens had decided to take Marge and Dr. Smathers' advice and wore civilian clothes. A tan shirt with black slacks.

"Marge and my doctor recommended it."

"You should stick with it."

"Think so?" said Pickens.

"I agree," said Dunne.

"Then it's my new uniform."

When they were out of town, Pickens noticed the folder in Dunne's lap.

"What's in the folder, Sergeant?"

"After you left yesterday," Dunne replied, "we had Lu run further background on Goodloe and her son Jake."

"Anything interesting?"

"Goodloe owns another vehicle, a 2003 four-door Camry. Lu found a birth certificate with Jake's name. He had a kid with a girl named Sandy Parks in 2007."

"And?" said Pickens.

"Guess where Parks' last known address is. Same as Agatha Goodloe's."

Pickens' interest piqued.

"Told you guys Lu was good," said Ellison. "Tell JD what Lu found on Jake's partner."

"I'm getting there, Ellison. Hold on," said Dunne. "Jake's wife, Adele's, last known address is the same as Goodloe's."

"So," said Pickens, "the gang all lives together under the same roof."

"Methinks the good captain will be surprised when we share it with her," said Ellison.

"That's if we share it with her," said Pickens.

"You're not going to tell her, Sheriff?" asked Dunne.

"Not at first. Remember what Bobby said about her sizing us

up? We'll hold this info and size her up. Let's see if she's willing to help us, first."

"Sounds like a plan," said Dunne. "You agree, Ellison?"

"Wholeheartedly."

"What else you got in that folder?" asked Pickens.

Dunne took out a sheet of paper. "The graphic artist finally got back to me. She apologized for taking so long. She was out of town on business and forgot to send this to me." Dunne showed Pickens the rendering the artist made. "Lu ran it through DMV and guess who it is?"

"Parks or Teeks?" said Pickens.

"Sandy Parks. She was the driver, and I bet Teeks was the shooter."

"We got them, JD," said Ellison. "The good captain will have to help us."

"Let's not get ahead of ourselves," said Pickens. "Let's see what the captain says first."

"I agree," said Dunne.

The drive to Bartow and Polk County had become very productive and they now had two promising suspects instead of just "persons of interest."

An hour out of Bartow, Pickens pulled off the road into a parking lot.

"Is this where we make a pit stop, JD?" said Ellison.

"No, my chest hurts." Pickens rubbed his hand over his heart. "Let's switch seats."

Pickens opened the door, and he and Dunne switched.

"I could take a turn if you want me to," said Ellison.

"Thanks, Bobby, but it's against regulations for a civilian to drive on official business."

"Right, regulations," said Ellison.

Pickens nodded his head, and Dunne got back on the road. He opened the file, took out a sheet of paper, and read it.

"What's this?" Pickens asked.

"I had Lu look up Captain Winslow," said Dunne. "I thought you might be interested in her background. She's a seventeen-year veteran and rose through the ranks. I'd bet she's savvier than we think."

Pickens looked at the photo of Winslow. "Probably. Don't take this wrong, Detective, but I bet she's all spit and polish like you."

"No offense taken," said Dunne. "If she is, then she and I will get along. Not sure about you two."

"If that helps us get her cooperation," said Pickens, "I'm okay with it."

They arrived at the Polk County Sheriff's Office in Winter Haven at eleven-thirty and were ushered into a conference room and sat around the conference table. At eleven-forty-five, the door opened and in walked Captain Leslie Winslow. She had a folder tucked under her arm.

"Good morning, I'm Captain Winslow. Which one of you is Sheriff Pickens?"

Pickens stood. "That would be me. Pardon the civilian clothes, but my doctor suggested them."

Pickens extended his hand and they shook.

"He got shot," said Ellison.

"Who's the civilian, Sheriff?"

"Names Bobby Ellison. I'm an underpaid consultant, a retired homicide detective, and a private investigator." Ellison offered her his card.

Winslow ignored the offer. Ellison set it on the table.

"This is Detective Sergeant Dunne," said Pickens. "She's heading up the investigation."

"Please to meet you, Detective," said Winslow and extended her hand. "We'll get along fine."

"I hope so," replied Dunne. "We came a long way to talk with you and our person of interest."

Winslow ignored Dunne's comment.

"I see you brought a folder, Sheriff. Care to share its contents?"

"You have one, too, Captain," said Pickens. "Will you share its contents, first?"

"We'll see."

"I thought we were going to have lunch, Captain?"

"I hope you won't mind, but I took the liberty of ordering sandwiches." She pointed to a credenza. "They're on the credenza. I ordered the same kind for all of us and sodas. One of my investigators will be joining us."

Ellison didn't wait for Pickens response. He grabbed a sandwich, a soda, a cookie, and sat at the conference table.

The door opened, and in walked an officer dressed in uniform.

"Ah," said Winslow, "just in time. Meet Sergeant Ronald Archer, my investigator."

Archer shook hands with Pickens and Dunne but ignored Ellison since he was busy eating.

"Shall we have lunch first? We can talk while we eat," said Winslow.

"Might as well," said Pickens, "since you're buying."

All four got a sandwich, a soda, and a cookie, and sat.

Winslow waited until everyone finished lunch before explaining why they were meeting in the conference room.

"I took the liberty of having Sergeant Archer do some digging on Agatha Goodloe and her son," said Winslow. She moved the file over to Archer. "Tell us what you learned, Sergeant."

Archer opened the file.

"Besides a Cougar, she owns a 2003 Camry. She's a part-time bartender."

Archer went on to tell them what they already knew about Goodloe, her son, Parks, and Adele Teeks.

"I shared, now you share, Sheriff," said Winslow.

Pickens scratched his chin, considering what to share.

"I'll let Detective Dunne share since it's her case."

Pickens slid the file to Dunne. She didn't open it as she knew what was in it.

"We essentially learned what you learned," said Dunne politely so as not to annoy Archer. "But we have a visual to share with you." Dunne opened the file and removed the image of the Cougar's driver. "A reporter captured the driver at the hospital after Sheriff Pickens got shot." Winslow and Archer's brows hiked. "That was the first time."

"The first time?" said Winslow.

"The second was yesterday," said Pickens. "Two teenagers supposedly joy riding according to their mother. Hence the civilian clothing. My wife and doctor suggested I lose the uniform since it made me a walking target."

"I see," said Winslow.

"The picture wasn't very clear, so we had a graphic artist work with it. She enhanced it and came up with this."

Dunne slid the picture across to Winslow.

"We compared the picture to DMV records, and it matched Parks' driver license photo." Dunne slid the photocopy of Parks' license to Winslow.

"As you can see," said Pickens, "she's now a suspect."

"We believe," said Dunne, "that Adele Teeks was the passenger and the shooter, and Goodloe, a conspirator."

"Give us a moment," said Winslow.

"Take all the time you need," said Pickens.

Winslow and Archer stood and left the room.

"I'm loving this," said Ellison. "Methinks, you got the Captain in a bind, and she'll cooperate. I hope so because I got a case of my own I have to deal with."

"Are you abandoning Sergeant Dunne, Bobbie?"

"For a few days. I still have an office and upkeep. Lu will still assist Sergeant Dunne with whatever she needs."

They waited patiently for Winslow and Archer to return.

"What's taking them so long?" said Ellison. "Think they went to Goodloe's without us?"

"No," said Dunne. "Captain Winslow wouldn't do that. She's probably getting authorization to do so."

Pickens squirmed in his seat.

"You okay, Sheriff?" said Dunne.

Pickens exhaled. "No, it's the damn bandage. It's too tight and uncomfortable."

"Maybe we should do this another day."

"No, Sergeant Dunne, I'll manage. I wish Winslow would return."

Finally, the door opened, and Winslow and Archer returned.

"Sorry about that," said Winslow. "Sheriff Pickens, I can't sanction an arrest of Goodloe, Parks or Teeks without a warrant."

"I have the county prosecutor on speed dial," said Pickens. "I can call and have one faxed to you, Captain Winslow." Pickens was beginning to get angry.

"That won't be necessary. I'll get one to search Goodloe's property for the Cougar and question her, Parks, and Teeks."

"Also, for a .38 revolver," said Pickens. "That's the weapon they used to shoot my deputy the first time."

"The first time?" said Winslow, shocked.

"And a .223 assault rifle," said Pickens. "That's what they used to kill my deputy, shoot up my office, shoot me, and probably used it in Eustis and God knows where else."

"I'll get my warrant. It will take until Friday. You come back with yours, and we'll piggy-back them," said Winslow. "No one is going anywhere. In the meantime, Sergeant Archer will head up surveillance on the Goodloe residence. If anyone tries to use a Cougar, we'll arrest them based on your BOLO." Winslow paused. "How's that work?"

"Works for me," said Pickens and turned to Dunne. "What about you, Sergeant Dunne?"

Pickens shifted again. Dunne knew he was uncomfortable and possibly in pain.

"Works for me, too," Dunne replied. "Who gets to make the arrest if there is one?"

"I'll ask our county prosecutor. But, I have no qualms against you doing it, Detective Dunne."

"We'll see you Friday, Captain," said Pickens. "Thank you and thank you, Sergeant Archer. We look forward to working with you."

"Same here," said Winslow and Archer.

"Hold on," said Pickens. "Here's a photo of the tire tracks from the first shooting." He handed the photo to Winslow. "It might match the tire treads on the Cougar."

Winslow glanced at the photo and said, "I'll hang on to this."

Pickens nodded, then he, Dunne, and Ellison left the conference room and walked to Pickens' SUV. Pickens tossed the keys to Dunne.

"You drive, Sergeant." He pointed his thumb. "Back seat, Bobbie."

"Yeah, regulations," said Ellison.

"A good day, after all, Sheriff," said Dunne.

"A good day, Detective."

When they arrived at the sheriff's office, Pickens and Dunne agreed to meet Friday in Warfield and then Dunne and Ellison left for Warfield in Ellison's vehicle.

Pickens decided to stop by the high school to check on practice. First, he called Marilyn Nudley, the county prosecutor.

"JD," said Nudley, "I heard you got shot, again. You okay?"

It seemed everyone Pickens knew had heard about him getting shot, again.

"I'm fine. Thanks for asking. Marilyn, I need a warrant."

"What for this time?"

"To search property in Bartow and hopefully make an arrest."

"In Bartow? That's not your jurisdiction."

"I know, but the suspects are there. The ones that shot me and killed my deputy. Will you help me?" Pickens waited for Nudley to answer. "Marilyn, you still there?"

"Yeah, I'm here. It won't be easy, but I'll get a judge to issue one. You sure make my life difficult, JD."

"Hey, that's what old boyfriends are for."

"Goodbye, JD."

Pickens wanted to pump his fists, but his chest hurt. He smiled and drove to the high school.

CHAPTER 36

Bartow, Florida

SANDY PARKS, AGE thirty-three, was getting ready for her waitress job at a roadhouse restaurant in the southern part of the county. She lived with her son's grandmother, Agatha Goodloe. Sandy's son's father, Jake, was incarcerated for attempted robbery and wounding a state trooper. His partner, Bobby Teeks, was shot and killed by a state trooper. Teeks' widow, Adele, age thirty-four, was left to take care of their two daughters, Brandy and Mandy.

Since Sandy and Adele had known each other since high school, Agatha invited her to live with her. Adele worked as a clerk at a local hardware store.

Goodloe's home had three bedrooms. Agatha slept in one, Sandy and Adele slept in another, and Adele's daughters slept in the third. Sandy's son slept on the couch in the den.

They only had one vehicle available for use. Another stayed parked in the garage. The two women were dressed and ready to leave. Agatha would make sure the kids were on time at the school bus pickup.

"You two going out this weekend?" said Agatha.

"No," said Sandy. "We did enough last time. We're going to stay home for a while. Maybe in a couple of weeks."

"You gonna see Jake Saturday?"

"Maybe. We'll see." Sandy waved goodbye to her kids. "We gotta go. Ready, Adele?"

"Soon as I kiss the girls."

"Ah, Mom," said Brandy. "We're too old for that."

"No, you're not. Come here."

Both girls strolled over and kissed their mother.

"Thanks, babies. You two be good for Gramma Goodloe."

Since they all lived under the same roof, and Agatha treated Adele and her daughters like family, Adele had her daughters refer to Agatha as Gramma.

Sandy and Adele left the house and got in Agatha's 2003 four-door Camry, unaware they were being followed and that Agatha's house was under surveillance.

CHAPTER 37

WHEN PICKENS ARRIVED at the office Thursday, Amy, Billy, and Hubbard were in front of the murder board. Pickens noticed the changes. The names of the participants in the get-togethers were in groups. Several had a circle around them, and there was a list that was labeled commonalities. At the top of the list was *Palmera*. Pickens was also pleased to see that all three were working together again.

Pickens went right to the board and wrote *Vanilla*.

"Vanilla?" said Amy. "What's that mean?"

"Bare Vanilla perfume," said Pickens. "Zeke remembered he smelled it when he entered the Buxton' kitchen." He left out the part about the gift for Jackson's wife.

"Okay," said Amy, "what about it?"

"Mrs. Buxton or Mr. Buxton's killer wore it," said Hubbard. "It's a clue."

"Right," said Pickens. "What do we do with it?"

Pickens searched Amy's eyes. He could tell wheels were turning behind them, and she would come to the conclusion he had.

"Call Palmera and ask if his wife used it," said Amy. "Or if any of the other women wore it."

"If we learn who wore the perfume, we might get a solid lead as to a suspect," said Hubbard.

Pickens was pleased to see his detectives back in action and working together to solve the Buxton homicide and possibly the others. He was also glad he had provided the clue obtained from Jackson. His teams were performing perfectly with him on the sideline except in the shooting case. In that one, he was assisting Dunne and Ellison.

"You call Everly," said Amy. "I'll call the Tampa detective and ask if she smelled vanilla."

Hubbard glanced at Pickens, who made a slight head shake. Hubbard got the message.

"Why don't I call Palmera and ask if his wife wears the perfume?" said Hubbard. "If she does, we might have a suspect, and Palmera wasn't honest about him and his wife discontinuing the sex group."

"That's a better idea," said Amy.

Pickens made a slight head nod, turned, went to the board, and wrote *Possible suspect*.

Hubbard called Palmera and asked if his wife used the perfume. Palmera put Hubbard on hold while he spoke to his wife.

"Theresa said she'd never wear cheap perfume like that. I don't remember what any of the women wore, but Theresa's thinking about it. If she remembers, I'll call you."

"Thanks, Mr. Palmera," said Hubbard.

"Hey, no problem, but call me Vinnie."

"Okay, Vinnie," said Hubbard.

"No luck?" asked Amy.

"Yeah," answered Hubbard and told her what Palmera said. "Didn't hurt to call though."

"I had no luck with Tampa. The only smell she remembered was of several days of decomposing corpses. Let's try Everly. You call him."

Hubbard called Everly and got the same result. After the call, his phone rang.

"It's Palmera."

"Put it on speaker," said Amy.

Hubbard pressed speaker and answered.

"That was quick, Vinnie. I hope you have something."

"I do," said Palmera. "Theresa remembered that younger woman who was here just that once wore perfume that smelled like vanilla, but none of the other women did. We both remember that this woman had sex with all the men and women, too."

Amy mouthed, "Who were the frequent attendees?"

"Say, Vinnie, any chance you could tell me who frequently attended your group?"

Palmera said the Tampa couple, the Buxtons, and another couple from Orlando. Their names and numbers were on the list he emailed and had put an asterisk next to their names. He also said the Buxtons and the Tampa couples attended other get-togethers, but he and his wife preferred to stay within the group.

"Thanks, Vinnie," said Hubbard. "I don't want to scare you, but I think you and your wife should be careful who you invite into your home."

"You think someone's after the group?" asked Palmera.

"Two of the couples that were in your group were murdered. Does that answer your question?"

"Holy shit!" said Palmera. "Maybe Theresa and me should take another vacation."

"Not a bad idea, Vinnie. Anyway, thanks for your help."

Hubbard ended the call before Palmera could respond.

"Mind if I make a suggestion, Amy?" said Hubbard.

Amy looked at Pickens. He nodded, hoping she'd let him.

"You're the experienced detective," she said, "so I'm listening."

Hubbard stepped up to the board.

"Let's put the names in clusters starting with the Palmeras, Buxtons, the Tampa couple, and the Orlando couple." Hubbard inserted the names into one of the circles. "Broward goes in another circle." He wrote *Broward*. "We'll leave the other clusters empty until we get more names. And, we'll add STD as the common denominator."

"I like it," said Amy. "We compare the frequently called numbers, especially the Broward couple's phone. It's possible one of those numbers belongs to the killers. We're close."

Pickens was pleased they were making progress in the investigation. It would free him up to work with Dunne and Ellison.

"I've got an idea," said Hubbard.

Amy raised her eyebrows. She was curious.

Hubbard took out his phone and dialed.

Before he could say who he was calling, Palmera answered.

"Hey, it's Vinnie. I was gonna call you."

Hubbard heard the faint sound of waves in the background.

"Where are you, Vinnie?"

"On the beach somewhere. Theresa and me decided to take that vacation you suggested. Anyway, Theresa remembered the guy's name."

Hubbard put the call on speaker.

"Let's have it," said Hubbard.

"It was Larry. She couldn't remember the last name but definitely Larry. I wish I could remember the woman's name."

"That's good, Vinnie. If you remember it, call me." Hubbard paused to reflect. "Say, Vinnie, by any chance did you record the get-togethers?"

"You mean like videotape them? Are you crazy? What do you think we're perverts? Of course not."

Everyone, including Hubbard, had to restrain themselves from saying yes.

"Why'd you ask that?" said Palmera.

"Because the Buxtons did."

"No, shit? Damn, they were perverts."

Hubbard again had to restrain himself from replying.

"Vinnie, if I email you images of women from the tapes, would you and your wife look at them and see if you recognize them?"

"All of them?"

Hubbard knew what Palmera meant.

"No, just their faces."

"Okay, but I got a better idea. Text them to me. I don't have access to a computer."

"Thanks, Vinnie. If you recognize any of the women, call as soon as you do. One of them might be a person of interest."

"You got it," said Palmera and ended the call.

"Great idea, Hubbard," said Amy. "We might get lucky."

"Hope so," replied Hubbard.

"It looks like you two don't need me, so I'm going over to the high school," said Pickens. "I won't be in tomorrow. I'll be with Sergeant Dunne and Ellison. They got two suspects."

Pickens turned and left before Amy or Hubbard could ask any questions.

Billy printed copies of the women that were in the videos and cropped just their faces. He'd chosen the ones that were the least grainy and sent them to Hubbard's phone. Hubbard texted the images to Palmera.

Thirty minutes later, Palmera called. Hubbard put the call on speaker.

"Hubbard," said Palmera, "good news. Theresa recognized one of the women. She was in our group. She and her husband were from Orlando You got their names on the list I sent you."

Hubbard interrupted Palmera. "We haven't gotten ahold of them yet, Vinnie. We've left messages."

"Oh, oh," said Palmera, "that doesn't sound good. You think maybe they . . . ?"

"Don't go there, Vinnie. They may be out of town like you were."

"Okay, if you say so."

"What about the other woman?" said Hubbard.

"Sorry," said Palmera, "Theresa couldn't make out who she was, but she remembered the name of the woman who wore the cheap perfume. Her name was Vivian because it sounded like Vinnie. Get it, Vinnie, Vivian."

Hubbard shook his head.

"Did we do good, Hubbard?" said Palmera.

Hubbard and Amy smiled.

"You did great, Vinnie. Thanks, and make sure you use plenty of suntan lotion."

"Gotcha. Take care, Hubbard. Call me when we can go home."

Hubbard pressed end. He and Amy turned to Billy to give him instructions. But Billy was busy on his computer searching phone numbers for a Larry or Vivian in the list obtained from the phone records of the deceased attendees of the get-togethers. They already had the names of the Orlando couple, Richard and Arlene Dalrymple. Now, they needed to make contact with the Dalrymples.

"Any luck, Billy?" asked Amy.

Billy shook his head and exhaled. "No. It's frustrating. It would be a lot easier if you could talk to the Orlando couple, or get their phone records."

"Can't you get their records?" said Amy.

"I tried, unfortunately, I couldn't. Phone company wanted a subpoena."

"Okay," said Hubbard, "I'll call my contacts in Orlando and ask to have someone visit the couple's home and get them to call us. How's that?"

"Makes my life easier," said Billy.

"Mine too," said Amy.

Hubbard made the call and was able to get a buddy of his to send an officer to the Orlando address.

*   *   *

Three hours after Hubbard made the call, his buddy from Orlando called him.

"Any luck?" said Hubbard.

"No one answered the door, so the officers checked the neighbors," said Detective Charlie Murdock. "They were concerned they hadn't seen the Dalrymples in weeks. The officers called the alarm company. They were told the alarm was off. The officers tried the door. It was unlocked. They announced themselves, entered, and found the Dalrymples' bodies." Murdock explained that the scene was similar to the Buxton scene. Mrs. Dalrymple in the bedroom, and her husband in the kitchen.

"What kind of shit did you get yourself into, Hubbard?"

"It's a long story," said Hubbard.

"Give me the short version," said Murdock.

Hubbard described the relationship between the Palmeras, the Buxtons, the Tampa couple, and the Dalrymples. He left out the specifics from the Buxtons' video.

"A group of swingers," said Murdock. "Someone transmitting an STD and someone after revenge."

"You could say that."

"Investigators are processing the scene as we speak," said Murdock. "It's my case. I'll let you know more after I get the autopsy."

"Any chance the first on the scene smelled vanilla when they entered?"

"Vanilla? No. Hubbard, you have any idea what a body smells like after it's been dead several weeks?"

"I do, but I had to ask," Hubbard told Murdock about what Jackson smelled.

"I need a favor, Murdock, the Dalrymples were the fourth set of victims in a case I'm working, and there might be more."

"Are you serious, Hubbard?"

"We have a pair of serial killers and believe their first names are Larry and Vivian."

"Damn, Hubbard, I thought you were retired. What are you doing working a serial killer case?"

"I'm acting as an unpaid consultant."

"Does Donna know?"

"Of course, she does. Murdock, I need access to the Dalrymples' phone records. Can you get me them?"

"I'll try or at least go through their cell phones and send their contact list to you. But not today. It may be tomorrow or next week. I'll see what I can do. Does that help?"

"Yeah, thanks, Murdock. Say hello to Anna."

"Will do. Why don't you and Donna come over? We'll have dinner, see a show, and you could stay overnight."

"Or," said Hubbard, "you and Anna could come here. There's a lot less traffic." Hubbard wanted to say and less crime, but under the circumstances, it didn't fit.

"I'll think about," said Murdock and signed off.

Hubbard explained the call to Amy.

"How long do you think before he gets back to you?" she asked.

Hubbard hunched his shoulders. "Hard to say when investigating a homicide. Maybe tomorrow, or sometime next week." Hubbard turned his palms up. "Gotta be patient."

"I'm out of patience," said Amy.

"I know, I am, too. But what choice do we have?"

Amy was about to pound her fists on the nearest desk, but paused and took a deep breath instead.

"Yeah," said Amy, "you're right. Might as well call it a day unless you got any more suggestions."

"I'll keep trying to get more names, said Billy. "Maybe I'll get lucky." Billy hunched his shoulders. "Can't hurt. You two go home and let it go until tomorrow."

Hubbard tilted his head toward Amy.

"Works for me," said Hubbard. "I could finish some chores for Donna."

Amy shrugged. "What the hell. I'll stop at the library and get a book."

Billy smiled and watched as Amy and Hubbard left.

CHAPTER 38

On Friday, Pickens and Dunne arrived at Winslow's office in Winter Haven. Winslow waited with Archer and five investigators. After introductions, Winslow explained the reason for the investigators.

"I got a search warrant for Goodloe's house, garage and its contents, and the property," said Winslow. "I also have a warrant to interview both her, Parks, and Teeks. If we discover evidence that links them to the shootings, I also have an arrest warrant. What did you get, Sheriff?"

Pickens held up two sheets of paper.

"I was able to secure an arrest warrant for Parks and Teeks based on our evidence, and I got an extradition order should you make an arrest."

"Then let's get this show on the road," said Winslow.

The group left Winslow's office and headed for the parking lot.

"You two are welcome to ride with me, Sheriff. If there's an arrest of Parks and Teeks to be made, it won't be at Goodloe's. They're both at work according to my surveillance team."

Pickens looked at Dunne. "You okay with riding in the back seat, Detective?"

Dunne grinned. "I'm certainly not going to sit up front between you two."

"I like that woman," said Winslow suppressing a laugh.

"Yeah, she grows on you," said Pickens.

Dunne grinned and got in the backseat.

The drive from Winter Haven to Goodloe's residence took thirty-five minutes.

Goodloe's property was in the country. Her nearest neighbor was at least a couple of hundred feet away. The exterior needed a paint job, and there was no curb appeal. There was a detached two-car garage. Scattered about was a football, a soccer ball, and an old pair of ladies high heels—all signs that children lived in the house. Pickens expected to see chickens milling around the yard.

The convoy of three sheriff's vehicles parked facing the house. Four patrol cars were already there.

Everyone except the deputies in the patrol cars exited their vehicles.

"Now what?" said Pickens.

"Sergeant Archer will take two investigators and search the garage, its contents, and the property. You're welcome to go with him, Sergeant Dunne."

"Detective Dunne," interrupted Pickens, "is in charge of our case. She goes with me."

Pickens crossed his arms as did Dunne.

"Fine," said Winslow. "I'll take the other three investigators, and we'll execute the search warrant and search the house. You two stay behind us and don't touch anything."

Pickens acknowledged Winslow's order with a nod.

"If Archer or my team discover any evidence, we'll collect it and process it. You're welcome to sit in on the interview," said Winslow.

"What about Parks and Teeks," said Dunne.

Winslow pointed at the three patrol cars.

"If we decide to arrest Parks and Teeks," replied Winslow,

"two cars will go to their POBs and make the arrests. Anything else, Detective?"

Dunne raised her palms. "We're good," said Dunne.

"Sergeant Archer," said Winslow, "if you find anything, call me on the radio. If the garage is locked, cut the lock or break it open. I don't care how you get in."

Archer acknowledged Winslow's request with a salute and headed for the garage.

Winslow walked up to the front entrance and knocked on the door. The three investigators stood behind her and Pickens and Dunne behind them.

The door opened, and Goodloe peered out.

"May I help you?" said Goodloe.

"Are you Agatha Goodloe?" said Winslow.

"Who wants to know?"

"The Polk County Sheriff's Office. I'm Captain Winslow, and I have a search warrant for your house, property, garage, and its contents. May I come in?"

Goodloe opened the door.

"I wanna see your warrant first."

Winslow handed Goodloe the warrant, then barged past her with the three investigators hot on her heels. Pickens and Dunne waited.

"I didn't say you could barge in," said Goodloe.

"Read the warrant," shouted Winslow.

Goodloe looked at Pickens and Dunne.

"You two coming in? If not, I'm closing the door. I can't afford to waste electricity."

Pickens and Dunne entered.

The interior was as bad as the exterior. A couch had a rumpled sheet and a pillow on it. Pickens guessed one of the kids slept on it. A round table with seating for six, and a direct site line to the kitchen still had breakfast bowls and a box of cereal on it. Goodloe must not have had time to clear the table in time to get the kids to the school bus. Dirty dishes were piled in the sink and on the counter.

Winslow had sent the investigators to search the bedrooms while she prepared to interview Goodloe.

Winslow looked around for seating and decided to use the table.

"Mind if we sit at the table and talk?" said Winslow ignoring the mess.

"Suit yourself," said Goodloe arrogantly and did not attempt to clear the table.

Winslow shoved aside a breakfast bowl and sat.

Pickens and Dunne joined her.

"We can do this while you stand there," said Winslow, "or you can join us, whichever makes you comfortable."

Goodloe huffed, went into the kitchen, poured a cup of coffee, returned with a pack of cigarettes, and sat across from Winslow. She lit a cigarette, inhaled, and blew smoke at Winslow.

Winslow ignored Goodloe and continued. "So, who sleeps on the couch? Sandy's son or one of Adele's girls?"

"That's none of your business," said Goodloe and took another drag, inhaled and blew the smoke at Winslow.

"Sandy and Adele live here, don't they?"

"So?"

"Which one of them drove the Cougar?"

Pickens noticed Goodloe blink, but her demeanor didn't change. He suspected she'd been grilled in the past by one of her ex-husbands.

"No one. It's in the garage for my grandson for when he's old enough to drive."

"So you say," said Winslow.

An investigator came out of the bedrooms holding a set of keys.

"Captain, we found these in the bedroom on the dresser," said the investigator.

Goodloe's head jerked towards the investigator.

"Which bedroom?"

"Not the master," said the investigator, "it was in the one where the two women sleep. We could tell because there were," the investigator paused, "personal things that belonged to two women. The keys are for a Cougar."

"Bag them," said Winslow, "and keep searching, including the kids' room."

Goodloe gasped. "There's no need to search their room."

"It's part of the house and included in the warrant," said Winslow. "Read it."

Pickens glanced at Dunne. She was paying strict attention to Winslow as she interrogated Goodloe. He hoped Dunne was learning tactics from Winslow.

"If the Cougar was for your grandson, why were the keys in Sandy's room?"

Goodloe took a sip of coffee and crushed her cigarette in the saucer.

"I must have left them there accidentally when I was in the room."

"Uh-hmm," said Winslow, then her radio squawked. "What is it, Sergeant?"

"We found the weapons in the trunk," said Archer. "Both of them."

"Good. Print them and the vehicle."

"Being done as we speak," said Archer. "Also, the tire threads are a close match to the tire marks in the photo."

Winslow grinned at Goodloe.

"So, Agatha, if the Cougar was for your grandson, why were the keys in Sandy's bedroom and why are there weapons in the trunk?"

Goodloe bit her lip and inhaled.

Pickens felt they had her.

"Care to explain?" said Winslow.

Goodloe leaned back in her seat and folded her hands against her chest.

"No," said Winslow. "Do the weapons belong to you, or Sandy or Adele? I'm sure they don't belong to the kids."

Goodloe glared at Winslow and looked like she would explode from anger.

Dunne was grinning.

"Okay," said Winslow, "can you tell me who this is?"

Dunne took the photocopy from the file and gave it to Winslow. She cleared a space in front of Goodloe and set the photocopy down.

Goodloe glanced at it.

"Don't know who that it is. Never saw her."

"A reporter took the picture in a hospital parking lot of the Cougar's driver after the passenger shot Sheriff Pickens." Dunne gave Winslow the copy of Parks' driver's license photo. "And this is her driver's license." Winslow placed the photo in front of Goodloe. "It's for Sandy Parks, and the address is . . . same as yours." Dunne gave Winslow the license photo for Teeks. "And this is Adele Teeks license. Oh, oh, the same address. Care to explain?"

Pickens was loving it and grinned.

"Go to hell," said Goodloe and lit a cigarette.

"Then, I'll explain. Sandy and Adele have been driving the Cougar and ambushing law enforcement officers. They killed one of Sheriff Pickens' deputies. The thing is, Agatha, they tried it in Eustis but failed. However, the Eustis police fired at the car and hit it."

Pickens' brow furrowed. He wasn't aware that had happened.

"My investigators will match the dent to a bullet from one of the weapons." Winslow wasn't sure they could, but she wanted Goodloe to think they could.

Winslow's radio squawked.

"Captain, we found boxes of 9mm shells hidden in the kids' closest."

"Good work," said Winslow. "Keep searching and tear every room apart."

Goodloe's color drained.

"Gotcha, Agatha, you're under arrest for harboring suspects in a murder. Stand up," snapped Winslow.

"Go to hell," shouted Goodloe.

"Detective Dunne," said Winslow, "would you help me?"

Dunne nodded, stood, helped Winslow get Goodloe up, frisked, and cuffed her, then Mirandized Goodloe.

"Wait," said Goodloe, "what about the kids? I'm supposed to be here when they get off the bus."

"A deputy will meet them. They'll be in good hands." Next, Winslow radioed the deputies that waited outside in patrol cars. "Pick up Parks and Teeks and take them into custody." Winslow escorted Goodloe out of the house. She waved to the remaining patrol cars.

A patrol pulled up, and a deputy got out.

"Take her into custody," said Winslow.

The deputy put Goodloe in the backseat.

Winslow turned to Pickens and Dunne.

"Satisfied?" she asked.

Pickens nodded. "Well done, Captain."

"Excellent," said Dunne.

"Good, now let's get the hell out of here. Wait," said Winslow, "on the way back, you can buy me that lunch you promised Wednesday."

"Pick your place," said Pickens.

Winslow smiled and signaled to the female deputy in the last patrol car who was assigned to meet Parks and Teeks' kids when they got off the bus. Then, they got into Winslow's car, and she drove toward Winter Haven.

In Winter Haven, Goodloe, Parks, and Teeks were taken into custody. Goodloe was being held for illegal possession of firearms and suspicion of aiding and abetting Parks and Teeks in the murder of Conlon and the shooting of Pickens. Parks and Teeks were held over for the killing of Conlon and shooting of Pickens until Monday.

The Polk County sheriff wanted a judge to sign off on Pickens extradition order before releasing Parks and Teeks into Pickens' custody.

Winslow agreed to transport Parks and Teeks to the county jail for Pickens first thing Monday morning.

*   *   *

Billy still hadn't discovered a connection to the Dalrymples with the names Larry and Vivian. Amy and Hubbard were disappointed and anxiously paced the floor hoping Murdock would call. Unfortunately, near the end of the day he hadn't.

"I don't think he's going to call today," said Hubbard. "I've got dinner plans with Donna, so I'm heading home."

Amy took a long breath and exhaled. "Yeah," she said, "it's frustrating. I'll call JD and update him. Will you be in tomorrow, Hubbard?"

"No, I'll see you on Monday. You and Billy take the weekend off and try to relax. Billy, don't you have a girlfriend?"

Billy smiled. "Yes." He checked his watch. "We're going to

the game tonight. I'm going to wrap it up early and go home and change clothes."

Hubbard grinned and left.

Amy called Pickens and gave him a progress update. Pickens was on his way to the high school and acknowledged her call but didn't mention that he and Dunne had solved the Cougar case. He didn't want to upset Amy.

CHAPTER 39

ATURDAY, AFTER PICKENS had informed Marge the Cougar shooters were behind bars, she was ecstatic. One less worry about Pickens getting shot again. Marge decided to surprise Pickens. Instead of bringing Sarah to dinner, she got a sitter, so they could go dancing later at The Bucket and Boots.

Pickens and Marge were first to arrive at Leroy's Bar-B-Que Pit. They received VIP treatment and the best table near the window. Leroy's wife, Liana, seated them.

The Duprees arrived shortly after and were seated by Liana.

After Liana took their orders, Leroy came from the kitchen and greeted them.

"Hey, JD," said Leroy. "We missed you last night. How's the arm? You up to fishing tomorrow?"

Leroy's restaurant was a hot spot on Friday nights after football games. Pickens always made an appearance after games to keep the celebration to a minimum and also helped serve.

"Sorry about that," said Pickens and rubbed his right arm and chest. "Still sore. Maybe another weekend."

"Let me know when you're ready. Enjoy your dinners, folks," Leroy said and went back to the kitchen.

"Still sore, huh?" said Connie Dupree, "the arm or the chest? I heard you got shot again. What now?"

"A couple of teenagers supposedly joyriding," said Pickens and gave her the short version.

"You going to send them to jail?"

"Yes. Connie, they shot me. I could have died. What else should I do?"

Marge placed her hand on Pickens' thigh to calm him.

"I was just asking," said Dupree. "What about the Cougar case?"

Pickens exhaled. "I'm glad you asked. We solved it, and the suspects will be transported to the county jail Monday." Pickens briefly explained what happened.

"Mrs. Conlon will be glad to know," said Dupree.

"She will. And speaking of Conlon, any word on getting me two replacements?"

Dupree shook her head. "I thought this was a dinner date, not an interrogation. You don't let up, do you? You have an appointment Thursday with the commissioners to plead your case. Don't screw it up."

"Thanks. What about Conlon's widow?"

"She'll get all the benefits due to her by the end of the month. Satisfied?

Pickens smiled. "Yes."

"Good. Here comes our dinner. Can we enjoy it in peace?"

Another smile. "We sure can, and after dinner, Marge and I are going dancing at the Bucket and Boots. You and hubby want to join us?"

"We'd love to," said Mr. Dupree.

Their dinners arrived.

"Now, can we enjoy dinner, JD," said Marge, "without any more shop talk?"

Pickens picked up a rib and bit into it. The others did the same.

CHAPTER 40

Monday, September 10

PICKENS WAS ON his way to meet the county prosecutor and Dunne at the county jail to process Parks and Teeks when he got a call from Deputy Abrue.

"Sheriff," said Abrue, "Mr. and Mrs. Brantley are here and making a scene. Mr. Brantley wants to know why his younger son was cuffed to the bed and wants to take him home. What should I do?"

"Hold your ground, Abrue. I'll be there in twenty minutes."

Pickens called Dunne. She was on her way to the county jail.

"Sergeant Dunne, I've got a situation at the hospital. The Brantleys are giving Abrue a hard time. I'm going there. You'll have to meet the prosecutor without me. She has the paperwork."

"You want me to send Deputy Jackson there? If there's an emergency, he has a radio and can respond."

"Good idea. Abrue may need backup."

"Got it," said Dunne.

Pickens arrived at the hospital, parked next to Abrue, and headed for the Brantley boys' rooms.

When he stepped off the elevator, Pickens saw Abrue and a hospital security guard in a heated exchange with the Brantleys.

"That's enough," yelled Pickens loud enough that everyone,

including Abrue, the guard, the Brantleys, the hospital staff, the patients, and the visitors froze.

Pickens walked up and got in Mr. Brantley's face.

"I don't know what your wife told you," said Pickens, his face a bright red, "and I don't care. Your younger son is under arrest, and your other son will be when his condition improves."

"For what," said Mr. Brantley, "a joyride?"

"Joyride hell," yelled Pickens and unbuttoned his shirt, exposing his bandaged chest. "See this? Your boys shot me. That's not joyriding. That's attempted murder of a law enforcement officer." Brantley's color drained. "The only place they're going is to jail for a long time. You'll be able to visit them there."

Mr. Brantley looked at his wife.

"Why didn't you tell me?" he said. Mrs. Brantley's face blanched.

"Take your wife and go home," said Pickens. "Until a judge says they can, your boys won't be allowed to have visitors. Deputy Abrue, escort the Brantleys out of the hospital."

Abrue and the security guard escorted the Brantleys to the elevator.

Pickens clutched his chest and sat in the nearest chair.

A gentle hand touched his shoulder, and he looked up.

"You okay?" said Dr. Smathers. Pickens tried to breathe. "Short breaths, JD. Nice and slow." Pickens breathed. "That's it. Is the bandage still on?"

"Yes. You didn't say to take it off."

Dr. Smathers reminded Pickens that she had. She said Marge could do it or he could come to the hospital and she would.

"Has this shortness of breath happened before?"

"Saturday night when I was dancing."

"Dancing?" said Smathers, "and you were out of breath?"

"Yeah, why?"

"JD, I might have made a mistake. You need to come with me. I want to x-ray your chest. There might be a cracked rib."

Pickens wanted to say, "You made a mistake, and you're admitting it?" However, now wasn't the time for jokes.

"I have to wait for my deputy to get back."

"I'll wait with you. JD, you're not going to like this, but the whole hospital heard you. Word will spread about your temper tantrum."

"It wasn't a tantrum, dammit, I had to make a point."

"Whatever you say but calm down. Please, JD."

Pickens exhaled. "Okay, this is me being calm."

Abrue, Jackson, and the security guard arrived.

"Zeke, you and Abrue make sure the Brantleys don't return."

"Got it," said Jackson.

"Okay, JD," said Smathers, "let's go."

Pickens stood, then sat.

Smathers signaled an orderly to get a wheelchair.

"I'm not getting in a wheelchair," said Pickens.

"It's either the chair or a gurney," said Smathers. "Your choice."

Pickens stood, then sat again.

"Fine, the wheelchair."

Smathers wheeled Pickens to the x-ray room, where he had his chest x-rayed, and then wheeled him to her office. She displayed the x-ray so Pickens could see it.

"There's a small crack in the left third rib, JD. I'm sorry I missed it when I checked you."

"Do I need surgery?"

"No, but you'll need to be bandaged again and be careful not to do anything strenuous, including dancing and throwing a temper tantrum." Pickens was about to object, but Smathers raised a palm. "Getting upset won't help. Try meditation. It will help you keep calm."

"Meditation? Like sitting on my butt and humming?"

"Whatever works for you. Just keep calm. When the rib heels, you can do whatever you please. Ask Marge to meditate with you." Smathers smiled.

"Yeah," said Pickens. "You and Marge would love to watch me meditate. Can I drive?"

"If you don't feel a tightness in your chest, then you can. JD, a cracked rib could lead to other problems, so please heed my words."

"Yeah. Thanks, Doc. Can I go now and without a wheelchair?"

"Bye, JD," said Smathers with a smile and a wave.

∗   ∗   ∗

Amy and Hubbard hoped Murdock would call. Billy still hadn't found anything on the names Larry and Vivian.

Hubbard's phone dinged.

"Hubbard, it's Vinny." Hubbard immediately pressed speaker. "Theresa and me were worried after we spoke to you about the Dalrymples, so I called my security company. We got cameras at the entrances to all the fitness centers and our house. I asked if they could send me the feed from Friday and Saturday."

"Did they?" said Hubbard. He and Amy were hopeful for anything.

"No. I got an app on my phone that allows me to check it. Guess what?" Hubbard and Amy anxiously waited. "They were at the house on Friday evening."

"Who was, Vinnie?" said Hubbard.

"Larry and Vivian. I swear it's them."

Amy mouthed, "Can he send the feed to us?"

"Vinnie, any chance you could send the feed to my phone?"

"I'm not sure how to do it. Let me call the security company and ask. You wait, Hubbard, I'll call you back."

"That's hopeful," said Amy.

"Maybe the break you wanted," said Hubbard.

"What break?" said Pickens, who had arrived from the hospital.

"JD," said Amy. "We heard about you're a . . ."

"Don't say it, Amy," said Pickens. "I'm not supposed to get upset. I got a cracked rib and need to meditate. Whatever that means."

Hubbard grinned.

"Not funny, Mitch," said Pickens. "What's the break?"

Hubbard told Pickens about Palmera's call.

"Any chance the Dalrymples had cameras at their entrance?"

"Good idea," said Hubbard. "I'll call Murdock and ask."

Hubbard's phone dinged.

"Hubbard, it's me again," said Palmera. "It's too complicated. The security company is gonna text it to you. I did good, right?"

"You did great, Vinnie. Thanks."

Hubbard dialed Murdock.

"Now what, Hubbard? I don't have the phone records for you yet."

"That's okay," said Hubbard. "I need something else. Did the Dalrymples have security cameras at their front entrance?"

"Yeah."

"Did you check them?"

"We're getting to them. Why?"

"The killers might be on the feed. Another couple did, and I'm waiting for the feed from their security company. Murdock, the killers might be on the feed."

"Which means we'd have identification of them. Gotcha. I'll send someone to the house. I'll get back to you as soon as I know. Good catch, Hubbard."

"Let's hope so. Thanks, Murdock."

Pickens and Amy waited for Hubbard's answer.

Hubbard's phone dinged.

"It's the text," said Hubbard and opened it. "So that's Larry and Vivian. Billy, if I text it to you, can you print it?"

"Absolutely," said Billy.

Hubbard forwarded the image. Billy opened it and printed a copy.

"I saved it to the hard drive," said Billy. "In case you want more copies."

Pickens, Amy, and Hubbard viewed the printout.

"If Murdock gets a video of them," said Hubbard.

"We have our killers," said Amy. "Billy can run the facials through DMV, and we'll have full names and addresses."

"I can do it now," said Billy.

"No, wait until we hear from Murdock," said Amy. "I want to know if we got our serial killers."

Pickens sat on a nearby desk and formed a steeple with his fingers. He was satisfied that Amy and her team had made progress and would soon identify the killers, but he felt they could do more.

"Amy," said Pickens, "why wait? Why not let Billy start his search? If Murdock does or doesn't get a feed, at least you'd have a head start."

Amy mulled over Pickens suggestion and looked to Hubbard for guidance. Pickens was pleased she did. Hubbard hunched his shoulders.

"What the hell," said Amy. "We finally got a break. Go with it, Billy."

Billy tapped on his keyboard and logged into the DMV.

Pickens, Amy, and Hubbard got coffee and stood in front of the board. Amy tacked the printout under the names Larry and Vivian.

"Won't be long before I can add the last names," said Amy.

"And move them from perps to susspects," said Hubbard.

Pickens tapped the board. "You two have done an excellent job and make a great team."

"Does that mean you'll pay me for what I'm worth?" said Hubbard.

"You're already overpaid. Tell you what—I'll buy lunch today. How's that?"

"Aren't you the big spender," said Hubbard. "Let's go."

"Bring me back a sandwich," said Billy.

Pickens, Amy, and Hubbard returned from lunch, and Hubbard's phone dinged.

"Any luck, Murdock?"

"Yeah. The Dalrymples had cameras at the front and rear entrances. I contacted the security company and asked if they could review the feeds as far back as six weeks. Any idea what we're looking for?"

Hubbard gave Pickens and Amy a thumbs-up.

"We got a printout from another couples' camera. I'll send it to you. Have the security company look for anyone that matches the pair in the printout."

"Nice work, Hubbard. If there's a match, we got our killers. Got a name?"

"Larry and Vivian. We're checking DMV for the last name."

"We'll do the same on our end. Talk to you soon."

Amy faxed the printout to Murdock.

Next, she stood behind Billy.

"Anything yet?" she said.

"No, and I can't work any faster with you breathing down my neck."

"Excuse me," Amy snapped.

Pickens was worried the exchange between Amy and Billy might have been from left over anger.

"Amy," said Pickens, "when Murdock calls back, have Mitch ask him if they got a DNA sample."

"Yeah," she said. "You got that, Hubbard?"

Hubbard glanced at Pickens. "Go with it," Pickens mouthed.

"Got it, Detective," said Hubbard.

Hubbard's phone dinged.

"It's Murdock." Hubbard pressed speaker. "That was quick."

"I don't have an answer yet, but I have a question. Did your people get a DNA sample?"

"Yeah, but no match in CODIS."

"I just heard from my people. They got a match. Unfortunately, it was to your sample and Broward's."

"At least we know we're looking for the same killers."

"Yeah, there's that. Hold on. I got a call."

Hubbard took his phone off speaker.

"Maybe it's the security company," said Hubbard. He put the phone to his ear then pressed speaker.

"Hubbard," said Murdock, "the security company went back six weeks and got a match. They could be our killers."

"I'd bet they are," said Hubbard.

"I'll have my people work faster to identify this Larry and Vivian. If you get anything, let me know. Been a long time since we worked together on a case."

"Actually, Murdock, it's Detective Sergeant Amy Tucker's case. I'm just consulting."

Hubbard glanced at Pickens. He nodded.

"When do I get to speak to the detective?" said Murdock.

"She's listening as we speak. Say hello to her, Murdock."

"Hello, Detective Tucker. It's good to know you're keeping Hubbard in line."

"I'm doing my best. Nice to meet you, Detective Murdock."

"Let's catch those sick bastards. Sorry."

"No need to apologize. My sentiments exactly."

Murdock ended the call.

Pickens placed a hand over his heart and took a deep breath. He walked over to the nearest chair and sat.

"You okay, JD?" said Amy.

Pickens took several breaths. "It's my chest. I think I'm going to go home and rest. You don't need me. If the county prosecutor or Sergeant Dunne calls, tell them I'll call them back."

Pickens got up and left. Amy, Hubbard, and Billy's brows wrinkled as they worried about Pickens.

"I hope he's okay," said Billy.

"Yeah," said Amy.

CHAPTER 41

PICKENS DIDN'T GO home. While Amy and Hubbard talked to Murdock, he texted Marge. She arranged a session with his therapist. Dr. Phyllis Wainwright wasn't a physical therapist; she was a psychologist who was counseling Pickens in dealing with the aftermath of getting shot, and Pickens' anger management. Pickens' recent outburst at the hospital worried him and Marge.

Dr. Wainwright cautioned Pickens against confronting Parks and Teeks at the jail.

"I'll think about it," said Pickens.

After he left Dr. Wainwright's office, Pickens called the county prosecutor.

"JD," said Nudley, "that's a bad idea. Besides, Parks and Teeks are lawyered up and won't talk to you without an attorney."

"You're the second person to tell me it's a bad idea. I want to ask them why they attacked my deputies and me."

"Sergeant Dunne already did that. I'm a lady, and I won't repeat what they called her. Wait until their arraignment or trial. You'll get your chance then. Besides, after your tantrum today, I don't want you anywhere near Parks and Teeks."

Pickens exhaled. "It was just a misunderstanding, not a tantrum, and it won't happen again."

"Whatever. Sorry, JD, I'm not taking any chances you'll jeopardize my case. You want a conviction just as much as I do, so stay away from Parks and Teeks. Don't you have football practice or a game you could go to?"

"No. I'm banned from football for the next three days."

"Then get a newspaper and do the crossword puzzle or take up needlepoint. Anything to keep your mind off Parks and Teeks. Do I make myself clear?"

"Yeah. Thanks a lot."

*   *   *

Soon after Pickens left, Billy threw his hands up.

"Gotcha," he shouted.

"Got what?" said Amy.

"I got a hit in DMV. Take a look."

Amy and Hubbard got behind him.

"Meet Larry and Vivian Voight from Clermont, Florida."

Amy and Hubbard studied the license photos.

Hubbard's phone dinged.

"It's Murdock," said Hubbard and answered and pressed speaker. "You got something, Murdock?"

"Yeah. Larry and Vivian Voight. We got a hit in DMV. They live in Clermont. Larry owns a 2014 BMW. Vivian owns a 2016 Ford Taurus."

"We got the same info," said Hubbard. "Any advice, Murdock?"

"We can't arrest them for visiting someone. We need evidence they committed the crimes."

"The Voights paid a visit to a couple in Gainesville on Friday. The couple is out of town until I tell them it's okay to go home. We could have someone sit on the house in case the suspects return."

"Then what? Again, we can't arrest them for visiting, and

Gainesville's not our jurisdiction. We can't ask the Clermont police to do anything based on security videos and, again, no evidence of a crime. At best we have the Voights as a person of interest."

"What about a PI?" said Hubbard.

"You mean like Bobby Ellison?"

"You know Ellison?" said Amy.

"Sweetheart, everyone knows Bobby. Yeah, like him."

"I'd have to get the sheriff's approval. Besides he's on another case."

"Not according to Bobby. He said the case was over. Look, I'll call him. He owes me a favor."

"Thanks, Murdock," said Hubbard. "Keep us posted. The Voights are bound to make a mistake."

After Hubbard ended the call, Amy said, "I wonder why JD didn't tell us Sergeant Dunne and Ellison solved the Cougar case."

"Maybe because it wasn't your case," said Billy.

"Who asked you?" snapped Amy.

"Just speaking my mind."

"Well, keep your mind to yourself," snapped Amy.

"Detective," said Hubbard, "if you're going to snipe at your only investigator, then I'm out of here. I got better things to do at home. I'll call Murdock and tell him I'm off the case, and he's free to do whatever he wants. Tell Sheriff Pickens to call me if he has any questions."

Hubbard turned and left.

"Way to go, Amy," said Billy. "I got better things to do, too." Billy stood and left. On his way out, he said to the dispatcher, "Stacey, if you need me, you have my number."

Stacey Morgan, the dispatcher, lowered her head to avoid any contact with Amy.

Amy frowned, sat at her desk, and regretted her actions.

She'd lost Hubbard's experience and Billy's investigative prowess. She felt sure Pickens would fire her.

Alone at her desk, Amy needed someone to talk to. She could call a counselor friend of hers, but she preferred someone with a personal attachment. Amy started to dial Iris Janson, the forensic accountant she'd become close friends with, but changed her mind. Instead, she decided to call Pickens but got his voicemail and didn't leave a message.

Pickens noticed while he was on the phone with the prosecutor, someone called and didn't leave a message. He recognized the number as Amy's, so he called her back.

When Amy's phone rang, and she saw it was Pickens, she hesitated to answer. She considered letting the call go to voicemail, but then picked up.

"JD," said Amy, "sorry, I didn't answer right away. I was on the computer. What's up?"

"What's up? You called me. Is something wrong, Amy?"

Amy exhaled and considered hanging up. "Yeah, I screwed up royally."

"Now, what did you do?" Pickens had an idea it had something to do with Billy. "Did you and Billy disagree again?"

Amy cleared her throat. "Yes, and with Hubbard. They both walked off the case."

"What?" said Pickens without shouting. "What's wrong with you, Amy?"

"I don't know. Maybe the case has screwed up my mind, and I can't reason. Maybe I should resign."

Pickens knew he had to control himself. He didn't want another outburst like the one at the hospital, and he didn't want to lose Amy. She was not only a good detective, but also a good friend.

"Are you still at the office?"

"Yeah."

"Stay there. I'll be right there."

Pickens turned his SUV around, and instead of going home, he headed for the office.

* * *

When Pickens arrived, he glanced at Stacey Morgan. She shook her head. Pickens walked up to Amy and put his hand on her shoulder.

"Let's talk in my office," said Pickens.

Amy stood, followed Pickens, and he closed the door.

"I'm sorry, JD."

Pickens held a hand up.

"Take a seat. I'll do the talking." Amy sat. "When I assigned the case to you, I knew it would be difficult. Especially since it was the first time you were on your own. You had nothing to prove for my sake. I trusted you, and Hubbard was your backup and Billy your investigative support. Everything you've done so far made me proud; I let you handle the case."

Pickens reached out and put his hand on Amy's shoulder.

"Amy, it's a tough case for anyone. Even Mitch would agree. You're taking it personally. Don't. It's not about you, it's about the case. You're not only my lead detective, but you're my friend. Both Marge and I love you."

Amy sniffled. "How come you didn't tell me Sergeant Dunne and Ellison solved the Cougar case?"

"Because I didn't want you to think you were competing with them and take it as a loss. Remember when I assigned the case to you, I said it wasn't a competition between you and Sergeant Dunne. Unfortunately, I think you took it as a competition. I talked to Mitch. He told me you solved your case. You did a great job and got a solid pair of suspects."

"He did?"

"Yes. I told Hubbard to call Murdock and have him hire

Ellison to tail the Voights. Bobby's supposed to report to Murdock and you if he learns anything which I expect he will. Bobby's good at what he does."

"He is. Thanks, JD. It won't happen again. I promise."

"Don't make promises you know you won't keep. Just try to keep your cool and take short breaths before you let your mouth get ahead of your brain and say something you'll regret."

Amy's brows hiked. "Where'd that come from?"

"It's a long story. My doctor told me to do it. I'm also in counseling, and my counselor said to do it. It's the new me."

"I don't know what to say."

"Say you agree with me."

"Can I hug you?"

Pickens smiled. "If you promise not to kiss me."

Amy stood, hugged, and kissed him.

"Sorry," said Amy. "I guess I can't keep a promise."

They both laughed.

"Call Billy and Mitch and apologize. Call Billy first. I'm going home and don't call me. I'll see you tomorrow."

CHAPTER 42

Clermont, Florida

THE LAST TIME Larry Voight felt this much anger was when someone rear-ended his 2014 BMW and caused thousands of dollars in damage. His insurance company considered the BMW totaled and reimbursed him for it, minus the deductible. The other driver's insurance company paid the difference.

The BMW was Larry's dream car. He worked long hours and saved his money to buy it. It was the first new car he owned, but with the insurance money, he was able to replace it. However, the new BMW didn't feel as good as the old one.

With his wife, Vivian, it was different. Someone had infected her with an STD. The doctors said it was treatable and she could continue to enjoy sex with him. But it wasn't about sex for her. It was what the STD did to her. Because of it, Vivian couldn't have children.

Yes, he agreed to attend a couple of get-togethers and enjoyed watching his wife have sex with other men and women, and he enjoyed sex with other men's wives. But neither he nor his wife expected someone would infect her.

The car that was destroyed he replaced. But the scars on his wife's psyche from the STD couldn't replace the woman he loved. On the outside, she was still the beautiful woman he married, but inside, she'd turned ugly. Hate and rage consumed her, and she wanted nothing but revenge and was hell-bent on getting it. So much, that not even an eye for an eye would satisfy her. She wanted lives for what they did to her. And Larry had to support Vivian no matter what she wanted even though, at first, he was reluctant. But Vivian reminded him that he could have prevented her from catching the STD by refusing to attend the get-togethers. They could have remained in the wife-swap with the couples they shared bedrooms with numerous times.

Larry could have reminded his wife that it was her idea to attend the get-togethers and insisted on it, even threatened separation if they didn't. Now he was a party to Vivian's acts of vengeance and hadn't expected he would enjoy it, especially with the women.

Larry purchased a .22 and a serrated knife for Vivian. She preferred the knife. He took pleasure in using the .22.

Four couples had felt Vivian's revenge and soon another would, and then another after.

CHAPTER 43

TUESDAY, PICKENS WAS pleased to see Billy at his desk working on the computer. Hubbard was studying the board and holding a cup of coffee.

"Good morning," said Pickens. "Where's Amy?"

"She called and said she'd be late," said Billy. "She had an appointment."

Pickens knew where Amy was. Marge was able to get Amy an appointment with Dr. Wainwright.

"Anything new on the case?" said Pickens.

"Um," said Billy and glanced at Hubbard.

"Since Amy is the lead, we're waiting for her to start," said Hubbard.

Pickens took two short breaths.

"Cut the bullshit," said Pickens. "I know what happened yesterday. Amy called me, and we talked about it. She's sorry and . . ."

"Dealing with some unresolved issues," said Amy who had arrived. "I talked about them with my psychologist."

Billy and Hubbard's jaws dropped.

"I'll be seeing her every Tuesday for the next six weeks or until I don't need her. First off, I've been struggling with the fact that I could have died if JD hadn't saved me. And I resent that it wasn't me who spent a week in the hospital. Second, because of those feelings, I've been taking my anger out on you two." Amy took two short breaths. "I won't promise it won't happen again because I don't want to make a promise I may not keep." She smiled at Pickens. "I will promise that I'll take short breaths and let my brain think before I open my mouth and say something I'll regret." She winked at Pickens. "A wise man told me to do that. Now that I've said my peace, what's the latest from Murdock?"

Pickens acknowledged Amy's comments with a nod, then sat on a nearby desk.

"Murdock hired Ellison as a consultant," said Hubbard. "He'll sit on the Voights and follow them. If they get invited into someone's home, Ellison will call Murdock. He'll alert whatever law enforcement agency's jurisdiction the home is in, so they can be prepared to take action if necessary."

Pickens raised his hand. "Who gets to arrest the Voights for murder?"

"That's a good question," said Amy. "What's your thought, Hubbard? So far, there are four counties where the Voights may have committed murder."

Hubbard pursed his lips. "Hmm," he said, "that is a good question. JD, can you get an arrest warrant for the Voights?"

"Based on what? Palmera's identification that they attended a party at his house, and they were at the Dalrymple's. No DNA match, no fingerprints, and no witnesses. The prosecutor would enjoy laughing at me. We need something I could use."

Hubbard shook his head. "I'm lost for ideas. You got any, Amy?"

"May I?" said Pickens.

"Please do," said Amy.

"Were there any security cameras at the Broward scene?"

Amy looked at Hubbard.

"We didn't ask," said Hubbard.

"We should have," said Amy. "I'll call Everly and ask. If there were and the Voights were on camera, then we got three incidents that they're POI's in."

"That should be enough to get Clermont to let someone talk to the Voights," said Hubbard.

Amy called Everly while Pickens and Hubbard waited.

"Unfortunately," said Amy, "no security cameras. Any other ideas?"

"I have one," said Billy.

"Let's hear it," said Amy.

"I did some research on the Voights. Larry was involved in a paternity suit in 2010."

"So?" said Amy.

"A paternity suit usually requires a DNA test," said Hubbard. "The results don't necessarily get posted on CODIS."

"I was reading about DNA databases," said Billy. "I found several that deal with paternity cases and genealogy. There's one in Clermont and Orlando. A tiny Florida site helped track the Golden State Killer, Joseph DeAngelo. Maybe we could find out the one used in Voight's paternity suit."

"Where the hell have you been, Billy?" said Amy. "That's an excellent idea."

Billy smirked. "I've been here since however long you have."

"Yeah," said Amy, "and you deserve this." She put her arms around Billy and kissed him.

"Does that mean we're engaged?" said Billy.

Amy, Pickens, and Hubbard laughed.

Amy's phone rang.

"It's Murdock." Amy pressed speaker. "What's up, Murdock?"

"Great news. One of our techs got an idea and checked DNA databases. There's one in Clermont."

"We know that," said Amy.

"Did you know that Larry Voight was involved in a paternity suit and had to submit to a DNA test?"

"We considered checking the suit."

"We already did. And guess what? We got Voight's DNA results, and they match ours, yours, and Broward's. We got the sonofabitch."

"That's great, Murdock," said Amy. "Now, what do we do?"

"You sit tight. I'm going to call Ellison and have him talk to Clermont. I bet Bobby knows someone in their police department. I want him to get their cooperation first. Then I'll get an arrest warrant and get Clermont to help expedite it."

"Murdock, Sheriff Pickens here. See if you could get an extradition order, too."

"Good idea, Sheriff. I'll let you guys know what happens."

"Thanks, Murdock," said Amy and ended the call.

"You look disappointed, Amy," said Pickens. "Something bothering you?"

"Yeah. What else do we know about the Voights, Billy?"

Billy worked his fingers on his keyboard.

"Voight owns a photography studio," said Billy. "And . . . whoa, that's his wife on the website."

"She's a model," said Hubbard. "When someone mars a model's *vanity*, she gets *revenge*."

"Spoken like a man," said Amy. "In this instance, you're correct. It goes to motive."

"You still don't look satisfied," said Pickens.

"I'm not. What about our case and Broward's and Tampa's?"

"Does it matter who makes the arrest and puts the Voights behind bars?"

"It does. What if something goes wrong? Murdock wouldn't be this far if it hadn't been for us. The Voights went after the Palmeras and will probably do it again. Who knows who else they'll go after? I started with this case, and I don't intend to sit on my ass and wait for Murdock."

"What do you suggest?" said Pickens.

"We get our own copy of the paternity case DNA results. We share it with Broward, and Tampa then put out a BOLO on the Voights as persons of interest and get Clermont's cooperation."

"Murdock's not gonna like it," said Hubbard.

"Screw Murdock. I don't like leaving our case unsolved. You got a problem with that, Hubbard?"

Hubbard rubbed the back of his neck. "What the hell. Get me a subpoena, JD. I'll hand-deliver it to Clermont and wait until tomorrow if I have to."

"I'll go with you," said Amy.

"I'll get the subpoena," said Pickens. He stepped away, called the county prosecutor, and explained the situation.

"Well?" said Amy.

"Pick up the subpoena at Nudley's office. Take Amy's patrol car, so it's official."

"I'll call Donna and tell her I might not be home for dinner tonight."

"If you have to stay overnight, get separate rooms," said Pickens.

Amy and Hubbard smiled.

"What do we do now?" said Billy.

Pickens checked his watch.

"How about lunch? I'm paying."

Billy glanced around the office.

"I can't leave Stacie alone."

"Stacie," yelled Pickens, "did you bring your lunch today?"

"I did, but if you're buying, I'll take something."

"Lydia makes a great panini," said Billy.

"Stacie, a panini from Lydia's okay with you?"

"No thanks, Sheriff, but I'll take an order of their bread pudding."

"Let's see," said Pickens, "one panini, one bread pudding, and something for me."

"Lydia's bread pudding is awesome. You'll love it," said Billy.

"Okay, one panini and two bread puddings. I'll be right back."

Pickens returned from Lydia's Bakery and gave Stacie her order and Billy his. He sat at Amy's desk to eat his bread pudding. He managed to enjoy several mouthfuls when his phone chirped.

"What's up, Zeke?"

"Sheriff, Mr. Brantley is here and wants to visit his sons. He promised there wouldn't be a scene like the other day. Poor guy looks like he's lost a son, not visiting one. I think we should let him."

Pickens took two short breaths.

"Is his wife there?"

"No, sir."

Pickens took two more short breaths.

"Okay but frisk him first."

"I already did. He's clean. Thanks, Sheriff."

"Call hospital security to back you just in case."

"Already here."

"Keep me posted."

Pickens hung up and went back to his bread pudding.

Later, Amy called and said they got the DNA results and were on their way back. Since it was late, Amy said she'd contact Broward and Tampa in the morning then take care of the BOLO and call Clermont.

Pickens said he'd see her in the morning and went home.

After dinner, Pickens told Marge about the paternity suit, the DNA results, and allowing Brantley to visit his sons.

"That was a good thing you did, JD."

"Yeah, I guess so."

"About the DNA results, I should have thought about an alternative DNA website."

"You didn't know about the paternity suite. We only learned about it today. Amy is hell-bent on finishing the case. She's done a hell of a good job so far, so have Billy and Hubbard."

"You got a great team, JD. They did it without you."

"Ouch, that hurt. You're right and thank goodness I only have two more days before I can get back on the football field."

"And there's that. Think you could manage a little scrimmage tonight?"

Pickens rubbed his chin. "I'll give it a try."

CHAPTER 44

On Wednesday, Pickens was about to enter the sheriff's office when his phone chirped. It was Marilyn Nudley, the county prosecutor.

"JD. Parks and Teeks got lawyers. There's a hearing scheduled for Friday morning in front of Judge Mathis at ten-thirty. If you plan to attend, be on time. Mathis is a stickler for promptness."

"What's the hearing for?" said Pickens.

"The usual, dismiss the charges, bail, and change of venue."

"Change of venue? Where to?"

"Who knows. It's what defense lawyers do if they can't get the charges dismissed."

"I'll be there. Do I get to ask questions?"

"No. I'll do the talking. You listen. If you open your mouth, I'll have you evicted from the courtroom."

"See you on Friday."

Pickens walked into the sheriff's office, waved to Stacie, and strolled up to the board. Amy, Hubbard, and Billy huddled around it. Amy was writing something under *Voights.*

"You got the DNA results," said Pickens, "now what?"

"We were just discussing it," said Amy. "Since we had time yesterday, we decided to stop at the Clermont police department."

Pickens brows hiked. "You what?"

"We talked to their chief. After we showed him the DNA results and described the murders, he agreed to provide as much help as possible."

"Such as?" said Pickens.

"If we issue a BOLO and get an arrest warrant, he'll handle it, provided we send someone from our office."

It was the same tactic Pickens used in the Cougar case.

"Does it need to be me, you, or both of us?"

"It's your decision, JD, but I'm definitely going."

Pickens looked at Hubbard. He nodded.

"We'll both go but not Friday. I have to be in court."

"He's right, Amy," said Hubbard. "Sheriff to Police Chief."

Amy shrugged. "Far be it for me to disagree in this instance."

Pickens and Hubbard were surprised by Amy's indifference.

"I'll set it up," said Amy. "Hubbard, you call Broward, and I'll call Tampa. Once we send them the DNA results, we'll issue the BOLO."

"I'll get the arrest warrant and an extradition order," said Pickens. "I might have to do some fancy footwork to convince Nudley."

Pickens dialed the county prosecutor.

"What now, JD?" said Nudley.

"I need an arrest warrant and an extradition order, and I need them fast."

"Again? Does this have anything to do with yesterday's subpoena?"

"Yes. Trust me, Marilyn, this case is the worst of the worst."

Pickens described the murders and the suspects' motive.

"How the hell do I explain that to a judge?"

"Not my job. Mine is to make the arrest. Can you do it, Marilyn?"

Pickens heard Nudley exhale.

"Yeah. I have to find a judge that can handle it. I'll let you know when I've got the warrant and extradition order. But, JD."

"What?"

"You realize it's another *capital felony*, and I've already got one."

"So?"

"Orlando might be better equipped to handle it. I'm not sure I can handle two. Think about it."

"I will and thanks for the heads up."

Pickens ended the call.

"Any luck?" said Amy.

"She has to talk to a judge. Then she'll let me know. Cross your fingers."

"What if Orlando beats us to it?" said Hubbard.

"We'll deal with it," said Amy.

"There's something you should know, Amy," said Pickens. "Nudley's not sure she can handle two capital felonies. She thinks Orlando might be better equipped."

"What are you saying, JD? You want me to back off?"

"Who would you rather Nudley try, the Voights or Deputy Conlon's killers? Remember he was one of ours."

Amy was suddenly quiet.

"Well?" said Pickens. "Who?"

"I need to think a moment." Amy sat at her desk and drummed her fingers on it. "It's a tough decision."

"Amy," said Hubbard, "a capital felony warrants the death penalty. The Voights crime was heinous enough to be considered one, but the deliberate murder of Deputy Conlon was definitely one. If it were up to me, I'd let Orlando have the Voights. They have the resources to try the case, and Murdock will seek the death penalty."

"What's tough about it?" said Billy. "Let Orlando go after

the Voights. Let Nudley concentrate on Conlon's killers. It's that simple."

"But it's my case," said Amy. "I have to finish it."

"Finish it hell," said Billy. "You let your ego get in the way, and Conlon's killers get off, or get off easy, no one in this office will work with you. You'll be a pariah."

Amy took several short breaths and exhaled.

Hubbard's phone dinged.

"It's Murdock." Hubbard pressed speaker "What's up?"

"What's up?" said Murdock. "I told that detective to sit tight. I'd handle the situation. What part of sit tight, didn't she understand?"

"Calm down. I get it, you're angry. It was my idea to talk to the Clermont police chief."

"Why? Don't you trust me?"

"Hold on, Murdock, I got you on speaker. I want to talk to the detective without you shouting." Hubbard took his phone off speaker and covered it with his hand. "Now what, Detective?"

Amy looked from Hubbard to Pickens, and then to Billy.

Billy's nostrils flared.

"Tell him we'll back off," said Amy.

"Murdock," said Hubbard, "we're sorry. We'll back off, but you better go after the Voights on a capital felony, nothing less."

"What the hell did you think I was gonna do? I want them as badly as you do. Go ahead and issue a warrant and send it to Clermont. We already delivered ours. Tell that detective to trust me."

"Will do, and thanks."

Hubbard ended the call.

"What did he say?" said Pickens.

Hubbard repeated what Murdock said but tempered it with the okay to send a warrant to Clermont.

"Satisfied, Amy?" said Pickens.

"Yeah," said Amy and exhaled. "Sorry I let my ego get the best of me, Billy."

"Hey, I understand," said Billy. "I'm sorry I got emotional."

"I'll call Nudley and tell her we don't need the warrant, yet."

Pickens dialed Nudley and explained that he was letting Orlando make the arrest and try the capital felony.

"Nudley was glad," said Pickens. "She's got enough on her plate with the Conlon shooting."

"It's better that way," said Amy. "Thanks, Hubbard, you didn't have to take the blame for yesterday."

"It was the right thing to do, and you would have done the same for me."

Pickens checked his watch.

"I think we all deserve a lunch break. Any takers, lunch is on me," said Pickens. "I know a place that serves great bread pudding and paninis."

Amy and Billy ordered paninis; Hubbard and Stacie ordered bread pudding, as did Pickens.

"I'll go with you, JD," said Hubbard.

Outside the office, Pickens said, "Something on your mind, Mitch?"

"Yeah. You made the right decision. Amy was too caught up with solving the case and lost her objectivity. I should have said something yesterday in Clermont."

"Amy is still dealing with the fact that I got shot and she almost did. Plus, it's her first capital felony. Hell, it's mine. The same for Nudley."

"Next time you'll both get it right."

"Never mind next time. There better not be a next time."

"Technically, there already is."

Pickens jaw dropped. "What are you talking about?"

"The Brantley boys. They shot you, remember?"

"Shit. I'll talk to Nudley and see what she advises. Let's get lunch and forget about crime for the rest of today."

"I agree. Hopefully, we can."

Hubbard's phone dinged.

"It's Palmera," said Hubbard and hit speaker. "What's up, Vinnie?"

"Hey, is it safe to go home yet? I got a business to run, and a payroll to meet."

"Hold on, Vinnie." Hubbard pressed mute. "Should we take a chance?"

"It's up to him," said Pickens, "but tell him to be careful."

Hubbard pressed speaker.

"Vinnie, it's up to you. You're safe at your business, but at home, be careful and don't open the door if the Voights show up. Call the police. They'll be on the alert."

"Hey, no problem. Hubbard, I got an idea. What about planting someone in my home and running a sting operation?"

Hubbard narrowed his eyes as did Pickens.

"A sting? Where'd you get that idea from?"

"Hubbard, we watch television. We saw it on Blue Bloods. Whaddaya think?"

"No, that's a bad idea. Do as I said. Call the police if the Voights show up. Take care, Vinnie."

"You, too."

"It would have been a good idea, JD,"

"It's too much of a stretch," said Pickens. "Besides it's Orlando's problem."

"Yeah, it is."

After lunch, Hubbard went home, and Pickens went to the high school to meet with the coaches and strategize for Friday night's game.

*   *   *

Thursday morning, Pickens met with the county commissioners. He argued his case for three more deputies. He cited the need since he'd lost Deputy Conlon and the increase in crime. Pickens also reminded the commissioners that Conlon was hired based on the grant from the state. Therefore, his position should automatically be filled. The extra two deputies would help protect the citizens of the county by providing more deputies available to patrol the county.

The commissioners agreed to replace Conlon but argued against adding another two deputies.

Pickens unbuttoned his shirt and showed the commissioners his wound from a recent shooting, and said, "It was the second time. Also, Detective Amy Tucker had nearly gotten killed during the shooting. Seven deputies in total were nothing compared to most counties throughout the state."

In the end, Pickens prevailed but got just one additional deputy plus a replacement for Conlon. It was a bitter victory, but Pickens accepted it with the condition he could immediately hire the two deputies. The commissioners agreed.

Satisfied, Pickens took the rest of the day off and went to the high school to participate in football practice.

CHAPTER 45

Friday, September 14

PICKENS GOT TO the courthouse at nine-thirty and parked. Dunne and Jackson arrived and parked next to him.

"Zeke, what are you doing here?" said Pickens.

"Miss Nudley called me," said Dunne, "and asked me to get him here in case she needed him."

"Fine," said Pickens. "You ready for this, Detective Dunne?"

"Yeah, it's for you, Conlon, and Jackson."

Pickens nodded.

"Let's do this."

Pickens, Dunne, and Jackson crossed the parking lot. Pickens looked left then right, checking for vehicles lying in ambush. Seeing none, he proceeded. He and Dunne entered and went to the trial room. Nudley was there preparing her case.

"I'm glad you're all on time," said Nudley. "Deputy Jackson, thanks for coming after such short notice." Jackson nodded. "Take seats behind me and don't speak unless I call you to the stand. Is that clear?"

Pickens, Dunne, and Jackson nodded.

"You might not have to testify, but I want you present just in case," added Nudley. "I've got all the evidence I need including the bodycams, dash cams, and Noseby's video. I might not need them, but I came fully prepared."

The defense councils entered, and Nudley acknowledged them.

Next to enter were Conlon's widow and his parents. They sat three rows back.

Nudley lowered her voice. "Don't look at them. Stay focused on the judge. Understood?"

Pickens, Dunne, and Jackson nodded.

Next, Parks and Teeks were escorted into the courtroom and seated next to their attorneys.

The bailiff entered and announced that the court was in session and all were to rise.

Judge Warren Mathis entered and took his place.

"Be seated," said the bailiff.

Parks' defense lawyer stayed standing and said, "Your Honor, the defense moves for dismissal."

"Dismissal?" said Mathis. "Counselor, we haven't started yet. Sit down. Motion denied."

"Then we move for a change of venue," said the attorney.

"Counselor, you're trying my patience." Mathis pounded his gavel. "Motion denied. Now sit down."

"Your Honor . . ."

"I said, sit down, Counselor, now."

The attorney sat.

"Miss Nudley, are you ready to proceed?" said Mathis.

Nudley stood.

"Yes, Your Honor, I am."

Nudley stated what evidence she had that would prove the defendants committed the crimes, especially the image of Parks from the reporter's video taken at the hospital. Defense counsel objected, but Mathis overruled him. It was like a circus with defense counsel objecting and Judge Mathis overruling. Finally, Nudley was able to finish her presentation.

"Your Honor," said Nudley, "the prosecution has shown proof the defendants are a flight risk. We intend to try the case as a *capital felony* as it resulted in the death of a sheriff's deputy and wounding of the sheriff. We plan to convene a grand jury. The prosecution recommends no bail."

"Your Honor," said defense counsel, "we renew our motion to have the case dismissed or a change of venue."

"Sit down, Counselor. Your motion is denied, as is bail. Please remove the defendants from the courtroom."

Parks and Teeks were escorted from the courtroom.

Judge Mathis pounded his gavel.

"Court's adjourned," said Mathis, stood and left the courtroom.

The defense counsels left in a huff.

Conlon's widow mouthed, "Thank you," and left with his parents.

Nudley nodded then turned and opened her arms.

"Not bad for a novice," said Nudley smiling, "and I didn't have to call any of you as witnesses."

Pickens, Dunne, and Jackson grinned.

"What's next?" said Pickens.

"Next, the county finds a dozen or more citizens capable of serving on a jury panel, and I plead my case to a grand jury."

"How long does that take?" said Dunne.

"Hard to say. Hopefully, two weeks, maybe more. I'll let you know. Right now, savor the victory as I am."

"Thanks, Ms. Nudley," said Jackson, "Jason would be pleased."

"Yeah," said Pickens, "we all are. Good job."

"Next up," said Nudley, "the Brantley boys. Have you decided what to do about them, JD?"

"I'm thinking about it, but they shot me. Does that constitute a capital felony?"

"We'll talk about it another time when you're ready. Let's go. I've got other matters to attend to."

Nudley packed up her things and followed Pickens, Dunne, and Jackson out of the courtroom.

When Dunne and Jackson were in their vehicles, Nudley pulled Pickens aside.

"I heard you're looking for two deputies, JD," said Nudley.

"What? I just met with the commissioners yesterday. How do you know?"

Nudley waved her hand. "In case you forgot, this is a small community. Word travels fast. Besides Connie and I are old friends. So, is it true?"

"It's true, and I'll need another patrol car. Quick question, are all my ex-girlfriends friends?"

Nudley smiled. "All that live here, and some that don't, but we don't kiss and tell."

Pickens shook his head. "Yeah, I bet. You going to the game tonight?"

"I wouldn't miss it. I'll be in the stands whooping and hollering for you."

"I'm not playing, Marilyn, I'm coaching."

"That's okay. I'll still cheer." Nudley smirked. "Maybe I'll shake my pompoms, too."

"You would. I gotta go. Thanks for today."

"You're welcome and, JD, think about the Brantley boys."

"Maybe. See ya, Marilyn."

When Pickens entered the sheriff's office, the first thing he did was say good morning to Stacie, the dispatcher/emergency operator. Then he approached Amy and Billy.

Billy was at his desk, researching something on the computer. Amy was at her desk, playing solitaire. Both looked forlorn.

"Hey, why so gloomy?" said Pickens. "I got good news."

Amy and Billy looked up. "The Cougar shooters were denied bail."

"That's great news," said Billy.

"Yeah," said Amy.

"Plus, I got approval to hire two deputies," said Pickens.

"Does that mean I have to give up my patrol car?" asked Billy.

"Temporarily until I get another one. It won't have all the bells and whistles, but you don't need them since you spend most of your time here."

"You're right."

Pickens looked at Amy. She seemed disheartened.

"Amy, it's over," said Pickens, "forget about it. You did your best. Move on."

Amy pressed her lips tight.

"Why don't you take some time off?" said Pickens.

"You won't mind?"

"No. It might do you some good. Call your friend in Tampa. Maybe you could visit her."

Amy smiled. "I'll call her tonight." Amy's friend was Iris Janson, the forensic accountant that had worked on the Wilson case last spring.

"Good. I'll be in my office. I have a few calls to make. Then I'm going to the high school for lunch with the coaches and prepare for tonight's game. You guys going?"

"I am," said Billy.

"I'll be there," said Amy, "unless I go to Tampa."

One of the calls Pickens made was to Marge to apprise her of the results of the morning's preliminary hearing. She already knew about the deputies.

.

CHAPTER 46

FRIDAY NIGHT, THE entryway to the Palmeras' front entrance was lighted by a string of outdoor lights. The front door was lit by two sconces attached to the wall on each side of the door.

The Palmeras returned from their stay away from home earlier in the day. They stopped at their gym so Vinnie could do the payroll and pay some bills. Theresa planned the workout schedule for next week.

Vinnie called two friends and had them meet him and Theresa at a restaurant for an early dinner. Then all went home to Vinnie's house and settled in.

At nine o'clock, the doorbell rang. Vinnie checked the security monitor and recognized his visitors. His guests went to their places, and Theresa stood in the kitchen.

Vinnie opened the door.

"Hey, we're here to party," said Larry Voight.

"Gee, we just got home and we're tired. Maybe another time," said Vinnie.

Larry waved a small packet in Vinnie's face.

"What the hell. Come on in."

Vinnie stepped aside so the Voights could enter.

"I'm Larry, and this is my wife, Vivian."

"Hi, I'm Vinnie. Theresa is in the kitchen."

Larry and Vivian Voight entered. Vinnie walked behind Vivian and admired her curves and tight dress. She strolled like a bathing suit model.

Man, she's got all the right moves, and she smells like vanilla, Vinnie thought to himself.

In the kitchen, Larry dropped the packet on the top of the kitchen island.

Vinnie joined Theresa, and they kept the kitchen island between them and the Voights.

"Hey," said Larry to Theresa. "You ready to party?"

"Always," answered Theresa in her best sultry voice. She checked Larry up and down, then licked her lips. "But let's dispense with the powder, and you and I go to the bedroom."

"I like your style," said Larry. "Let's go."

Larry followed Theresa to the bedroom and closed the door behind him.

Vinnie stayed in the kitchen and kept the island between him and Vivian.

Vivian picked up the packet.

"Shall we?" said Vivian.

Vinnie felt tempted.

"You go ahead. I'll wait for Theresa."

"We could skip the powder, too, and I'll do you on the counter. How about it?"

Vivian moved to her right.

"Um," said Vinnie and moved to his right.

Vivian moved farther to her right, so did Vinnie, keeping the island between him and Vivian.

"Don't you want me to do it?" said Vivian seductively.

Vinnie eyed her. He had a hard time believing her pretty face was the face of a killer. Under different circumstances, he'd be up on the counter with his belt unbuckled, but he had to stay focused.

"Yeah, it's just . . ."

"Didn't you enjoy it the last time?"

Again, Vivian moved to her right. Vinnie did the same. Vivian stalked Vinnie like a tigress did her prey. They had completely circled the island.

Vinnie started to sweat. Vivian's looks were alluring, and when she spoke, it was like a spider luring its prey into its web.

"I did, but I got this problem."

The look in Vivian's eyes changed from alluring to anger and caused a knot in Vinnie's stomach.

"So, you're the one," screamed Vivian. Her face was no longer beautiful; it was now grotesque and repulsive, and she foamed like a rabid animal.

It almost made Vinnie flee, especially when the knife suddenly appeared from nowhere.

"You, sonofabitch."

Vivian lunged but was immobilized and dropped the knife when hit from behind by 50,000 volts from a taser gun fired by Detective Elena Gardener, who had emerged from her hiding place. Gardener immediately cuffed Vivian, grabbed the knife by its tip, and bagged it. Next, she radioed for backup.

Detective Don Brady emerged from the bedroom with Larry cuffed. Theresa was behind Brady.

"Nice work, partner," said Brady.

"You too," said Gardener. "Did he have a gun?"

Brady held up an evidence bag.

"Yeah, a .22, but he never got to use it. I was on him before he got to unzip his pants."

Two uniformed Gainesville police officers entered the kitchen.

"They're all yours," said Gardener.

The officers led the Voights out of the house and put them in separate police cars.

"Funny thing," said Brady, "he looked almost relieved to be arrested."

"Not her," said Gardener. "You two were lucky. We'll be back later for your statements."

"What was she like?" asked Brady.

"Crazy," said Gardener, "and she overdid it with cheap perfume. Let's get out of here."

"Did you see the look on her face?" said Vinnie. "She was gonna slit my throat. You okay, Theresa?"

"Yes, Detective Brady took good care of me."

Vinnie wrapped his arms around Theresa, hugged her tight, and kissed her.

When the detectives had left, Vinnie called Hubbard.

"It's over, Hubbard," said Vinnie. "We did exactly as we were supposed to. Thanks, Hubbard."

"I'm happy for both of you," said Hubbard. "Now you and Theresa can relax. Take care, Vinnie."

"You, too," said Vinnie and hung up.

Hubbard waited until he was sure the game and celebration were over then called Pickens.

"I won't keep you, JD, I know you're busy. Everything worked out as it was supposed to. I'll tell you about it on Monday over lunch. You're buying."

"You're on. Thanks, Mitch."

The phone calls that Pickens made earlier in the day were to Hubbard and the Gainesville police chief. Pickens told Hubbard to contact Ellison and set the sting up. He told the Gainesville police chief of the plan and that Bobbie Ellison would be in touch. The chief assigned two deputies to be part of the sting. They were the friends Palmera contacted for dinner.

Hubbard had also called Murdock and alerted him of the plan. Murdock wasn't happy, but he'd agreed to it.

Pickens called Amy but got her voice mail and left a message.

"Amy, just checking if you took my suggestion. I guess you did. Don't return my call. I'll talk to you whenever."

"I take it you got good news," said Marge.

"I got great news. I'll tell you tomorrow."

"Wonderful. Now give me something good." Marge removed the sheet that covered her.

"I'll do my best," said Pickens and he smothered her with kisses.

*   *   *

Saturday after breakfast, Pickens told Marge about the sting in Gainesville. Later he went to the sheriff's office to see if he was needed. Since he wasn't, he told the dispatcher to call if anything happened.

Sunday morning, Pickens, his father, and Leroy Jones went bass fishing. Later, the Pickens and Jones families grilled the morning's catch at Pickens' parents' house.

Other than running out of beer, the rest of the weekend went without an incident requiring the need of Sheriff JD Pickens.

CHAPTER 47

ONDAY, WHEN PICKENS greeted Stacie, the dispatcher, she seemed more jovial than usual.

"Great weekend, Sheriff," said Stacie. "I bet you're glad."

Pickens' forehead wrinkled. "Uh, yeah, I am." He had no idea what Stacie meant.

"Billy's waiting for you."

Pickens frowned and walked over to Billy's desk.

"Good morning, Billy."

Billy stood. "Good morning, Sheriff. I bet you're glad."

Pickens narrowed his eyes. "What am I glad about?"

"The Voights. They were arrested in Gainesville Friday."

"What? How do you know?"

"It was on the news. The Gainesville police chief even mentioned you and Amy. I bet she's glad. Did you see it?"

"No. I don't watch the news."

"You should. Anyway, I bet you and Amy are glad. Has she called you?"

"Not that I'm aware of. She's on an extended weekend."

Pickens' phone chirped.

"It's Amy," Pickens answered. "Hey, did you get my message?"

"I did. Did you see the news?"

"No. Billy told me about it. You satisfied?"

When Pickens called Hubbard and the Gainesville police chief, he asked that Amy get credit for the sting operation.

"Kind of. Thanks for giving me credit. I owe you."

"No, you don't. How's it going?"

"Great. I'll see you on Friday. Sorry, gotta go."

"Was she satisfied?" asked Billy.

"Yeah. I'm having lunch with Mitch Hubbard. I'll be in my office. Tell Stacie to let me know when he gets here."

"Will do."

Pickens went into his office, closed the door, and called Marge. He wanted to tell her about the newscast, but she had already heard about it from her staff.

"Have you decided about the Brantley boys now that the other cases are solved?" asked Marge.

Pickens took two short breaths, exhaled, and said, "I'm still thinking about it. Don't forget if my phone wasn't in my pocket, I might be dead or still in the hospital. I can't let them get away without punishment."

"When you look at it that way, I have to agree with you to some extent, but they are teenagers. And teenagers . . ."

"Don't go there, Marge. Teenagers or not, you and Sarah could have ended up without me. Let's not discuss it any more. I don't want to get upset."

"Sorry, sweetheart, we won't. Are you having lunch with Mitch?"

"Yeah, he should be here any minute. And, Marge, I love you."

"Same here. Enjoy your lunch. Tell Mitch I said hello and for him to tell Donna, hi."

There was a tap on his office door.

"Come in," said Pickens.

"Sheriff, Mr. Hubbard is here," said Stacie.

"Thanks, Stacie."

Pickens stood, left his office, and went to greet Hubbard.

"Ready, Mitch?"

"Yep. Did you see the news?"

"No, but everybody else did, and they've let me know. I don't want to hear anymore about it. Let's go."

Hubbard grinned, then he and Pickens went to lunch.

Over lunch, Hubbard described what had taken place Friday night at Palmera's house.

"Murdock wasn't pleased when I called him, but he agreed with the plan. I wonder which county will get to prosecute the Voights?"

"Multiple counties, multiple capital felonies. Might be the state attorney's office."

"Yeah, but which one?"

Pickens hunched his shoulders. "Beats me. That's up to the lawyers. All I care about is that they get prosecuted."

"Me, too. Let's enjoy lunch and talk about anything but crime."

CHAPTER 48

THURSDAY, SEPTEMBER 27, Nudley had a jury—twelve females and eleven males. Nudley presented the evidence and called Pickens, Amy, Dunne, and Jackson as witnesses. Conlon's widow addressed the jury and explained that Conlon's death left her as a widow with three children, one still an infant. If it hadn't been for her mother, she wouldn't have been able to care for her children. Conlon's widow made an emotional appeal for justice for her husband.

The grand jury decided that the evidence was strong enough for trial and issued a true bill charging Parks and Teeks with a capital felony.

While Nudley awaited a jury trial for Parka and Teeks, the Brantley brothers recovered from their injuries, and a hearing was set with a judge to determine their punishment. Mr. Brantley pleaded for leniency for his sons and promised it would never happen again. He even agreed to take shorter trips out of town, so he was home more often to discipline the boys. Pickens argued that a show of leniency would do nothing to prevent the brothers from committing another crime, possibly shooting someone else.

Yielding to requests from Nudley, Marge, Ellison, and others, Pickens finally relented. He agreed to a term of ninety days in the juvenile detention center, followed by nine months of probation and supervised community service three hours daily except on Sundays. Pickens also insisted on a seven o'clock curfew. The brothers' sentences would be a blot on their permanent records. Mr. Brantley appreciated Pickens' decision. Mrs. Brantley was a whole different matter. Suffice it to say, she wouldn't vote for Pickens the next time he ran for re-election.

A month later in October, the jury trial for Parks and Teeks was set.

During the hearing on pre-trial motions, Nudley announced the prosecution intended to seek the death penalty for Parks and Teeks.

Nudley presented a compelling case with Pickens, Amy, Dunne, and Jackson testifying. Conlon's widow's address to the jury was heartbreaking.

Defense counsel argued that Parks and Teeks were single parents and sentencing them to death would leave their children without a parent.

Upon deliberation, the jury sought advice from the judge. Although Nudley presented a strong case, the jury had difficulty with who actually shot Conlon. There was sufficient evidence to prove both Parks and Teeks drove the Cougar, handled the weapons, and took part in the shootings. The reporter's video showed that Parks was the driver, and most likely, it was Teeks that shot Pickens. As to who shot Conlon, the jury was unsure whether it was Parks or Teeks.

The jury also considered the impact on Parks and Teeks' children if sentenced to death. Instead of the death penalty, the jury recommended a felony of the first degree and a sentence of thirty years in prison. The judge agreed with the jury, and Parks and Teeks were sentenced to serve their terms at the women's correctional institution in Marion County.

Parks' husband would be released from prison before she

was. Her parents, who lived in Alabama and hadn't had contact with Parks in more than a decade, took custody of her son.

Teeks had an aunt that lived in Georgia and she took custody of Teeks' daughters.

In a separate instance, Agatha Brackett got five years for her part in the shootings.

Pickens never got an answer to why Parks and Teeks went on a rampage. The only plausible explanation was the timeline of their shooting spree coincided with Brackett and Teeks crime spree—which ended with Brackett behind bars and Teeks dead. Parks and Teeks were seeking revenge against law enforcement for what happened to their men. Conlon and Pickens simply happened to be in the wrong place at the wrong time.

A month after the trial of Parks and Teeks, Conlon's widow moved to Lake City to live with her mother.

Larry and Vivian Voight were tried and convicted of multiple capital felonies. The prosecution wanted the death penalty, but the jury recommended multiple life sentences. Unfortunately, the judge agreed. During the sentencing, it was necessary to restrain Vivian as she ranted and raved. At one point, her wailing sounded like a banshee. Larry was sentenced to serve his life terms in a prison cell. Vivian was sent to a mental facility, confined in her self-imposed solitary confinement.

Jimmy Noseby, the local newspaper reporter, covered both trials. Hubbard, Ellison, and Lu refused to be interviewed or have their names mentioned. Amy and Dunne gave brief interviews and credited good police investigation and luck for the capture and convictions of the killers. Noseby used the trials as a means of writing career building articles.

When asked, Pickens commented, "The hard work of Detective Sergeant Amy Tucker and Detective Sergeant Mia

Dunne resulted in two pairs of killers behind bars, and the county and its citizens were safer."

When asked about his injuries, Pickens said, "My family and I are grateful for the doctors that took care of my injuries." When pressed for more, Pickens replied, "No further comment."

EPILOGUE

WITH THE TRIALS over and the killers behind bars, Pickens and his deputies could get back to doing more normal things. Like answering calls that someone's cow had wandered onto the highway or that teenagers were speeding on the roads after high school, or something else other than murder.

Pickens was back on the field coaching and had completed his counseling sessions, so had Amy. Both were dealing with PTSD from the shootings but had their anger under control.

Mitch Hubbard had time to take Donna and Harley Baxter, Donna's friend, quail hunting with Bo Tatum.

Bobbie Ellison was back at private investigating. He and Lu had lunch together when he was in town. Lu accepted a dinner date after work. She wasn't ready to socialize with Ellison on the weekend.

Pickens got a thanksgiving present from the county. The commissioners came through, and Pickens hired two deputies. Both were fresh out of the academy. One was a cousin of Zeke Jackson. The other, Carla Bosnik, was assigned to Detective Sergeant Mia Dunne. Zeke's cousin, Dwayne Lansing, was paired with Deputy Ritchie Ortiz because Pickens still hadn't received the new patrol car yet.

After the Christmas holiday, Pickens, Marge, and Sarah

took a cruise vacation to the Caribbean. It was the first real vacation they had taken since their honeymoon, as the sheriff's and medical examiner's work always seemed to get in the way.

Pickens and Marge rang in the New Year in the ship's ballroom.

The next day, Pickens, Marge, and Sarah were relaxing on the deck.

"Isn't it great we didn't have to think about crime for a whole week?" said Marge.

"Yeah, and it's great that if something did happen, no one could contact us here."

"Excuse me, Mr. Pickens," said a steward, "there's an urgent phone call for you."

AUTHOR'S COMMENTS

THE EVENTS THAT took place in this book weren't part of any actual criminal cases. They were derived from my imagination. Any resemblance to actual events, locales, or persons, living or dead was entirely coincidental.

I'm grateful for the numerous websites that gave me an enormous wealth of information, making it easier to do research.

My thanks to those who anonymously provided information relevant to the sequence of events portrayed in this book.

A special thanks to Heather Whittaker for editing my work and her sage advice.

Thank you for reading my book. I hope you enjoyed it and will recommend it to family and friends. If you feel like it, I'd appreciate a review on Amazon or a post on my website www. georgeencizo.com.